FAMILY
BONDS

Other Books by
CANDICE POARCH

Family Bonds

Loving Delilah (Coree Island series)

Courage Under Fire (At Your Service series)

Lighthouse Magic (Coree Island series)

Bargain of the Heart

The Last Dance (Nottoway series)

Shattered Illusions (Coree Island series)

Tender Escape

Intimate Secrets (Nottoway series)

The Essence of Love

With This Kiss (Nottoway series)

White Lightning (Nottoway series)

Published by BET/Arabesque books

FAMILY BONDS

Candice Poarch

BET Publications, LLC
http://www.bet.com
http://www.arabesquebooks.com

ARABESQUE BOOKS are published by

BET Publications, LLC
c/o BET BOOKS
One BET Plaza
1900 W Place NE
Washington, DC 20018-1211

First Printing: October 2005

10 9 8 7 6 5 4 3 2 1

Printed in the United States of America

Acknowledgments

My sincere thanks go to readers, book clubs, booksellers
and librarians for their continued support.
As always, profound thanks go to my family
and my critique partner, Sandy Rangel.

Chapter 1

Seattle's constant rain showers chased Taylor Harrison into the hospital. He wiped the water off his face and headed to the elevator that took him to his grandfather's floor. As he walked down the antiseptic-smelling corridors, he jockeyed for a clear pathway with harried nurses and orderlies. Everywhere he went, heart monitors beeped. Finally, he found the right room. The older man was resting peacefully, while Taylor's mother gazed out the window.

"What did you find out?" Ralph Johnson asked from his hospital bed. "Do you think he was dating her?" The tangle of tubes had finally been removed, and he was out of intensive care.

Taylor eased into a chair beside the bed and took a photo out of his pocket. "Why else would Palmer Wainwright give a woman a check for four hundred grand? She attended the funeral, but she certainly wasn't distraught."

Melia Lucas. Gorgeous brown hair, nutmeg complexion, and vivid brown eyes that seemed to pierce Taylor's soul. *What are your secrets?* he wondered. There was something definitely appealing about her. He'd detected that quality at the funeral.

He tossed the photo on the table. The young beauty had hypnotized the much older Palmer Wainwright, all right. Vying for Melia's attention must have made Palmer, who had taken over Ralph Johnson's law practice ten years ago, abandon his principles and jeopardize his career. Ultimately, he'd lost his mind and attempted to kill Taylor's grandfather—all in an effort to do something outrageously illegal to keep Melia Lucas. Palmer's car had careened off a cliff, plunging him to his death.

"What did you find out about Ms. Lucas so far?" his grandfather repeated.

"Other than what we already knew, very little. She has a local Saturday morning cooking show. She also teaches cooking classes in a gourmet shop. She isn't hurting for money. She has virtually no debts." Raising an eyebrow, he added, "I also discovered she's throwing a party in a couple of days."

"I suppose you're going to crash it?" Taylor's mother rose from a chair in the corner and straightened the covers around her father. Phyllis Harrison had been glued to her father's side since the accident.

"Of course."

"I'd like to know what the relationship was between that girl and Palmer," Ralph said, his anger elevating his blood pressure. "Palmer was a good lawyer. He clerked for me. I owe him that much."

"You don't owe him a darn thing," Phyllis said, angrily. "That man tried to kill you, and you're acting like it was nothing."

"Calm down, honey. My heart's still ticking."

"No thanks to him."

A wise man knew when to be quiet.

She took his empty water pitcher and left the room.

For more than a week after the automobile accident, Ralph had clung to life by a thread. He then spent two weeks in critical care. Now the washed-out hue of his brown face gave the appearance of a man much older than eighty-three, as a few strands of black hair stood out among the gray. Although his face had aged, he still made women's heads turn. Taylor's mother often spoke of the neighbor who visited her father daily.

The woman had been working on marrying him since his wife died five years ago.

Guilt nagged at Taylor. Using every spare moment to build a legal practice, he hadn't spent nearly enough time with the older man since he graduated from college. His hard work had paid off financially while building his career, but family was important, too.

Taylor studied his grandfather. He'd exchanged his hospital gown for the loose-fitting royal blue pajamas Phyllis had brought to the hospital. She had found them in the back of his dresser drawer at home. She'd probably cut the sales tags off before bringing them to the hospital. Taylor supposed his grandmother had probably placed them in the drawer years ago, while she was still alive.

Taylor thought of Melia again. Indeed, a cunning woman could get a good man to do just about anything, especially if he was in love. So far, he hadn't found an insurance policy. But Palmer had declared the money was hers, and he'd make sure she received it.

"What's this about money she was due?" Taylor asked.

"Palmer left her a letter. Enclosed was a check for four hundred grand. Something about money from an insurance policy she never received."

"Was it legitimate?"

Ralph shrugged. "Who knows, but the question is why would he give it to her at this late date," he asked, "when her parents died several years ago? I think he used that as an excuse to leave her a nice windfall."

Many questions and few answers, Taylor thought, considering how he could get closer to Melia. "Don't you own a condo in the building where she lives?"

"Should be on the same floor as hers. All the investors' condos are on that floor."

"She invested in it?"

"Her adopted family did." Ralph spoke dryly. "Leticia

Sims wouldn't have settled for just anything. That woman is a deal maker if I ever saw one."

"You don't usually invest with that group. What changed your mind?"

"Palmer talked me into it. Said it was sure to make a huge profit. And he was right, of course. The value has almost tripled."

"I suppose someone is renting your unit now."

'Actually no. The real estate agent told me the last tenant moved out just before the accident. Need to rent it out again. Haven't gotten around to contacting her."

Taylor smiled with satisfaction. "Leave that to me. Shouldn't take me long to rent some furniture and move in. Can't think of a better way to meet this Melia," Taylor said.

"Don't get too involved in this mess. It's dangerous. Palmer was desperate. I've never seen him that spooked." Ralph closed his eyes at the memory. "I'll look into it when I recover. Besides, you can't neglect your own practice."

Phyllis entered the room and set the pitcher on the tray. "He just closed a huge case," she said with pride. "It made the news even in Seattle. And he promised to take a vacation to spend some time with us."

Phyllis had come to Seattle as soon as she heard about the accident. She was now staying at her father's house while she waited for him to be released from the hospital. Now that Ralph was mending, the worry lines around her eyes and mouth had eased.

Taylor held up his hands. "I'm on vacation. My schedule is clear."

"For the first time in five years," his mother muttered. "After you uncover whatever is going on, I'm hoping you'll start looking for a wife."

"Was almost there once. Didn't work out," Taylor countered.

"Who could blame her?" Phyllis said. "Try spending some time with the next woman."

"What's important now is Granddad. Why did Palmer try to kill you?"

"Our last conversation was about a complaint letter the office received from a woman questioning how Palmer handled her estate. He had power of attorney for several seniors who had been declared incompetent to handle their own affairs. Some are in nursing homes."

"Complaints aren't unusual considering many of these people are suffering from some form of dementia. If everything was on the up and up, all he needed to do was prove the expenses were necessary or bills were paid on time. Even if he were guilty of something, he's a lawyer. More than likely he could find a way out without trying to kill you. So why such a drastic step? Unless he felt you were going to dig deeper—find something else?"

"That's my concern." Ralph gazed at his hands, then into his grandson's face, his expression fierce. "The office still bears my name. I want this mess cleaned up." Then Ralph's tired eyes searched his. "Some vacation," he said in a hoarse voice.

"Don't worry about me," Taylor said. "You just get well. I'll take care of everything."

Taylor's mother approached him. At fifty-six, her hair held only a few strands of gray, and only a few thin lines fanned out from the corners of her eyes. Her smooth skin barely held a wrinkle. She was still a very attractive woman, but worry was present in her eyes.

"Be careful, son."

It was Wednesday, Taylor thought. It shouldn't take him more than a couple of days to settle into the apartment. The first order of business was getting a cleaning crew in there. He'd call one as soon as he reached the office. Then he'd call a furniture rental company. He had a lot to do and a small amount of time in which to get it done.

Wednesday was a late-night closing for Modern Gourmet. The last salesclerk had just left. It was nine, and Melia Lucas was waiting for Jessica Bell, while the owner, Mark Fisher, was in the back room counting the money. She and Jessica had known each other since they were children. Before Jessica could lock the door, Mark came out. Jessica was the sales manager, and Mark was dating her. Neither Jessica nor Melia understood why he came by every night or why he wouldn't let Jessica close the shop at least some nights. Jessica excused his actions by saying that he was overprotective and that he expressed that same caring in their relationship. But this nightly business was carrying safety a bit far. After all, he didn't walk all the employees to their cars. He usually told them to exit in pairs, so no one would be alone in the parking lot. Melia thought he was a control freak.

"I'll walk you ladies to your cars," he said to Melia and Jessica.

"The two of us can leave together just like the salesclerks," Melia said. "Jessica and I are parked near each . . ." She stopped in midsentence when the door burst open with a force so hard it hit the window. It was a wonder it didn't shatter into a million pieces.

"Don't move!" shouted a ski-capped man brandishing a gun.

Jessica screamed. Her heart tripping, Melia stood as rigid as stone.

"Shut the hell up!" another man said, approaching them waving another gun. There were two of them, but Melia's eyes were glued to the guns. The size of the guns didn't matter, Melia thought. She didn't know a thing about guns except that they were deadly. The last thing she wanted was one pointed in her direction.

"Oh, my God. Don't kill us," Jessica said, backing away, while the guns kept Melia hypnotized.

"Your next step will be your last one," one of the men said.

He grabbed Melia roughly by the arm and turned her around. Suddenly, she came back to life. Melia yelped, and the man cut her scream off with a beefy arm pressed to her throat. She felt a gun's barrel against her head and nearly fainted.

"Move and she gets it first."

Melia was trembling so hard, it was a wonder the gun didn't go off from her body shaking.

"Just take it easy," Mark said calmly. "We'll give you anything you want. No need to hurt anyone."

"Give us the money. All of it," the other man said.

Mark held up both hands. "Okay, okay. Just don't hurt anyone." He seemed unusually calm, while Melia was scared speechless. She could smell the man's sweaty fear and wondered if he could smell hers.

Melia couldn't tell what race they were—only that they were light in complexion. She had barely glimpsed the hazel eyes of the one who was holding her in his iron grip.

Salespeople were always warned that holdups could occur. They happened all the time. But in the four years she'd worked at the gourmet shop, this was her first.

Poor Mark. He was so out of his element. Perhaps his geeky appearance was an advantage. They'd see he wasn't a threat to them and wouldn't hurt him. *Please God, protect us,* Melia prayed silently.

Jessica was visibly shaking, her hands covering her mouth. Melia wasn't fairing much better. She felt as if her legs were going to give way, and she was going to melt into a puddle on the floor.

Jessica stumbled back a step.

"I said don't move," the man holding Melia shouted. Sweat beaded up around the other man's lip. Both of them wore gloves so that even their hands were covered. Jessica moved again, and the gunman waved his gun at her. The two of them hovered there as the other man disappeared into the back room with Mark.

A fleeting thought passed through Melia's mind: how did the men even know that Mark counted the money in the back room? But she was more worried about whether they would live through the experience.

Melia's eyes were trained on Jessica. The man holding Melia was breathing rapidly in her ear. He was as fearful as they were, she realized. Surprisingly, she smelled mint on his breath. It would have been almost funny, if the situation wasn't so dangerous. A gunman taking the time to chew a breath mint before a robbery.

"Why are you doing this?" Melia croaked.

"Shut up!" he snapped and whacked her on the head with the gun.

She saw stars. Her knees buckled, and suddenly they were both on the floor. The man pulled her to her feet, screaming something in her ear.

Jessica screamed again when he shouted, "Shut up!"

Finally, the first gunman appeared behind Mark.

"If you follow us, we will kill her," he said to Mark as he pointed at Melia. Then he jogged to the door.

"You have the money. Leave me here. We aren't going to follow you."

The other man ignored Melia's plea and dragged her with him to the door and then outside. *My God. They have no reason to keep me alive*, she thought. She could hardly breathe because of the tight grip he held her in.

"Please let me go," Melia pleaded.

The man remained silent and just kept dragging her until finally an SUV appeared around a corner and its door burst open. He shoved Melia forward, knocking her to the pavement, and jumped into the SUV. Tires screeched as the driver sped off. Melia picked herself up as quickly as she could and saw Mark jogging down the street after the SUV.

Was he crazy? He wasn't Arnold Schwarzenegger. Didn't he know he couldn't outrun a car?

Suddenly, Jessica burst through the door of the Modern Gourmet, her cell phone in her hand. "Are you all right?" she asked Melia. Then she hugged her. "Thank God they didn't take you with them."

Mark jogged back to where they stood. "You okay?" he said in an absent manner.

Melia nodded. Her mind had gone blank with fright, and words eluded her.

"I called the police," Jessica said.

"Did you get the license number?" Melia managed to ask Mark.

"No," he said, shaking his head. "They were too fast." He put an arm around each woman and ushered them back inside.

Melia could have sworn Mark had repeated the numbers out loud. Still recovering from her brush with death, she hadn't listened closely. Right now, she didn't see fear in him, but rather a deep, abiding rage.

In the distance, she heard sirens. When the police arrived, they took everyone's statements and examined the shop.

After the police left, Melia was still teetering on the edge of hysteria. She couldn't drive home. She sat at the stoplight in a daze, contemplating what had happened until a horn beeped behind her. Then she turned and drove toward the Sims's house, and Earl Sims's soothing presence. The Sims were her surrogate family, and tonight she needed their warmth.

It was amazing how quickly things got done when you greased a few palms, Taylor thought. It had been two days since he put his plan into action. His grandfather's condo was almost furnished—at least as much of it as he wanted furnished.

He struggled to the elevator with the last of his boxes. Suddenly, his path was blocked by the very woman responsible for his moving there. She wore an outfit straight out of the roaring twenties. She was coaxing another woman onto the elevator. Impatiently, Taylor stood behind them, waiting for them to move.

"Just one more step," Melia said. Her soothing voice wrapped around him like sweet honey. "I'm with you. You're not alone."

Obviously, the other woman had a problem with elevators. As Taylor waited, he focused on Melia. Four-inch strands of sequins adorned the bottom of her shimmering, off-white flapper dress, grazing her shapely calves. A matching silk scarf was tied in a band around her head, leaving her long hair flowing down her back. From Taylor's vantage, he could see the shape of a striking brown face.

"Excuse me, please," Taylor said, trying to pass them.

"Hold the elevator for me! Hold it," said another woman, as she ran up behind Taylor. She was dressed in a headache-inducing psychedelic sixties-style dress, an Afro wig at least half a foot high, four- or five-inch stilettos, and long, dangling earrings that extended to her shoulders. "Sorry I'm late, ladies," she said.

The two women in front of Taylor stepped gingerly into the elevator, but not quickly enough to stop the other one from falling against Taylor's back. He stifled a curse when the heavy box in his arms tilted forward and went crashing to the floor an instant before he lost his balance. Melia grabbed at him as if she could stop his momentum and wound up flat on the floor beneath him.

Lifting himself on his elbows, Taylor stared down at her. His body immediately responded to the soft curves beneath him. He tried to think with his brain, but his body was more persuasive. Rolling off her, he knelt beside her.

"Are you okay? Did you hit your head?"

Her eyes stared back at him as she gasped for breath.

"Take it easy," he said softly.

"Oh, my God. Is she dead?" said the neurotic woman, now braced against the corner wall as if she were wallpaper.

"Melia, Melia?" the psychedelic called out.

"Got the wind knocked out of her. That's all. Stand back and give her some room," Taylor said. By then the elevator buzzer blared.

"Let me out of here," the other woman, who was obviously claustrophobic, said. "We're going to crash."

"You're okay," Taylor told her. Her saucer-like eyes looked as frightened as a spooked horse.

Melia struggled to breathe.

"She's coming around," he murmured.

The claustrophobic woman moaned in the corner.

"Take it easy," Taylor said to both of them. As Melia gasped for breath, he helped her sit up before helping her to her feet.

"I . . . I . . . ," the claustrophobic woman stammered.

"What in the world? You tackled me like a linebacker," Melia finally wheezed out.

"Sorry." He wrapped an arm around her to steady her. Then he kicked the box to the side, blocking the claustrophobic woman so other people could enter the elevator. His attraction to the soft woman in his arms, staring at him with accusing brown eyes, stunned him.

"I'm so sorry. You okay, Melia? These damn heels. Always getting . . . well, who did I catch this time?" the psychedelic woman who'd knocked him into Melia asked, slowly turning to him. She was jostled when a giant of a guy resembling a longshoreman entered the elevator.

"Are you going to take all day?" he demanded. He seemed to take up most of the available space.

"I . . . I . . . ," the claustrophobic woman plastered against the wall repeated.

"What floor?" Taylor asked Melia in a steady voice.

"Fourteen," the psychedelic woman responded. "We're going to her place. I'm Lisa, by the way. What's your name?"

"Taylor."

"For the love of . . . ," the longshoreman started, "Can we move it?"

"Be patient," Lisa snapped, effectively shutting him up.

She glanced at the box. "Are you moving in?" she asked Taylor.

"Yes."

Lisa was pretty, with raven eyes and hair that was too black to be natural.

The elevator moved.

"Help!" the claustrophobic woman breathed out in a weak gasp.

Melia shoved Taylor aside and nearly fell. Taylor held her firmly.

"It's okay, Christina," Melia said in a soothing voice and patted her arm. "I fell. That's all."

"Help!" Christina said weakly again as if she were about to faint.

The longshoreman turned around. "What's the matter with you? You sick or something?"

"We'll be there in a minute," Melia continued in that same comforting voice. "Think about something else, like the wonderful time you're going to have."

The longshoreman sighed and turned back around.

"I have to go back down," Christina said, struggling to get the words out.

"But not before you enjoy great food, wine, and company. Besides, Blair's playing the sax."

As she continued to talk to Christina in that soothing tone, Taylor listened closely. He hated that he remembered vividly the soft curves of her body, and that he'd responded. Even worse, she seemed caring and sweet.

"You and Melia are going to be neighbors," Lisa said to Taylor, changing the subject.

"Really?" The elevator stopped. Christina hurtled over the box, nearly causing another collision. Everyone cleared a path, including the giant, as she bolted out of the elevator like a horse out of a starting gate.

Taylor looked at Melia. "May I help you to your apartment?"

"I'm okay now, thanks. I can make it on my own," she said, and followed the frightened woman. A corner unit, he noticed.

Already he missed the warmth of her body pressed against his.

Lisa grasped his arm after he'd fished his keys out of his pocket and picked up his box.

"We're having a party tonight." She plucked his keys out of his hand. "I'll get the door for you. Which one?"

Before he could respond, the door Melia and Christina had disappeared behind opened and a blast of Louis Armstrong's horn floated out. Taylor and Lisa walked down the long corridor. After he gave Lisa his apartment number, she opened the door for him. Even with the furniture and posters, his place was still stark and uninviting. Maybe a few personal items and books might help it seem more livable.

"I have to unpack," he said.

As soon as he slid the box onto the foyer table, Lisa took hold of his arm again and dragged him out of the door.

"Lovely place. But enough work for one day. It's Friday. Time to party," she said, and opened the door to Melia's condo.

The Chinese-style chairs that flanked an 19th-century Victorian table in the foyer created a striking entrance.

"I agree," Taylor said, tilting his lips into a smile. "I need to relax." Lisa was giving him exactly the opening he needed to forge an inconspicuous introduction to Melia.

"Melia prepares all the food, and everyone always eats too much. Most of the people are singles and really pig out. So you've got to grab the food as soon as you arrive, or else you might not get away."

"Her cooking is that good?"

"The best. Has her own local cooking show. You've probably heard of it. 'Cooking with Melia.'"

When he shook his head, she said, "Are you from around here?"

"Oregon."

"That explains it. Melia's very popular here. She's trying to get with a national cable food network. And she teaches a few classes at one of the gourmet shops. They are always packed."

"You've persuaded me." Everyone seemed to be standing around with plates in hand listening to music.

"See what I mean?" Lisa said.

Taylor nodded as they headed to the buffet.

As he took in the surroundings, he understood how Palmer

had gotten into trouble if he had to keep this woman in style. Her condo, a designer showcase, was twice the size of his, and all the eighteenth-and nineteenth-century furniture mixed with modern pieces certainly weren't bargain basement specials.

Surprisingly, her home radiated romance, elegance, and sophistication, yet it managed to be inviting and warm. A comfortable home.

In the dining room, significant headway had already been made into the food, and Melia directed someone to refill the platters. She was as cool as a cucumber, as if she were the queen of the manor.

A man playing the sax to a Coltrane CD stood in a corner, as an audience gathered around him. Christina was sitting closest to him and staring into his face as if the moon and stars were shining on him alone.

People were dressed in a mix of period outfits and modern clothing, blue jeans, suits, and business casual attire. Taylor felt like he'd walked into a costume party.

He focused on Melia again. Although she still looked shaken, she carried on as if nothing had happened.

The music turned mellow and the sax player leaned into the rythm as if he were one with the instrument. The slow, sensual melody carried Taylor on a potent wave where everything faded to darkness except Melia and the music. She started to sway to a beat that transported him to hot, sultry summer nights where the air was so thick he could barely breathe and her skin shimmered with sweat mixed with the heady aroma of her perfume. The beads of her white dress beating against her long, shapely legs tantalized him. In rhythm with the long notes of the sax, his hands stroked the curves of her body, tasted the nectar of her sweet mouth as he slid the sensual fabric up her body until she stood before him in her bra and panties, her skin glistening in the moonlight. He was hot. He was ready.

The last notes of the song faded away, releasing him from its spell.

Damn, he was in trouble.

Melia felt Taylor's eyes on her whenever she moved. She tried her best to keep from blushing, but the memory of his soothing arms supporting her and his steady heartbeat wouldn't abate.

"I got him in here. The rest is up to you," Lisa whispered as she snagged a plate. Taylor was selecting food from the other end of the table.

"I'm meeting my Internet pal next Friday, remember?"

"This one's in-hand—just in case. His name is Taylor, by the way."

"I heard."

"How are my favorite ladies?" Audie Sims approached them and linked his arm around Lisa before he kissed her on the cheek. Then he kissed Melia.

"I don't know. Where are they?" Lisa asked.

"One day you're going to be eating out of my hand," he said so only Melia and Lisa could hear.

"In your dreams," Lisa said and approached Taylor.

Audie's eyes followed Lisa as she headed for the great room. "Why are you women always trying to play so hard to get?" he said to Melia. "When are you going to marry me?"

"Audie, I can't date my brother. Besides, what kind of life would we have when you're pining for another woman?" Melia said, referring to Lisa. Audie and Melia weren't actually related. But since their parents had been best friends and the Sims had taken Melia in when her parents had died when she was in college, they had always thought of each other as family.

Audie finally focused on Melia. "There's no blood between us, baby. It would please Mom if we were to marry. And I love you."

Melia sighed. "Do we have to go through this every time I see you?"

"I'm worried about you." He cupped her face in his hand. "Dad told me about the robbery. You okay?"

"I'm fine," she said.

"Do they know who did it?"

"Not a clue."

"As long as you're okay. You should have called me." He held her close before he let her go. What would she do without the Sims, Melia wondered, grateful that they were a part of her life.

"Fix yourself a plate, Audie. I have a new dish I've been working on. I think it's almost there. Tell me what you think."

"Anything for you, baby," he said as he grabbed a plate and began to pile food on it. Audie's handsome face and tall stature were a perfect complement to his trim build. He wasn't a complicated person. Not like his brother, Blair. But Melia had other worries. And for the most part, the party distracted her. But this constant nagging about marriage annoyed her.

"Help yourself to a plate while I freshen Taylor's drink," Melia said. She approached Taylor with a bottle of wine. "May I top your glass?" she asked.

After pouring his wine, she sat on the ottoman next to Taylor's chair. The CD changed to a Miles Davis hit, and Blair segued into the new routine. He looked innocent. Was h᷈ as innocent as he appeared, or was Blair part of some plot?

Of course, she was being silly. There wasn't a plot to steal her land. Leticia was always involved in some real estate deal, and so was Audie. It didn't make Leticia a criminal.

She was worried and had no one to turn to. In the past she could talk to the Sims about anything. But she couldn't approach them now, and she had no other family to speak of.

"So tell me, what are you celebrating?" Taylor asked, drawing Melia back to the present.

"Once a month, a group of friends and I have music night

here at my apartment. Just a chance for friends to get together," she explained. "We choose a style of music each month. This month it's jazz. I dug out my Louis Armstrong, John Coltrane, Miles Davis, Ella Fitzgerald, Billie Holiday, even threw in some Wynton Marsalis."

"Did you choose jazz? You seem like a jazz kind of woman. Slow, serious."

"My mother loved jazz, and I developed a healthy appreciation." Taylor was a handsome man, Melia thought. Over six feet tall, close-cropped black hair, wide shoulders. But his raven eyes were . . . secretive. Everything about him was polished and controlled.

"Are you from here?" Melia asked.

"Portland."

"What brings you to Seattle?"

"Business. That sax player is a good musician," he said, obviously changing the subject. She'd let him get away with it . . . for now.

"Blair is very good."

"Christina seems to have recovered."

"I guess you gathered she hates elevators."

"But the food and the music are worth the trauma," he said.

After the party, Taylor hung around to help with the cleanup. Only Lisa, Blair, and Melia were left.

"Blair, it looks like you and Christina have a thing going on," Melia teased.

Blair blushed. "She's just a friend."

"Be interesting to see how this relationship goes," Lisa said. "She won't come upstairs, and you won't go downstairs. Do you talk on the phone or e-mail each other?"

Blair blushed even more.

"Have you thought about seeing another therapist, Blair?" Melia asked.

"It hasn't done Christina much good. She still won't come up the elevator alone," Lisa said. "She was moaning like a kitten."

"But at least she can get in the elevator," Melia said. "That's progress."

Blair checked the time. "I need to get home," he said.

"Is Christina calling you?"

"Stop teasing him, Lisa. Come on."

He hesitated at the door, holding his sax in a death grip.

"Just think about your conversation with Christina. That should get rid of the fear."

"Stop being mean, Lisa." Blair was agoraphobic, and after a year of coaxing, Melia finally convinced him that crossing the hall wasn't the same thing as actually leaving the building.

"Remember you're still inside the building," Melia prompted. "You're just walking to another room." With a tug, he leaned forward, and Melia opened the door. He exhaled deeply. Blair suddenly pulled back. But Melia managed to get him over the threshold and into the hallway by talking to him softly. The door slammed behind them. Melia walked Blair across the hall and into his apartment, where he felt safe in his cocoon.

While Melia was gone, Taylor and Lisa stood at the kitchen counter. Looking around the kitchen for the first time, Taylor noticed the six-burner industrial stove. Twice the cabinet space than in his place, two Sub-Zero refrigerators. Guess she needed all that to prepare for tonight's crowd. But why did she need all that the rest of the month?

"She can pick up the weirdest friends. Every misfit seems to land on her doorstep," Lisa said.

"She seems like a generous person," Taylor observed.

"To a fault sometimes," Lisa responded.

"Talk about me behind my back," Melia said as she walked in. "My friends aren't weird. They just have different fears from the rest of us."

Lisa rolled her eyes. "They're weird any kind of way you dress it up." She looked at Taylor. "It usually takes at least half an hour for her to coax Blair and Christina in here. But it was a great party as always. I'm leaving."

"Thanks for the invite and the company," Taylor said.

"Anytime. Don't forget next month. Oh, and leave ten dollars with Melia for the food. Don't be a stranger to your neighbors."

"I won't be."

When Lisa left, the atmosphere seemed more intimate. Taylor wasn't there to hit on Melia, as much as he wanted to. He was knocked for a loop. He never fell for women this quickly. Yes, he wanted an attractive woman just like the next man, but this was different. He had to get the heck out of there before he found himself just as ensnared as Palmer had been, or worse, before he compromised his investigation. He pulled out his wallet and handed her a twenty.

"You were our guest tonight. Just ten for next month," she said.

"With the menu we had here, ten is a bargain. Lisa said you prepare all the food," Taylor said, exchanging the twenty for a ten.

She nodded. "Most of the time. I prepare some of it ahead of time and freeze it. All I have to do is stick it in the oven. Sometimes I ask Lisa or someone to come a couple of hours early to help." She slipped the ten into a jar on the counter.

"Is there anything more I can help you with?"

"No, thanks. Everything's almost done." She walked him to the door, signaling that it was time for him to go.

As he left, he thought about the too-busy people—those who volunteered for committees and were loaded down with a mountain of tasks while small jobs were doled out to everybody else. He wondered if there was a reason for the madness. Was Melia one of those hyper people who couldn't stand to sit still for more than two minutes? Was she only testing recipes to use on TV, or was she trying to win friends and recognition?

The question was, who was Melia Lucas, and what was her connection to Palmer?

Chapter 2

Modern Gourmet was a quaint little shop located on a busy thoroughfare. As she approached the door, Melia watched as a bicycle nearly collided with a pedestrian. Bumper-to-bumper traffic made its way slowly down the street.

The store was always busy because nearby office workers frequented it for specialty items, as well as for the cooking classes Melia offered. The fact that she'd become a local celebrity was an added benefit. Often she mentioned the classes on her show, and people poured in wanting to learn how to prepare dim sum, or lobster in myriad ways, or even vegetarian meals.

The problem was that her boss, Mark Fisher, was missing an opportunity. She had to practically force him to make any changes. Sometimes she had to send customers to other shops for specialty items the store didn't carry. She'd warned Mark that customers would eventually begin purchasing more items at the other stores if he didn't stock what they needed. It had taken weeks for him to agree to stock edible flowers. Talking to him was like talking to at a blank wall. He was forty-five, far enough south of sixty to be flexible.

It was Friday afternoon, and Melia made her way into the kitchen where she taught her classes and began to finalize the preparations for her next cooking class. She dreaded what she had to face afterward. She'd been summoned to the Sims. Leticia wouldn't tell her why. But the woman's latest mission was to get Audie and Melia married. Melia tried to get out of going over to the Sims, but Leticia had been insistent.

Melia's parents had died several years before, and the Sims had taken her in as if she were part of the family. Every Sunday after church Leticia Sims served a brunch. Last Sunday Leticia had asked her if she'd be willing to sell her land to them. As much as Melia hated to say no to people who had been nothing but kind to her, she couldn't sell. A week later Audie proposed. She'd gently refused him with the brother-sister bit. But he hadn't given up. Every time she saw him, he renewed his offer. Even Melia knew he had no romantic feelings for her any more than she had for him. The proposals were at his mother's urging.

By themselves, each of those things meant little. But with the developer's offer, her parents' lawyer's sudden death, the Simses' offer, and Audie's sudden proposal, it was too much to be considered just a coincidence.

But she trusted Audie's parents. They treated her like their own daughter. Audie was a bit much at times but was always very kind to her. And she couldn't ask for a more compassionate brother than Blair Sims, Audie's younger brother.

Both men were tall—about six feet—but there the similarities ended. Audie inherited his mother Leticia's more outgoing personality, although he was more easy going than she was. Blair inherited his father's more gentle and serious temperament.

Melia was willing to do a lot for the Sims. But she was unwilling to give up her family legacy, and that meant she wasn't going to sell the last of the land her family had owned and passed down through generations.

Melia had almost finished her class preparations when Jessica joined her.

"You should get a look at the dish that came in with his niece," she said. "He's taking your cooking class."

"Oh yeah? Got him all picked out for me?" Melia asked.

"Bite your tongue. He's all mine."

Melia stopped taking the food out of the fridge and peered at Jessica. "What about Mark?"

Jessica flipped her long blond hair over her shoulder. Her blue green eyes were brimming with mischief that could easily turn into trouble. "We may be an item, but I'm not blind. And Mark's not giving me the attention I deserve."

"Girl, you work for him. Fooling around is going to put you in a precarious position."

"I know. I know. But I'm not serious about this guy. It doesn't hurt to look. Just"—she shrugged—"I don't know. I've been restless lately. I suggested to Mark that we needed some space from each other to determine if this relationship is right."

"Easier said than done since you work for him. What's wrong, Jessica?"

Jessica leaned against the edge of the counter. "I'm ready to settle down. I want some stability in my life. I want to know I'll wake up beside the same man every morning, and damn it, I want children."

"I'm assuming you want all these things with Mark."

"For all the good that does."

Melia never thought they were the perfect match that Jessica believed they were. And not because Mark was only an inch taller than Jessica's five-foot-eight. Jessica was usually attracted to more type A personalities. Mark was on the low side of type B. But who was she to criticize?

"Then talk to him," Melia said. "He seems easy enough to talk to as long as it's not about adding supplies or a new refrigerator case to the store. I'm speaking on a professional level, mind you, not personal. I know that men are not necessarily the same to their lovers as they are to employees and friends. But give him a chance. Have you asked him if he feels the same way about you?"

"He says he loves me."

"That's wonderful, isn't it?"

"Yeah."

"But?" Melia continued.

"He's wonderful as long as I fit into his program. I'm just ready to take what we have to another level. I mean he's fifteen years older than me. You'd think he'd be ready to settle down more than I am."

"You never know. Some men are confirmed bachelors. Has Mark ever been married?"

"Almost. Once. But the woman changed her mind at the last minute, he says."

"Well, a relationship is supposed to be two-sided. Some of your needs have to be met, too." Melia patted Jessica's arm. "Remember, he can't read your mind. You have to be honest with him." Melia dug into the depths of the refrigerator. "I don't understand you. Usually you're very vocal about what you want."

"I know."

Melia looked at her friend again. "Talk to him. *Before* you get tangled up in something with another man."

"Yeah, yeah, yeah. In the meantime, I'll stick around and help you. You need some help?"

Melia chuckled. "All I can get." Unfortunately, Jessica wasn't taking her seriously.

"So have you decided to go on that Internet date yet?" Melia had talked to a guy online for a while now, and he wanted to meet her.

"I think I am. Haven't told him yet, though."

"I have a friend who met her husband that way. I think it's the wave of the future."

"More people seem to be doing it, at least. And if I date him, Leticia will leave me alone about Audie. The poor guy's in love with Lisa, but Leticia doesn't feel Lisa will make a suitable daughter-in-law."

"Don't you hate mothers like that?" She touched Melia's arm. "That's him walking in now."

When Melia looked at the man, she understood the attraction. He seemed more Jessica's type. The niece was a petite redhead, but his hair was nut brown, his body was gorgeous, and his dreamy blue eyes were just the shade Jessica liked. They were both attractive people.

"Mark had better get his act together if he wants to hang on to you," Melia said and pulled out copies of the recipes for today's class, which focused on soups, stews, and salads. Seattle Crab Louis and roasted pepper, corn, and arugula salad with goat cheese croutons. Arugula, with its rich, nutty taste, grew wild in some parts of Washington, and some people even considered it a weed. Steamed clams in a Thai curry broth, oyster stew, and Pacific Northwest seafood stew would also be included in the class.

Melia had not eaten. Just thinking of the recipes made her even more ravenous.

Mercedes, Range Rovers, Cadillacs—more than a few upscale vehicles were parked in Leticia Sims's driveway when Melia arrived. When she had asked Melia to stop by that evening, Melia hadn't expected the woman to have company. She parked her modest Jeep Cherokee on the street so she could easily slip out. In three-inch heels she hiked up the stately driveway. The house was located on a steep hill, making the walk even more difficult.

The lawn gave new meaning to Seattle's nickname, the Emerald City. The grass and trees created a lovely green canopy under the Seattle sunset. Melia knew she smelled like the spices she'd used in her cooking class. She should have taken a shower first and changed clothes, but Leticia had insisted she come over right away.

Clara Holmes, the Simses' housekeeper, opened the front door. "How are you, Melia?"

"I'm fine. I see I arrived at a bad time. Maybe I should stop by tomorrow." At least the woman could tell Leticia she came and left.

"Mrs. Leticia is expecting you; just go downstairs," the older woman said.

"But she has company. And I don't want to interrupt them," Melia said hopefully.

"Some business doings. But she told me to tell you to join them as soon as you arrived. Here, give me your jacket."

Melia tugged her jacket tightly around her. "I think I'll keep it. I won't be here long."

"Just give it to me."

Melia had learned long ago not to argue with Clara. Melia handed her jacket over just as Audie made his way in.

"You were summoned, too, I see," Melia said.

"From the grand dame herself," he said, linking his arm around her shoulder and kissing her on the cheek. When he let her go, he grabbed Clara and hugged her, lifting her off the floor.

"Oh, boy, go on."

"You're still my favorite lady, Ms. Clara."

"They all are, you wild thing. When you going to settle down?"

"Just as soon as Melia accepts my proposal."

"You're gonna stay single forever?" she asked, knowing very well Melia wouldn't marry him.

"Don't do me like that."

"Go on downstairs. Your mama's waiting for you, too. You're late as it is, the both of you. You're never on time."

"If we're on time, we can't make an appearance." Audie linked an arm around Melia again. "We'll go brave the big bad dame together." They passed the tastefully furnished living room boasting several antique pieces and walked down a short hallway to the stairs.

"Do you know what all this is about?" Melia asked.

"Business, what else? Something about a new development they're starting up," he said as they made their way to the basement rec room.

Mark was sitting near the stairs, patiently listening to whomever was speaking. He'd purchased the gourmet shop two years ago, when the owner sold it to go back East to take care of his ailing mother. The man he purchased the shop from had also arranged the cooking show for Melia. Of course, his gourmet shop was well advertised on the show.

Mark smiled when he saw her. His brown hair was slicked back and gathered in a curly ponytail. Neat wire-rimmed glasses gave him a decidedly bookish air.

Sliding over, he made room for her on an ottoman large enough to seat two and patted the cushions. Audie sat on the steps.

"It's boring so far," Mark whispered as she settled on the seat.

"What are they talking about?" Melia asked.

"A new golf community they want to build."

"We don't have enough of them already?" she asked.

He shrugged. Melia almost felt sorry for him. Jessica had flirted with the man from the cooking class, the one who had brought along his niece. Melia had learned his name was Duncan Ford. Nothing got by Duncan's sharp eyes, Melia thought, while Mark reminded her of a sweet, clueless man.

Melia's attention was drawn to Leticia. She was pointing at something—a beautiful layout of houses and townhouses surrounding a picturesque golf course. A small lake was highlighted on the wall screen.

"Perfect setting for you. You love golf," Melia whispered to Mark.

"Too long a commute. They want to build it on an island."

Apprehension drew Melia's stomach into a tight fist. Palmer had been a member of this group, and he'd wanted her to sell her land to its members. So did Leticia. Melia understood why Leticia had asked her to stop by. The group of five men and four women would gang up on her to try to convince her to sell her land.

A few months before, Palmer Wainwright had approached her with an offer for her land from a developer. Melia had refused. It was the only piece of her family's land left. They'd purchased it in the late 1800s. The property that had been the site of their family home had been bulldozed and was now a shopping center and condo complex. It pained her to see her homestead become a shopping mall when her parents had vowed to keep it in the family. She was holding on to the last piece, which was located on Bainbridge Island, a ferry ride across Puget Sound from Seattle. Every so often Palmer called her with a higher offer, until a few weeks ago, when he'd died in a horrible accident.

Leticia had promised her a safe haven, yet Melia felt as if all eyes were aimed at her family legacy. She decided to escape upstairs, she was halfway off the ottoman when Leticia called out to her.

"Don't leave. Everyone, you know Melia, my adopted daughter. I'm so pleased you could join us, dear. I invited her here because this project might be something she will want to invest in."

"How thoughtful, Leticia," Melia said and reluctantly slid back into her seat.

Wearing a burgundy silk pantsuit that fit her trim figure well, Leticia held court. She visited the health spa religiously three times a week. But she was never the type to go jogging with the locals.

Mark patted Melia's hand and leaned close. "You don't have to invest, you know. Just endure the meeting like me."

"I'm thankful for small favors," Melia said. "But why are you here if you aren't interested in investing?"

He nodded toward the right, where Charles Wilson sat. "Charles owns the building where the shop is located. It's not a good idea to upset the management."

"In other words, you're forced into investing."

He shrugged again. "I did pretty well on my last deal with them. And their investments usually pay off handsomely. I'm all for making a profit."

"What does he do, gang up on all the tenants in the complex?"

He chuckled. "Not really. Not all the tenants are here."

Looking around the room at Leticia's husband, Earl, a gentle soul compared to his aggressive wife, and the clueless Audie, Melia felt as if the only family she had left was threatened. She knew exactly how Mark felt.

Melia suffered through another fifteen minutes before everyone was herded upstairs to the dining room and dinner. She'd already sampled the food she'd prepared in the cooking class. But this meeting was enough to make her lose what little appetite she had left.

Afterwards, Leticia hugged her and reminded her about the Sunday brunch, as if Melia could forget the weekly tradition. She couldn't leave fast enough.

Melia was lying in bed tossing and turning until finally she flung the covers back and turned on the bedside table lamp. She gazed at the framed photo of her parents that sat on the nightstand. Her mother had been a teacher, her father a manager at a local computer company. They were a warm, loving couple. And her world had felt safe and complete. But nothing had been the same since their deaths. She traced the outline of their images as if she could stroke their faces. Death was so final. As much as she needed them, as much as she longed to talk to them, hug them, those precious times were gone forever.

Melia stared at the photo for several minutes before she grabbed a robe and went out on the balcony. Standing at the railing and viewing the city lights, thoughts of her parents wouldn't go away. Although eight years had passed, she still missed them. How she missed them. At times the loss seemed an unrelentingly dull ache lodged in her heart. Most days were better than this.

Neither Leticia nor anyone at the meeting mentioned Melia's property that night, but the Bainbridge Island land hung in the air just the same. They conveniently mentioned a fifty-acre lot. They mentioned the artsy community and the cultural atmosphere of a college community. It was certainly an escape from the bustling city of Seattle. A place retirees would love to settle down in and play golf. If that didn't describe Bainbridge Island, then what did?

Perhaps Melia was holding on to the land for the wrong reasons. She hadn't been to the old place since she'd had it renovated. The memories were just too painful. Maybe it was time to go back. For a day, at least. She certainly couldn't stay the night. Too many ghosts from the past.

The next day, Melia's footsteps echoed in her empty apartment after work. After a shower, she sank onto her bed with her laptop and logged on to the Web. She had to admit she'd met some pretty interesting people through the Internet. Many of her friends at the party had gone on dates that way. A few were even lasting friends. Like Jessica said, it seemed to be the only way to find suitable men these days. Melia hated to admit it, but she hadn't been on a *real* date in more than a year. But she'd e-mailed "Standby" for a couple of months, and he wanted to meet her.

She stared at the ceiling. It was Friday night, and she was sitting in front of her laptop checking her e-mail. She was certainly representative of the average single black woman in her late twenties—twenty-nine to be exact. *What have I got to lose*? she thought as her hand hovered above the keyboard.

Another evening alone instead of with a man, her inner voice responded. And it would solve the Audie problem. If she was dating, perhaps Leticia would get the message that she wasn't going to marry him.

"I'd love to meet you," she typed. She figured she could e-mail any night.

"Wow," Standby typed back. "Dying to meet you."

She knew he lived somewhere around Seattle, which meant she didn't have to travel halfway across the country to meet him.

"I'm looking forward to meeting you, too," she responded. For a computer geek, he sounded like a pretty neat guy. After all, she lived across the hall from one. She knew their quirks, knew they loved spending hours on the Internet with only Twinkies and Mountain Dew for sustenance. She knew she'd get her computer fixed in a jiffy when it broke. And she knew she'd get the latest gadgets for gifts. From Blair, she had gotten the most technologically advanced toaster on the market. And that was no small feat, given that he didn't venture out of his apartment. The world came to him. She knew she wouldn't have to compete with other women, just machines. At this no-dating juncture, she could live with that. A breathing body won hands down over a laptop any day.

"Does next Friday work for you?" he asked.

She had nothing interesting on her schedule, but she was also cautious. It was the perfect venue for serial killers.

"I'll have to check my schedule, but it sounds like a winner," she wrote.

He named a coffee shop off East Madison.

"I know where that is," she responded.

"Seven okay?"

"How will I identify you?"

"I'll be wearing black jeans and a white sweater. My real name is Stan, by the way."

Even she knew that to men the color white ranged from bright bleach white to canary yellow.

"My favorite color is black," Stan continued.

She hadn't thought of what she'd wear, but . . .

"Stilettos. Tight black jeans . . . and a low cut black top." He typed in a smile. "I admit I'm a boobs man. I've been picturing you in that outfit for months. By the way, how tall are you?"

Who does this creep think he's meeting? A porn queen?

"I checked my schedule," she quickly typed. "Seems I have a late hair appointment. Need a touch-up," she said. "Badly," she threw in for emphasis.

"We could meet after."

"Hair appointments are like doctor visits. No telling when I'll get out. A friend's coming over. Got to go. Bye."

So much for Stan. Why did she get the creeps? Even though Luther Vandross was singing in the background, she heard that country-and-western song "On the Road Again" pounding in her head.

Suddenly, she thought of Taylor. She couldn't get him off her mind.

Melia saw Taylor practically every day as they stood in the hallway, talking for several minutes before they made their way into their respective condos. He invited her out to dinner one night, but she was busy. He was out of town right now. He'd left a key with her and asked her to water his plants while he was away.

His apartment was half the size of hers and was furnished with only the bare necessities, as if he planned to be there for only a short while.

An eight-by-ten photograph of what must have been his family was displayed on the foyer table. Mother, father, several siblings, and smaller children. She wondered if any of the children were his.

She placed the picture back on the table and went to water his plants.

She was like one of those wanderers, cruising through life with no real direction. All her friends were models of modern-day career women. Lisa owned her own accessory shop. Another friend was an artist who created impressive sculptures; one was a geriatric specialist who enjoyed the wisdom of those who had lived long enough to know what they were talking about. One was an administrative assistant who hung on to her boss with the grip of a tick. She expected to hear about a divorce any day now. To these women, their work wasn't just a job, it was their passion. All these women knew what they wanted. And they went after it—their careers and other things—with the dedication of an army drill sergeant. Even Blair, a certifiable nerd had known his calling since kindergarten.

Not her.

She dabbled in one thing then the next, hoping to find something that would make her job worth going to each morning. Although she did enjoy her cooking classes, she had never thought that much about it. She just fell into it.

She left Taylor's place and went back home. The view from the balcony windows drew her nearer. A steady flow of cars crawled on the two floating bridges in the distance. The beautiful vistas of Mount Rainer emerged in the background. People below were water-skiing in Lake Washington, where two divers had recently found a World War II torpedo bomber that had crashed during a training exercise.

Springtime in Seattle. The flowers were bursting with color. Perhaps that was what she needed—to drive to the country. Feel the breeze on her face. And look at miles and miles of gorgeous flowers. Besides, she wanted to check out a supplier of edible flowers.

The phone rang, shattering her thoughts. Melia pulled off her earring and answered it.

"I thought I heard someone."

"I just got in, Blair. How are you?"

"Great, great."

She sat on the chair and sifted through mail. There was a letter from an attorney.

"Are you listening to me?"

"Sorry. I have a letter from an attorney."

"What's his name?"

"Palmer Wainwright. You know him. He died a month ago."

"Died? Why are you just getting his letter?"

"Someone from his office must have mailed it." She opened it and extracted a single-page letter with the name of the law office emblazoned on top. He was asking her to call and make an appointment to see him.

"I have to go," she said. Although it was Saturday, after hanging up with Blair, she dialed the office, expecting to leave a message for them to call her, but a deep voice answered the phone. The voice seemed familiar, but she couldn't place it.

After identifying herself, she said, "I received a letter from Mr. Wainwright's office asking me to call."

"Oh yes. Ms. Lucas. We have some unfinished business we want to conclude from your parents' estate."

It was still difficult to believe the avuncular man who'd handled her parents' affairs and made things so easy for her was dead.

"Someone will be here until one, if you can make it by today."

So much for her drive in the country. "I'll be there," she said and hung up.

Melia drove to a group of townhouse offices over in Madrona. The parking lot was nearly deserted except for an SUV parked directly in front.

The office was locked. She knocked on the door and waited. The surprise was that Taylor answered it, looking attractive in a green designer polo shirt and khaki slacks.

It took a couple of seconds for her to realize the implications of his presence, and then anger began to simmer in her like a slowly boiling pot. His voice on the phone had seemed so familiar, and now she knew why.

"Why didn't you tell me who you were at the party? Or at least at some point in the last two weeks?"

"I'd just arrived in town. I didn't know who you were until recently." He stepped back. "Please come in."

Melia didn't believe him for a moment. What was his game?

She marched through the reception area, where stacks of paper were heaped on a desk beside a computer and several file cabinets were lined up against the wall. Walking down a short corridor, she passed three offices, a water fountain, and a small kitchen before he led her into the room where he was working.

"Have a seat, please." He pointed to a chair in front of a huge cherry walnut desk. He settled into a burgundy leather chair behind the desk.

"I was told there was some unfinished business with my parents' estate." Fuming mad, she pressed her lips together and straightened her back.

"I have a check for you. There was an insurance policy check that was held in escrow."

"Why are you handling this?"

"Mr. Wainwright took over my grandfather's practice several years ago. Although he hasn't practiced in years, my grandfather is still the managing partner. Right now he's recovering from an accident, and I'm finalizing everything for him."

"My parents died eight years ago. Why am I getting a check now?"

"I don't know, Ms. Lucas. I'm researching the situation, but it will take time. In the meantime, I wanted you to get your check." He handed over the envelope.

"Why the formality? For two weeks you called me Melia. There's no reason to change that now."

Melia opened the envelope and pulled out a huge check.

"The office is obligated to pay interest."

"This seems more than the interest I made on the money I have in the bank. But I still don't understand why he held it so long."

"Believe me, I'm looking into it. As soon as I find something, I'll let you know."

"Thank you." Melia stood. "You must be very busy if you have to work on Saturdays."

"I'm leaving, too. May I take you to lunch?"

She gave him her best "drop dead" look.

"I don't really know many people here. I'm tired of my own company." His look was so heartrending that as angry as Melia was, she couldn't ignore the appeal in his voice.

"I had planned to drive out to the countryside to look at the fields of flowers."

"Flowers and food seem to be the big thing now."

"I use edible flowers in salads, and they always make a plate more beautiful. Food has to look good as well as taste good."

"I can't think of anything you do that isn't."

"Are you trying to charm me, Mr. Harrison?"

He tilted his head to the side. "What if I am?"

Melia thought a moment. He wasn't the only charmer around. "It might be working."

"Good." He let a heartbeat pass. "Why don't we go by Pike Place Market and pick up something for lunch and then take the drive together. Stop somewhere for a picnic."

Melia hesitated; then she nodded. She wanted to know what was going on with this man. She couldn't find out from a distance.

"I'll pick you up at your house in a half hour."

Pike Place Market was a bustling mass of confusion on Saturdays. A favorite tourist stop, the locals had to dodge them. Melia and Taylor selected smoked salmon, cream cheese, fruit, vegetables, and olives for their picnic. Taylor also selected a bottle of wine and bottled water. Before long, they were edging their way through the snarl of traffic out of the city.

"Tell me about your job," Taylor said.

She turned her head to look at him. "I work at a gourmet

food store. One of my duties is to teach classes on how to prepare gourmet cuisine, with a minimum of fuss."

"Are they popular?"

"Very."

"Have you considered trying to do a show on the Food Network?"

"That's my next step. It's difficult to get a spot."

"I don't see many black chefs there, not that I really watch it."

"I don't know if there are any right now. Those who actually teach cooking, anyway."

"Amazing that with the number of black cooks over the years, they can't find one for a cooking show."

"Isn't it though?"

They finally came upon a field of blooming irises, daffodils, and tulips, perfuming the air and forming carpets of vibrant colors. The vista rivaled Van Gogh's famous fields of Arles in the south of France. Melia forgot that she wasn't alone until she felt Taylor's gaze on her. She got a little tingle in her stomach. He parked beside the road to let her enjoy the view. Then he drove on and stopped at a picnic table in a little park beside the road.

"Is this okay?"

"Perfect," she said, her throat husky. What was his game? And why did she have this queasy feeling in the pit of her stomach, especially knowing there were secrets hidden behind his eyes?

Chapter 3

A month had passed since jazz night, and Melia finally accepted her first online date with Jeffrey. Not much of a date, really, since they were only meeting for half an hour over coffee at Starbucks. She wished she hadn't mentioned the date to Lisa, but she shared a lot with her friend. They'd met during Melia's first job out of college. They had both worked for one of the dotcoms that had littered the Seattle landscape. Like many others, the company went bust. That was when Lisa had taken her savings and opened her accessory shop, and Melia had started to teach cooking classes at Modern Gourmet.

"I'm going with you, girl," Lisa said firmly.

"I'll be fine. I don't want you to go out of your way for that."

"Girl, please. You didn't let me meet my date alone, did you? Even though he turned out okay, you never know."

"We're meeting in a very public place. People are always coming and going."

"You don't know him. Remember the weirdo that wanted you to dress like a hooker? I'll be there."

The night before the date, Lisa called saying she couldn't make it. Melia dressed carefully in a colorful blouse and jeans, opting for a casual look. As she stepped out of her condo, Taylor came down the hallway toward her.

"You didn't leave very much time to get there," he said, glancing at his watch. He, too, wore jeans, but with a sweater that emphasized the breadth of his shoulders.

"What are you talking about?"

"Your hot date." His glance slid rapidly over her body before he met her eyes. "You look nice," he said.

Goose bumps danced over Melia's skin, and she cleared her throat. "Lisa told you." It wasn't a question. The last couple of weeks she'd tried, unsuccessfully, to forget Taylor.

"Your bodyguard, at your service, madam," he said with a mock bow.

Melia couldn't figure him out. She still didn't know what he wanted from her. "Why are you doing this? You don't even know me."

"Thought it'd be the neighborly thing to do. Besides, who but you will fix delicious gourmet meals for me once a month?"

"I do it for the group. I get forty guinea pigs to experiment on." She glanced at him. "I can't take you on my date to meet another man," Melia complained.

The door across the hall opened. Blair tossed a paper bag toward her. She barely caught it before the door slammed shut so hard the walls shook. She was almost afraid to open the thing.

"What's in there?" Taylor asked.

She lifted out a can of pepper spray and a key ring with an alarm on it.

"You get into trouble, just press the button. It'll get him moving," Blair called through the door. He must have been peeking through the peephole.

"Thanks, Blair," Melia called out.

"Be careful."

Shaking his head, Taylor took her elbow and steered her toward the elevator.

"You must not date very often if he feels this occasion calls for an armored truck."

Melia ignored his statement.

"I'll just drink coffee and read a paper or something while I wait for you. I won't embarrass you."

"I appreciate the offer, but it's unnecessary. You and Blair are overprotective."

"Don't forget Lisa." As if Lisa's word was law, he gathered her elbow in his hand and steered her down the elevator and to his car. Enclosed in the confines of the new-smelling car with its cream leather seats, she was very aware of him, the scent of his cologne, and how he confidently maneuvered the SUV into the traffic.

The area in the U District was darker than she remembered. It had been a long time since she'd spent any time there at night. At least they had cleaned it up in the last few years.

"I'm going to go in first. A couple of minutes later, you follow me."

"Ashamed of me or something?"

"It doesn't seem right."

Taylor held up his hands. "Okay."

Melia opened the car door and got out; then Taylor went looking for a parking space. Parking was horrible. As she walked, Melia wondered about her date's personality and whether they would be as compatible as she and Taylor seemed to be. It was dark on that side of the building and she was so deep in thought that she didn't see the man approaching her until the last minute. She picked up her pace, but he walked quickly toward her. She searched in her handbag for her pepper spray, but she hadn't been careful about where she'd put it. Then she remembered it was in the paper bag. The paper crackled as she tried to retrieve it. All the while she became more and more aware of the man.

His hat was pulled low over his brow, and his collar was pulled up around his ears, covering most of his face. He might not be wearing a ski mask, and he was certainly more subtle than the men who'd robbed the gourmet store, but she still saw trouble coming. She should have waited for Taylor. At this point, she could either turn and walk in Taylor's direction or she could keep going. She started to jog, but suddenly the man sprinted toward her like a greyhound. Before she could break into a full run, he was upon her and she was struggling for her life.

She tried to yell, but his hand covered her mouth as he dragged her back. Dragging her feet on the gravel, she tried to slow his progress, but he was so much stronger than she was. The thought of biting his hand occurred to her, but the grip over her mouth was too firm.

Lord, why hadn't she waited for Taylor? Was her attacker going to rape her or kill her? *Don't panic. Stay calm*, she thought, but those words didn't mean a damn when she was in trouble. Panicking was the worst thing she could do, but how could she not under the circumstances? *Think, Melia, think!* Suddenly, she went slack. Surprised with carrying the full weight of her body, he almost fell, and Melia felt herself slipping as well. Then she felt the key ring with the alarm in her hand. She pressed the alarm button. The alarm's ear-splitting shriek rent the air.

The man's hand slipped from her mouth, and for a second he stood frozen. She drew in a deep breath and screamed at the top of her lungs, not realizing no one could hear her screams over the alarm. Quickly she crawled away and attempted to rise to her feet. He caught her, pulling her back, and hit her upside the head before he covered her mouth again. Melia was hitting and kicking at him, but her struggle didn't faze him. He was much heavier and stronger. But he couldn't stop the alarm, and almost immediately Melia heard footsteps.

"Hey!" Taylor's welcoming voice called out. "What the hell's going on?" And then his feet were pounding rapidly toward them.

Suddenly, Melia was tossed on the ground again. Trying to gather strength in her weak legs, she crawled toward Taylor.

He grabbed both her arms. "You okay?"

She felt like saying, "hell no." But she nodded instead.

Taylor looked ready to charge after her attacker, but she wasn't going to stand there alone. She grabbed onto him and held on with every ounce of strength. By God, if he left, he was dragging her with him. The piercing alarm also brought several people to the scene.

After the commotion died down and they made it inside the Starbucks, the proprietor called the police. *Another police report*, Melia thought. It seemed she was finding trouble all around. And it was a funny thing that her date never showed.

Melia was quiet on their way from the coffeehouse.

"I know everyone thinks the attacker was a . . . Well, did he seem familiar at all?" Taylor asked.

Melia shook her head before she realized his attention was focused on the road.

"No." She knew that most rapes were carried out by people the victims knew. But she didn't know that man.

"Are you sure?"

"Of course. If I knew him . . ."

"What is it?" Taylor asked.

"It's just, most of his face was covered. I couldn't see much except the blond mustache. The only other thing I saw was brown hair peeking above his collar."

Taylor nodded.

He turned on East Madison.

"This isn't the way home."

"I know."

"Where are we going?" Fear still clenched her stomach.

He reached over and gathered her hand in his. "Relax. I haven't had dinner. And I don't think you have either."

"I couldn't eat a thing." Just the thought of food made her want to gag.

Squeezing her hand, he said, "You need to relax. You're not alone right now. I know it was a harrowing experience."

"I don't want to be around people," she said. "I just want to go home. I'll fix dinner for you."

"Not in the shape you're in. We'll order in."

"For me, cooking is therapy." His hand was warm and helped chase away the chill racking her body.

Taylor sighed. "All right. We'll go home." But he wouldn't allow her to cook. He ordered Chinese.

Taylor was happy to see that Melia had an appetite after all she'd been through. She'd changed out of her torn jeans and had showered off the dirt. Except for her dazed eyes, she almost looked like her normal self again. When he'd heard that alarm, his heart had nearly stopped. He wanted to follow that piece of scum who'd been struggling with her and beat him to a pulp. But he couldn't leave her. She still wasn't ready to be alone.

"When did Blair's agoraphobia set in?" Taylor asked.

Melia placed her chopsticks on the table. "It started with panic attacks."

"What caused them?"

He saw the despair in her shoulders. "He was the one who found my parents."

Taylor frowned. "I don't understand."

"My parents died several years ago. The police recorded it as murder/suicide. They think my father killed my mother then shot himself."

"How horrible."

"Except I don't believe it." She boldly met his eyes. "Not for a moment."

He'd thought she was a kind and compassionate woman. Now he saw another side of her. Defiance.

"We never believe our parents are capable of doing something so horrible; otherwise, it's as if they didn't love us enough."

"It's nothing like that. Someone said my mother had an affair with another man. I know that isn't true. I know there are bad marriages. But my parents' was the best. They truly loved each other. I'm not saying they didn't go through the usual problems most marriages experience. I'm not that naïve. But they weathered the storms. They worked through them. They were each other's best friends. I felt loved because I knew they loved each other first."

"You're talking romance novels now."

"No I'm not. A lot of people put more energy into friendships than they do marriage partners."

When he nodded, she said, "Why is it so impossible to believe that the opposite sex can feel that way about each other? I mean I cook for a living. I'm expected to teach gourmet cooking techniques. If I don't work at it, it won't happen, and I'll lose my audience and my students. I'm always experimenting around here. I use my friends to test recipes. So why shouldn't I be successful? You're a lawyer. Are you telling me you don't do everything you can for your clients? Are you telling me you don't go above and beyond the eight-hour day to make your practice successful?"

"I do. But you're talking about . . ."

"So you say we can put that much effort into our jobs, but we can't put it into each other. The person we stand with before God, parents, other relatives, and friends, and promise to love until death. Is that what you're telling me?"

"You're making it too simple. Personalities clash. Don't forget pride. We practice what we learn from our families, our environment. And that's difficult, nearly impossible, to unlearn," Taylor said. "By nature, most people are stubborn. Emotions are different in our jobs. At home we're with the people we love. And whether you agree or not, we're less forgiving of spouses because our expectations are so much higher than with virtual strangers."

Her chin jutted forward. "That wasn't the way it was with my parents. They were there for each other. They wouldn't leave me an orphan, and they wouldn't hurt each other that way."

It was time to steer the conversation to another topic. There wasn't an answer to her parents' deaths. Death was final. Period.

"Do you have other relatives nearby?"

"No. Some distant cousin somewhere in the South. I've never met her. And you? Do you have siblings?" Melia asked.

"Three sisters and a brother."

"Do they live in Portland?"

"My sisters do. My brother is a stockbroker in New York."

She looked wistfully off into space. "It must be nice having siblings to fight with."

"I guess we're lucky, although growing up, we didn't always feel that way. But I love them and my nieces and nephews."

She smiled. "I bet you're the favorite uncle."

"Right now I'm on everybody's hit list. They accuse me of not spending enough time with them." He chuckled. "My mother is ready to disown me."

"Never."

Taylor had tried to get her to relax, and it was finally working, but he needed answers. His suspicion was that her Internet date was the attacker.

"Let's check your e-mail and see if your date sent a message."

"Sure." In the den she logged onto her computer and then clicked on her e-mail.

"There's a message from him," she said. "It was sent just before we left. He said a family emergency came up, and he wouldn't be able to meet me."

"How convenient."

Taylor was still in a quandary about the connection between Melia and Palmer. She seemed innocent. There was nothing about her that indicated she was using the older man as a sugar daddy. And now that he knew of her financial resources, he realized she didn't need Palmer's money. It was the other way around. Clearly, he'd used her.

She was one of Palmer's victims. How many other victims were out there?

"Who do you think attacked her?" Ralph asked.

Taylor settled on the chair beside the bed. "I don't know.

But in the morning's paper, it said a woman had been raped within a mile of the coffeeshop."

"My word. Thank God you were with Melia," his mother said.

"Yeah."

"Do you think it's a good idea to get to know this woman socially?" Ralph asked. His grandfather seemed stronger today. "After all, it could have been staged for your benefit."

"I don't think so. She was really shaken. He left marks around her neck." Then Taylor remembered the pepper spray and alarm that Blair had conveniently given her. As a single woman, she was out alone all the time. Why wait until then to give them to her? But she seemed truly shaken. Was she that good an actress?

"Getting to know her is the easiest way to keep tabs on her," Taylor finally said.

"Be careful. I'm an old man, but you have your entire life ahead of you."

"I'm careful. I'm still going through the records. It seems her parents sold land to a real estate investment group just before they died. A shopping center and condo complex is located there now. I'm looking up the investors."

"I remember Palmer talking about it years ago. Such a tragedy. It happened just before the daughter's senior year in college."

"According to Palmer's notes, the same investment group has been trying to get her land on Bainbridge Island. But she won't sell."

"I overheard a conversation about this one day when I was in the office. Palmer was really upset about it."

"Why? It was just another business deal. He was just the go-between. No reason for him to get personally involved."

"According to the paperwork, he invested with the group from time to time. He invested in Melia's parents' land, for example," Taylor said.

"A while back, there was some unfavorable talk about that investment group. It was over ten years ago, and I think some people were forced out. That was before Palmer became their attorney. As a matter of fact, I think it was because of their problems that they hired Palmer. I haven't heard anything since then." Ralph took a deep breath, then yawned. "I'm tired. We'll talk more about it later."

Taylor grasped the older man's hand. "Take care, Grandpa. I'll stop by later."

Ralph nodded, and before he tucked the papers in his briefcase, Taylor heard a light snore. He stood beside the bed fondly looking down at him and remembered summers of sightseeing, fishing, crabbing, boating, and camping out under the stars with his grandparents. With a busy law practice, how did he find the time? Ralph's life had slowed almost to a crawl since his wife died. Taylor should have carved out more time to spend with him.

Ralph's neighbor had stopped by earlier, and he had seemed more irritated than welcoming. Taylor thought it was a good thing the woman was interested in his grandfather. Left on his own, Ralph would whither away in that rambling old house of his. But the older man still pined for his late wife. They'd been married for more than fifty years. Her pictures were prominently displayed on his bedside table. My God, just the thought of being married to someone that long sent chills down his spine. On the other hand, they'd shared a lifetime of unforgettable memories. Experiencing new things had started to ease Ralph's grief. He'd started to play golf with retired lawyers, judges, and some of the members of his church.

Would he recover enough to play golf again, or any of the activities he enjoyed before the accident? Taylor also wondered how Melia fit into the equation. Last night, while listening to her talk about her family, he'd thought she was the most innocent person on earth. Was she as innocent as she seemed?

Seeing his grandfather so wiped out made Taylor return to the office, where he called a client who complained that one of his customers had missed a sizable payment.

"I understand how you feel," Taylor said, "but according to

your contract, the payment isn't late. If you go to court, you'll more than likely lose."

Taylor listened to the client explain the mistake another attorney had made on the advance fee his buyer was required to pay.

"I realize the contract was badly written, but both parties signed it, and it's binding."

Taylor listened some more.

"All right," he finally said. "If you want me to take it to court, I will. I just want you to be aware of what to expect."

The client paid Palmer a monthly retainer. If the client wanted to take the case to court, Taylor was obliged to do so, even though he thought it was useless. So when he hung up, he pulled out the contract and started on the suit. So much wasted time.

Hours passed before he could return to his research about the real estate investment group and locate a folder with some useful information.

"Finally."

He carefully scanned the pages. It seemed most of Palmer's questionable dealings were through the Sims, Melia, and the real estate investment group. It began eight years ago. The Sims' had purchased land from Melia's parents and had brokered a shopping center and condo deal. It seemed Leticia Sims had spearheaded the deal.

Melia had cooked up a storm that day, preparing the southern favorites her mother and she both had loved. Still upset over the assault, she had been restless and couldn't sleep. She needed the soothingly familiar routine and the pungent aromas of her "comfort food." She realized this was something she and her mother had in common. When her mother was upset, she would always cook.

A knock at Melia's door jarred her from her reverie. She

dried her hands on a paper towel and then opened the door to reveal Taylor and Blair.

Blair rushed past her, and she was so surprised that she stood in place a full minute before she closed the door. Blair didn't leave his apartment without help, yet there he was pacing her living room floor.

Taylor entered more slowly. He wore a dark suit.

"Recovering okay?" he asked.

"Much better."

They walked slowly toward Blair. He was taking deep breaths but managed to thrust a wrapped box toward Melia.

"What's this?"

"A gift. Open it." Blair's hair was in disarray. His shirt had a stain on it. And his eyes looked as if he'd pulled another all-nighter.

"What did I do to deserve a gift?" she asked.

"Nothing. You don't have to do anything." Blair glanced toward the kitchen. "I smell food."

"Have you eaten today?"

"Snack cakes. Maybe some peanuts."

"Come on in and help yourself. I fixed enough to feed an entire class."

She set the box on the kitchen counter. He'd gone to the trouble of having it wrapped. Carefully, she peeled the paper away. "Blair . . . I don't know what to say."

"Where's the salt?"

"Be still my beating heart. I hid it. You use too much."

Blair checked the cabinets until he unearthed it.

"Thanks for the gift," Melia said, shaking her head.

Blair grunted. With his plate full, he grabbed a soda from the fridge and pulled a barstool up to the counter.

"Homemade rolls," he said and groaned as he bit into the buttered bread. "Your mama's recipe."

Melia shook her head. She wondered about the depth of his and Christina's conversations. It took all kinds, she thought, then warmed. He cared enough to order her a gift. She approached him and kissed him on the cheek, then hugged him.

He looked at her curiously.

Five hours later, Audie rushed over to Melia's.

"Why didn't you call and tell me somebody attacked you?" he said angrily.

"I didn't want to worry you. Who told you?"

"Blair called. Said Taylor took you to meet some guy who stood you up."

"I'm grateful he was there."

"No more of this Internet dating. It's dangerous."

"Not always. Besides, the man didn't even show up. He canceled by e-mail just before I left, only I didn't check my messages."

"You still should have called me. I could have spent the night here."

"This is a secure building. I'm perfectly safe here."

"I got in. Secure buildings aren't as secure as you'd like to think."

"You're my brother. Security knows you. Blair even gave you a key to his apartment. Besides, I don't think of you as a mad attack dog."

"That's beside the point," he said only slightly appeased.

"Thanks for caring, Audie."

He frowned. "Of course I care. Why would you say something silly like that?"

Just as he was about to rip into her, the doorbell rang again. Still on his tirade, Audie answered it to find his parents.

"Pack your bags. You have to move back home with us. I don't know what I would have done if anything had happened to you," Leticia said.

"I'm fine, really I am," Melia answered. When she left Leticia's arms, Earl pulled her into his warm embrace. Melia closed her eyes against threatening tears.

Earl eased his hold and linked his arm around her shoulder as they walked toward the living room. "Now, dear. Leticia and I have talked it over. We think it's best that you move back in with us," he said.

When Melia started to protest, he said, "Just for a little while. Just to make sure you're safe and no one is after you. We live in a secure neighborhood. And I'll be there to protect you."

"You don't know what your offer means to me, but I'm safe in this building. I wasn't attacked here."

He smiled. "Well, think about it. We'll talk it over. Now what is that I smell? Have you been cooking again?"

She groaned.

"You're not as relaxed as you want me to believe," Earl said.

"I'm better now that I got it out of my system."

Again, there was rapid-fire knocking at the door before a key opened it. This time Blair burst through the door as if an attacker were after *him*. He had not been out of his apartment without Melia walking him to hers in years. Just the fact that he came to see her twice in one day was humbling.

"Well, now that you're all here, why don't you stay for dinner?" Melia swept her hand toward the kitchen. "I've cooked enough for an army."

"At least it will give us a chance to talk some sense into you," Blair said.

"Why don't you boys set the table while I show Melia this beautiful sweater I bought for her," Leticia said. "I went shopping today, and I know it will look absolutely darling on you."

"You didn't have to do that, Leticia."

"I wanted to." Giving Melia gifts seemed to give Leticia pleasure. It was always something: gold earrings, Coach and Gucci purses, or Hermès scarves. Leticia loved fine things, and when she bought gifts, they were never second rate.

Melia felt ashamed that she thought Leticia didn't want the best for her. Just because she wanted the land didn't mean she didn't care.

Chapter 4

Melia served after-dinner drinks in the library.

"The shipment arrived at last," Audie said.

"Well, great. Where are you going to sell them?" Melia asked.

"I know a guy who distributes leather goods in stores in several cities. He has agreed to distribute my share."

"What's this about shipments?" Leticia asked. "What are you selling?"

"A group of us pooled our money to have leather handbags made in a factory in Haiti. Their depressed economy is even worse after the hurricane, and we wanted to do something to help." Audie shrugged. "It's not a lot, but the woman who runs the factory serves lunch to the employees. And the employees are happy to get the work and a meal each day. The meal alone insures they'll show up."

"Especially since there's so little work to be had in Haiti," Taylor said. He'd arrived twenty minutes after Blair blew in the second time.

"That's for sure," replied Audie.

"Was the factory destroyed in the hurricane?" Earl asked.

"Luckily, no."

"Our church is collecting food and supplies for the Haitians and for the people affected in Florida. Let me know if we can do more," Leticia said.

After dinner everyone lounged in the library as if they were afraid to leave Melia alone.

"Are handbags the only thing you're selling, Audie?" Taylor asked, continuing their discussion.

"They're also making ladies underwear."

"Underwear, what little there is of it, is really hot right now," Leticia said. "I think you're going to succeed at something for the first time."

"Thanks for the vote of confidence," Audie said, his voice laced with sarcasm.

Audie's projects rarely panned out. Every year it was something new. He'd lost a fortune on different ventures. Luckily, his grandfather had left him a small fortune, or else he would be bankrupt by now. Even with his inheritance, Melia wondered how long he'd hold out. But he'd talked her into investing in this venture. Even if she didn't make a profit, it was for a worthy cause.

"Where will your distributor market the goods? Be nice if they could get a major department store," Melia said.

"We're working on that. I'm meeting a buyer for a national department store chain in California next week. In the meantime, we're hoping I can sell the batch I have pretty quickly. Then we'll finance another shipment. Either way, we can keep this little deal going for a while. Taxes are increasing. Economy's going down the drain. Folks are going to want inexpensive quality goods."

He sat beside Melia, elbowed her, and winked. "I'll give you anything you want for free."

"Let's not cut into your profits."

"That's what I like about you. A woman who understands business."

"Can't tell you how much that means to me," Melia said tongue in cheek.

"Taylor, Melia tells me you're from Portland," Leticia said.

"Yes."

"Do you have relatives here?"

"My grandfather lives here," he said.

"He was injured when Palmer had his accident," Melia said.

"How unfortunate. How is he?"

"Recovering well. He's going home tomorrow."

"That's wonderful," Melia said. "He established the law office where Palmer worked, although he retired years ago."

"Did he? Now I remember. An attorney named Johnson owned that practice. We tried to get him to represent our real estate investment group, but he'd already retired."

"Ralph Johnson. That's him."

"I never met him, but I've heard good things about him. It's the main reason our real estate investment group chose Palmer. Who is taking over?"

"I'm clearing up all the open cases. My grandfather hasn't chosen a replacement."

"You're a lawyer. Why don't you take over?" Melia asked.

Taylor was doing well in his practice back home. He hadn't considered moving.

"I'm sure you're established already," Earl said.

"Yes, well. I'm glad Audie and Melia are doing so well," Leticia said, smiling at them. "Neither of you are getting any younger. You're turning thirty this year, aren't you, dears? Got to start thinking about children. I'm ready for grandchildren, you two."

"Mom. I'm not a baby anymore," Audie piped up. "I don't need you to get me a date."

"She's not going to marry Audie," Blair said when he glanced up from Melia's computer. "Did you know you have a bug in here?"

"No."

"I don't see why not," Leticia said, somewhat offended.

"They don't feel that way about each other. Audie's in love with Lisa. Bug's gone," Blair said. "Now it's clean as a whistle."

"Forget the computer," Leticia said. "I thought you were through with that woman, Audie. What is he talking about?"

"What have you got against Lisa?" Audie asked with a sharp look at his mother.

"She's looking for a rich man. She doesn't love you."

"For crying out loud. You've never liked her. How would you know whether she loves me or not?" His face was pinched with anger. "Have you ever spent any time with her?"

"I can sense those things."

"Mom, stop," Blair said. "You can't choose for him."

"He could do a lot better."

"Don't get yourself worked up, dear," Earl said. "They're still young. They don't know what they want at this age."

"You and I were married at their age, for heaven's sake. We had children already."

"Things are different now, dear. This generation likes to live a little before they settle down. It's not a bad thing." He rose, gathered Melia in his arms, and kissed her on the cheek. He'd worn the same cologne forever, and Melia felt comforted by the scent. "It's time for us to leave," he said. "Are you sure you won't change your mind, Melia, and stay with us a few days?"

"I'm fine here. Thanks."

As Melia watched him, she realized that Earl was so unassuming that most times she could forget that he was even in the room. But he was a solid man. On the surface, it would appear Leticia and he were completely mismatched. But once you looked beneath the surface, it was apparent they achieved a balance. He was the rock that held Leticia up. And she was the excitement in his drab world.

"By the way, Melia, we're having another meeting in a week," said Leticia. "Do you think you can make it?"

"Not this time. I'm going to Bainbridge for a few days."

"You haven't stayed there since—"

"It's time," she said quietly.

Leticia touched her shoulder. "I can clear my schedule

and stay with you. I don't think your first time should be alone."

"Thanks for the offer, but I need to do this."

"Of course, you do," Earl said. "We'll be just a phone call away if you need us."

"You've been so kind. I don't know how I would have survived without you."

"You're precious to us," Leticia said. "It's not one-sided, either. You are the daughter we prayed for. As much as we love Audie and Blair, we wanted a little girl, but we weren't that blessed until you came along."

"And I always wanted a sister I could annoy and dis her boyfriends," Audie said. He kissed her on the cheek and left.

As Melia closed the door behind the Sims, she realized Leticia hadn't mentioned the land, but Melia knew she was disappointed that she wouldn't sell it to them.

"I think I'll be leaving, too," Taylor said.

"Me, too," Blair said, turning her computer off. "Been a long day."

"Thanks for the fabulous dinner," Taylor said.

"Stop by before you take your grandfather home. I'll send food. Is he on a restricted diet?"

"No. He'll appreciate it. He's been complaining about the hospital food." Taylor left, leaving Melia and Blair alone.

"Let me walk you home," she told Blair.

When Blair was comfortably behind the closed doors of his apartment and his heartbeat had returned to normal, he held Melia's arm. "Christina wants to come up here this evening, but she doesn't have anyone to ride the elevator with her."

"I'll be happy to bring her up. What time?"

"Anytime. I'll call her."

"So you two are doing fine in the romance department?"

"No, no. It's just, well, I'm going to show her some things about computers. She's nervous using them." The blush on his face revealed more than computers.

"If you say so." She laughed. "Tell her I'm on my way."

As Melia went to the elevator, she breathed a sigh of relief that she'd be alone soon. She didn't understand Leticia. Melia came from a tiny family, but her home was filled with love. Her parents would never dream of setting her up with a man she didn't love. Yet in the name of money, Leticia was trying to marry her son off to her. She didn't know where the hugs and kisses Audie threw around like spring rain came from, but she liked the fact that he was so affectionate. Leticia wasn't as outwardly affectionate as Melia's parents, but she loved them in her own way, and they knew it.

They caught the man who'd raped the Seattle woman Taylor read about in the paper. He admitted having sex with her, not raping her, mind you. But he said he didn't attack Melia. It turned out the woman knew him by sight. He lived in the same apartment complex.

Melia was called to the police station to identify him, and Taylor went with her for support. Several men shuffled out and formed a lineup. The bright lights in the room highlighted their every feature, but Melia had seen her attacker in the dark. She perused each of their faces, but she couldn't identify the man. All of them had mustaches, some of them obviously false.

"Officer, I saw only a blond mustache. I couldn't see the rest of his face."

"Look carefully, anyway. See if you can identify something."

Melia closed her eyes for a moment, trying to reconstruct the events of that night. Opening her eyes, she scrutinized the men again. None of them seemed to match the attacker.

"I only saw him in the shadows. It was dark in the parking lot."

"We'll lower the lights."

In the dim light, she studied the men, trying to remember what her attacker looked like. But she couldn't lie. As much as she wanted to identify the man, she couldn't.

"I'm sorry," she said. "I don't recognize any of them."

* * *

The summer season would soon begin, and Melia felt at loose ends.

When Taylor walked into the apartment after her, he noticed a packed duffle bag near the door.

"Are you going to be okay on the island alone?" he asked.

"Of course."

"How long will you be gone?"

"Most of the week."

He raised an eyebrow. "An entire week? What about your cooking show?"

"The next couple of weeks are already taped. I don't have any classes next week. They do reruns and specials part of the summer, so my schedule isn't quite as hectic."

"Come here," Taylor said, grasping her shoulders and tugging her close. He wrapped his arm around her and kissed the corner of her mouth. "You have had a tough time of it lately." Then he kissed her again. What he'd thought would be light and healing turned hot and heavy. She smelled heavenly, tasted sweet, and had cottony soft skin. He gathered her closer, pressing her curves against his hard length.

"Damn." He kissed her cheek, her forehead. "I didn't mean to do that."

"Why did you?" The husky timbre of her voice almost forced him to kiss her again. But he had never intended to kiss her at all, to feel anything for her. He released her, berating himself for the impulsive gesture. But he wanted to hold her again. Kiss her again.

"I'll see you when you return," he said instead. "Stay out of trouble." And then he was gone.

Soon Melia was on her way to spend the week on the very land the Sims wanted to purchase. The ferry from Seattle to Bainbridge Island was loaded with tourists and locals. Bainbridge Island locals often spent the night in Seattle for a taste of the city. Bainbridge Island was famous as an artist community, with quaint little shops where one could run into artists and writers. But in recent years it had become more populated.

Melia's house was situated on a fifty-acre plot right on the water in a quiet little cove on Puget Sound. The house had been built decades ago as a summer retreat. Three years ago she'd had the house completely renovated, including adding a heating system and insulation. She'd hoped to spend vacations there, but with so many memories of her family still strong, it was just too painful. As much as Leticia touted that she was family, sometimes Melia felt it came with a price. With real family, she didn't have to prove herself or bargain her legacy away. She felt alone, and she needed to be with her memories.

Melia took her suitcase to one of the two first-floor bedrooms and had just opened the windows to air it out when the doorbell rang.

Jessica, Melia's coworker, must have told her grandparents Melia was coming to the island because the Sieversons stood at her front door. Aslin Sieverson wore a chambray shirt. Suspenders held up his jeans. His wife Briana's long gray hair had once been blond. It was coiled in a braid, and several hairpins held it in place on the back of her head. Not a wisp fell out of place.

Mrs. Sieverson opened her arms, and Melia stepped into her warm embrace.

"It's so good to see you, child."

"Been too long," Mr. Sieverson said as he hugged Melia.

"Why didn't you tell us you were coming?" the older woman chastised, clucking her tongue. "I was at the market this morning having tea with Hattie. When I got home, Aslin told me you'd called no more than two hours before. He barely had a chance to cut the grass around the house. Can't have you wading knee-deep in weeds."

"Thank you so much," Melia said. "It was a last-minute decision. Come in. Come in."

"I made a little something for your first night. It's so good for you to be here. I was just saying to the Mr. that this has turned into a sad place. I think of the years you and your mama took long walks with our Jessica. The two of you always romping around picking berries and getting underfoot." She looked around the room. "This is a huge room. It's a house for living."

"It's wonderful to be back."

"The yard hasn't looked the same since your daddy took care of it. That man had a hand for growing things. Will you spend the summer?" Mr. Sieverson asked.

"I don't think so. But I'll be here for a week, anyway."

Mrs. Sieverson took the casserole she'd been holding to the kitchen. "Heat this in the oven," she said, coming back to the living room. "I froze it a couple months ago, when Aslin went hunting."

The couple helped her take the sheets off the furniture and dust.

"You really don't have to," Melia said.

"The quicker the work's done, the quicker you get to enjoy." Not very much was needed because Melia contracted for a caretaker to clean once a month and see to repairs.

"The sunporch needs furniture," Mr. Sieverson mused.

"Should be some pieces in the shed," Mrs. Sieverson added, pointing to the back of the garage.

"I believe there are."

"Well, let's move them here."

Melia found the key, and the three of them trekked to a small building that was nestled to the side and slightly in back of the house. It was a combination garage/storage area and had a small two-bedroom apartment on the second floor. The door squeaked on its hinges when she opened it.

Mr. Sieverson swung the door back and forth. "Gonna have to oil the hinges. I knew there was something here. We'll help you move the chairs and tables."

Melia stared skeptically at the dust and spiderwebs floating in the room until she saw the rocker her great-great-grandfather had purchased for his wife from one of the cargo ships that came to port. *How did such a fine piece end up here*? she wondered. Her grandmother had told her countless stories while she sat in that rocker shelling beans and snapping peas on warm summer evenings. Melia smiled and sighed wistfully.

"Let's take this piece first," she said.

"Fine workmanship. Don't make it like that today," Mr. Sieverson observed while carrying the rocker to the house. He set it in the great room.

Mrs. Sieverson looked at the pictures lined up on the fireplace. "I remember your great-grandmother. She lived to be a hundred. She was sprightly until the day she died. She used to tell me she was born the year after her parents moved here from California. Oh, the stories she'd tell about the Gold Rush. I'd sit at her knee while she shelled beans and listen for hours."

"My father told me those same stories," replied Melia.

"We came from the old country when I was just a girl," Mrs. Sieverson continued. "My parents left Sweden in the 1920s to work in the logging industry, leaving us with our grandmother and her sister. Later my aunt brought us children to America. On the voyage she met the man she later married.

"The last time I saw your parents together," Mrs. Sieverson continued, "was the weekend before they died." She shook her head. "They were walking along the water with their arms wrapped around each other. I said, 'Mr., they're going to have a good long life together just like you and me.'" Mrs. Sieverson set the picture she'd been holding back in place. "You never know."

After the Sieversons left, Melia warmed up the casserole and ate it on the glassed-in porch, which offered a terrific view of the water. The grassy and muddy shore led down to the water, and it was quiet as the fog began to roll in.

But Melia couldn't stop thinking about her parents. When she was finished with her meal, she returned to the porch and sat on a cushioned recliner. She revisited the many summers she and her mother had spent on the island. They'd dine on the porch and watch boats race by. Her father would join them on the weekends. They would walk through the forest. Mother would point out the names of different trees and flowers. She taught her to identify animal tracks. On an old tree were carvings of ancestors from generations back.

They also used to chase each other, making a path through the tall grass and up the lane to an island store for lunch or ice cream. *Fond memories,* Melia thought, with a stab of pain and nostalgia.

Now, although she could see the water, her view was partially obscured by an overgrowth of bushes and trees. She'd ask Mr. Sieverson to cut the bushes and trim the trees. It was too spectacular a view to have it partially hidden.

Being here made her feel warm and loved, as if she were wrapped in a heated blanket, Melia thought. And she didn't have to pay a price to enjoy it, the way she felt she had to with the Sims lately.

Melia yawned, and within minutes she had fallen asleep.

It was pitch dark when Melia awakened. She hadn't meant to sleep on the porch, but the quiet nighttime on the island was so different from the city. The lapping of waves, the chirping of crickets, and the singing of tree frogs soothed her. Stretching, she went into the house. Lights flickered from boats in the sound. Otherwise, unrelenting darkness surrounded her.

She was halfway across the room when she detected a strange odor. Several seconds passed before she realized it was gas fumes. With visions of houses exploding, she grabbed her cell phone and ran out of the house. When she was several yards away, she called the utility company.

"Ma'am, your valve was turned to the wrong position, which is extremely dangerous."

"But I haven't been anywhere near that heater. It was too warm to turn the heat on today."

"Someone turned it on."

After demonstrating how to operate the valve properly, the man left.

Since the fumes were now out of the house, Melia closed the windows, but she wondered how that valve got turned on.

Suddenly, Melia grew still. Who would gain if she was killed? She had no local relatives. Her mother had once mentioned some distant cousin who lived in the South. Melia had never researched the woman because she didn't know her. Melia didn't have a will, so if she were killed, her estate would be held in escrow practically forever until this person was found.

Melia knew she wouldn't be able to sleep, so she made herself a cup of tea and climbed the stairs to the second floor. There were five bedrooms and three baths on that floor. On the third floor, there were two dormitory style bedrooms. On the first floor there were two large bedrooms on opposite sides of the house.

She remembered how the house was filled with people in her grandmother's day. Her grandparents' friends spent summers and holidays at the house.

She descended the stairs and wandered into the great room. The furniture in the great room was arranged into sections, and there was an imposing stone fireplace along one wall. The adjacent dining room was large enough to easily seat thirty.

She sat in the great room in the rocker she'd dusted and polished earlier and selected an old photo album from a bookcase. Slowly, she looked at pictures of her parents. There were also pictures of her grandparents and other ancestors, and many of her. She came from a long line of strong men and women. She'd have to be sure to take the albums with her when she went back to Seattle.

Her parents had been very strong. They were *in* their marriage. Theirs was not like most marriages, where the couple drifted to separate lives. They were always together, really together, emotionally as well as physically.

The rumor that her mother had been seen going out with

another man was just as ludicrous as the idea that in a fit of jealousy, her father killed the woman he loved. Her father wasn't insecure, nor was he crazy. Melia glanced up from the photo album. She wondered what the Sims knew.

Losing her parents had devastated her, but she'd be damned if she'd make her bed there. Instead of crying in her tea about what she'd lost, she was going forward with what she had left—with or without the Sims. Right now she had the Sims, but she knew very well that might change. If their love could be purchased with her land, then it was as stable as the volcano on Mt. St. Helens. She always had the memories of her parents, her ancestors. But the Sims wouldn't be easy to forget. She loved all of them.

Looking toward the fireplace, she began to rock slowly in the rocker. She pulled an afghan around her shoulders. It was as if the rocker was waiting for her to tell stories to her grandchildren. This house was part of her roots, and she was going forward.

Melia put the photo album aside and checked the locks and bottom floor windows before she finally went to bed and quickly fell asleep.

During the week, she experimented with a bunch of recipes and made plans for more cooking shows. She rode her bicycle around the island and even invited the Sieversons to dinner one night. They reminisced about old times. She knew their grandchildren complained that they talked too much about ancient history. Even Jessica complained. But they were Melia's ties to the past. She remembered the old couple visiting her grandparents on many summer evenings, bringing Jessica over to play with her. She and Jessica had become close friends and had explored the island together.

About midweek, Mr. Sieverson showed up at the house early one morning, and he and Melia went clamming. With their catch, Mrs. Sieverson cooked a clam stew over an open fire outside.

She could never sell this house. This tie to the past. The

place where her ancestors settled decades ago. If she didn't
have ties anywhere else, she had them here. But she couldn't
help thinking that this house was built for families to enjoy.

In the week Melia was away, Taylor drove to a nursing home
in the direction of Mt. Rainier to visit a Mrs. Emerline Miles,
who'd sent a letter to his grandfather's firm a few days earlier stating she was being cheated. But when he met with Mrs.
Miles, he found her conversation disjointed. The nurses told
him that she was suffering from memory loss, which had been
the case with another person who'd complained about Palmer.
Taylor had spent the week balancing expenses against what
Palmer had drawn out of the account. All of the expenses had
been legitimate. So why did Mrs. Miles and the other woman
think they'd been cheated?

He drove back to town, wishing he could talk to Melia. He'd
grown quite attached to her lately.

On Sunday Melia awakened refreshed and packed her
bags. She had a mission.

After saying good-bye to the Sieversons, she made her
way to the ferry. After the ferry started across the water, she
bought a cup of coffee and watched the water from the rail.

As soon as the ferry landed, she drove directly to the
Simses' home for Sunday brunch. Originally, she'd planned
to skip it, but Leticia could fill in some of the blanks for her.

"My darling girl. How was your trip to the island?"

"Wonderful. Refreshing."

"Not too hard?"

"I needed to exorcise the ghosts, the fear of returning to a
place that had brought so much joy. I wasn't able to do that
before. The pain was too raw."

"You should have let me come with you." Leticia had
called her almost daily asking to visit her.

"I needed to do it alone."

"Now are you ready to put all that behind you?" she asked with a hopeful desperation in her voice. Melia had noticed from the very beginning that talking about her parents' deaths made Leticia nervous.

"I want to talk about my parents," she said.

Earl's fork clattered on his plate.

"What about them?" he asked.

"The state of their marriage before they died."

"They seemed the same, but people don't always talk about problems," Leticia said. "Not even to friends."

"But all couples go through their trials," Earl warned.

"Something seemed to be troubling your father," Leticia continued. She reached over and grasped Melia's hand in her own. "They didn't want to trouble you, because you were in college. Your mother didn't want to burden you with her problems when you were so close to graduating."

"How come I never noticed that?" Audie said.

"Sometimes you aren't quite as observant as you should be," Leticia informed him.

"We should have been more help to them," Earl said. "I should have talked your father into getting professional help. Taken him to the island to get away from the pressures of his job or whatever. But I thought he was just going through a phase. I've been through my own."

It was painful to even think about the next question, but it needed to be asked.

"There was talk that my mother was having an affair."

"Ah, come on. You don't believe that," Audie blurted out.

Leticia looked away. "Your mother was a dear friend. Think about the joy, the good experiences you shared with your parents. Don't dwell on the unpleasant. As much as we try, we aren't perfect, you know."

"They seemed just about perfect to me," Audie injected. "Your mama was a sweet woman. She wouldn't have done anything like that. And you can take that to the bank."

"He's right. My mother loved my father."

"Audie, honey. Could you get that carton of rocky road ice cream out of the freezer in the garage for me, please? I bought it for dessert, and I can see you've already finished with your meal."

When Audie left the room, Leticia said, "Sometimes feelings change. Especially when a woman goes through the change." She whispered "the change" as if it were a disease, some sacrilege too terrible to say aloud.

"Can't you tell me anything? I need reasons all this happened. It seems so unnatural, such a waste of a perfectly good life."

"They both loved you, Melia. That you can count on," Earl offered. "Sometimes we have to accept things. When death occurs that way, no answer is acceptable."

Melia could agree with that.

She skipped dessert, and a half hour later she was on her way to her condo with a plate for Blair. Poor thing. Because of his agoraphobia, he missed out on most family gatherings. Leticia had trotted in so many psychologists, Blair had threatened to lock her out if she brought any more. She'd finally relented, but Melia knew she still searched for a solution to Blair's problem.

On her drive she passed the property her parents had owned. The property where her parents' home had sat until their deaths. Just before they died, they'd sold the three acres to a developer. According to the Sims, they'd planned to move into the condo where Melia now resided. After Melia had moved out of the house, her mother no longer wanted such a large place to clean. And her father was tired of the grounds upkeep. But her father had told her he was looking forward to caring for the flowers. He was going to plant an English garden. Even then, he'd rise on Saturday and Sunday mornings and walk the grounds with Brownie, their dog, and a cup of coffee—rain or shine. He always said he was looking forward to the day he could do that on a daily basis. He was working toward his retirement. So why would such a man throw all that away even if his wife was having an affair? Why not at least try to patch up the marriage?

She was making too much out of this. Suicide wasn't out of the realm of possibility, but it didn't seem plausible for her family.

Going back to Bainbridge had been good. She'd enjoyed her conversations with the Sieversons. That piece of land was her roots. Maybe she wasn't as alone as she thought.

Leticia hadn't mentioned the land this time. Knowing how much the land meant to Melia, perhaps the older woman had finally given up on making her sell it.

Chapter 5

She was back. Taylor had worried all week that Melia would enjoy the island so much that she'd spend the summer there, which would really cramp his investigation. He was so relieved when she returned, he'd dropped by the florist shop for a bouquet. He wouldn't question his reaction. Of course, the kiss had a lot to do with it. She was no longer a suspect in his eyes, but Palmer was linked to her in some way, and he had to find out how.

He knocked on Melia's door a half hour later. The chic woman he was accustomed to greeting wasn't in evidence. A bandana and skimpy shorts revealing her gorgeous legs greeted him. He couldn't take his eyes off the top that barely covered her breasts. It was a moment before he realized she was talking to him. And she looked totally refreshed.

His eyes finally lifted to her face. "Umm," he stammered. He knew he was acting like a foolish teenage boy but couldn't help himself.

"Hi."

He finally thrust the flowers at her and fixed his mouth to say, "Welcome back."

"They're beautiful," she said, moving back to let him enter, "but I don't know what I did to deserve such a beautiful arrangement." She looked sunny and bubbly, as if she had never been attacked. The island was good for her.

"Let's just say you were missed. And I'd like to take you to dinner."

"I dined with the Sims today. They served a big Sunday brunch. But I can quickly whip up something for you."

"I won't put you to the trouble."

"No trouble. Remember, you're talking to the cook for the working woman."

He chuckled. Ordinarily, Taylor would refuse, but he'd use any opportunity to spend more time with her. He couldn't get his mind off her all weekend, and he didn't like that. When he left for Portland, he planned to do so with no regrets. For now he needed her. But only for now.

"You've twisted my arm," he said, closing the door behind him. He noticed the condo smelled of orange oil as he followed her to the state-of-the-art kitchen. He wondered if she used all the gadgets. She probably did since she was a chef with her very own cooking show. Any number of cookware companies would jump at the opportunity to have their brand name flashed across a television screen, even in a local market.

"Your grandfather settling in okay?" she asked. Her head was buried in the fridge, muffling her voice.

"Improving by the day. May I help you with something?" he felt obliged to ask.

She eyed him, then said, "Sure. Wash up. You know where the bathroom is. I'll get an apron for you."

After he scrubbed his hands, she put him to work washing and tearing lettuce leaves. His mom usually fixed salads with green leaf lettuce or bought the mixed greens already prepared. Melia mixed different lettuce shapes and colors herself and even threw in flower blossoms, like the upscale restaurants did.

"How was your week on Bainbridge? Did you rent a room in a B&B?" he asked.

"I have a house there."

"Lucky you."

"My great-great-grandfather built it. I had it renovated but never used it."

She handed him a washed cucumber.

"It's an English cucumber, so you don't have to peel it."

"You'll have plenty of time to spend there this summer."

"This week was the first time I've spent the night since my parents died," she said quietly.

"Too many memories?"

She nodded.

He sounded as if he really understood.

"The Sims want me to sell it to their investment group, but that land meant too much to my family, and I'm the only one left. My roots are there. I have nothing left but memories and that fifty-acre piece of real estate. I know it's only dirt." The relief at sharing her concerns with someone was instantaneous.

"Wars have been fought over dirt, and memories are powerful incentives. Is there any reason why you'd have to sell?"

She shook her head. "No."

"Then don't."

"I know I shouldn't feel this way, but I feel so guilty. The Sims have done so much for me, and I haven't given them anything in return."

"There's no room for checks and balances in relationships. We do what we can and let the rest go. We don't know what effect we have on people who pass through our lives. You think nothing of what you do for Blair, but if you didn't live across the hall, poor Blair would never leave his condo. He wouldn't have an outlet for his music. Now he plays for an audience, and more importantly, he enjoys it—thrives on it. He can sit for hours playing the sax. And if it weren't for you, he wouldn't have Christina, a woman who worships the ground he walks on. You buy groceries for him, even clothes. You do more for him than his own family," he said.

"You noticed."

"Impossible not to. As much as Audie loves his brother, he doesn't give him that kind of attention. Leticia and Earl do even less. Yet, you wouldn't think of asking Blair or the Sims for payment."

"I never thought of it that way because it's a two-way street."

"And look at Christina. The poor woman would never ride the elevator if not for you. You do so much for so many people." He caught her chin in his hand. "Yet you don't even see your value." He caressed her cheek. "We can't think of checks and balances before we take a step. The last thing you should worry about is whether you do enough for the Sims."

"Giving cuts two ways. I don't know what I would have done without their care after my parents died. They kept me sane. For a while I couldn't even function. I stayed with them for a year before I returned to school."

Melia never took credit for the things she did for others. That was one of the things he'd noticed early on. She was the quiet worker bee, while others lorded it over her as if they were the queen bees. She needed to be protected so people wouldn't take advantage. As far as he was concerned, he was the only one in her circle to do the job.

She hypnotized him with those adoring eyes. He didn't realize he was leaning toward her until his lips had touched hers. She tasted as sweet as he'd dreamed she would.

Her arms came up around him. Kissing and caressing her, his blood pressure spiked.

"Who are you, Taylor Harrison?" she asked, a bit breathless.

"A man who's bewitched by you," he said softly, then kissed her lips again.

"What's your connection to Palmer Wainwright?" she asked.

Taylor forced himself to pull back. "A better question is what is your connection to Palmer?"

"He was my parents' lawyer. He settled their estate. Now please answer my question."

Taylor rubbed the side of his face. He knew he had to

reveal his purpose sometime, and now was as good a time as any. "Palmer was my grandfather's partner. My grandfather was on his way to meet with him when their cars collided in the accident."

"What are you saying?"

"Palmer tried to kill my grandfather."

"My Lord, why?"

"That's what I'm trying to find out," he said. Taylor realized that he might be making a big mistake, and that he might be letting his body override his common sense, but for some reason he trusted Melia.

"Have you ever questioned the police's theory about your parents' deaths?"

"Over and over. I still don't believe my father murdered my mother and then committed suicide."

"Why did they come to that conclusion?"

"I guess because the gunshot to my father's head was close range. And they said there was gunpowder residue on his hand. But there were other things that didn't add up." She told him about her parents' decision to move into the condo and her other doubts. It was a relief to talk to someone outside the family who could offer an unbiased opinion. Someone who wasn't trying to make excuses or make her feel as if she was grasping at straws.

"You have to understand," she continued, "that my parents and I were close. They wouldn't have made a decision like that without telling me about it, even if it were a foregone conclusion."

"It's not too far out of the realm of possibility for parents to buy a smaller house after the children leave."

"My father loved that house, the yard even more. They always said they would retire there and spend their time between there and Bainbridge Island. That house was part of his heritage. His grandfather built that house. He wouldn't have sold it to a developer."

"Did the police look into your allegations?"

Melia sighed. "They treated me like a distraught daughter. And I was. I guess to people who deal with grief on a regular basis, I sounded like a babbling idiot. But they overlooked so many facts. Now a developer wants to buy my land, and I'm not going to sell it."

"It's your land, your heritage. Even I can see it means a lot to you. I commend you for taking your time, Melia. Listen to your instincts. Don't be coerced into making a decision you'll regret later. Once it's gone, there's no turning back."

The next day Taylor drove to a nursing home in Seattle. Maggie Allen's son had called from New York. Evidently, one of his mother's old friends had stopped by his office and informed him that some of his mother's valuable jewelry was missing.

The nursing home was rather upscale. The grounds were well kept and colorful. He introduced himself to the receptionist, and after a call to Mrs. Allen, he was allowed to go to her room.

"Did you say you're taking over for Palmer Wainwright?" she said, a little too loudly.

"Temporarily, anyway," Taylor responded.

"Who's taking over after that?" she asked.

"I'm not sure yet, but someone will contact you when the change occurs." He relaxed in the seat she'd offered him. "How are you, Mrs. Allen. Do you have everything you need?"

"They jail me here and forget me," she said.

"You aren't forgotten," Taylor informed her. "Your children are concerned."

"Humph. Rarely see them," she said, rubbing her already red eyes. "Spend the best years of your life raising them, and they forget you're alive until some jewels they're going to inherit go missing."

"About the missing jewelry," Taylor cut in. "When did you realize they were gone?"

"I just misplaced them. My son shouldn't have called you. He should mind his own business. If some of my jewels are missing, I know how to report it."

"Do you know exactly which pieces are missing?" he asked.

"Nothing's missing."

Getting information out of her was like pulling teeth. Why wouldn't she report her missing jewelry? Perhaps she was afraid.

Taylor changed tactics. "Do you feel safe here?"

She nodded. "Never had any problems."

"Are you being treated well? Because it's my responsibility to make sure you're comfortable."

"In the lap of all this luxury, why wouldn't I be comfortable?" she asked.

"Are you missing anything else?"

She stood. "I'm not missing a thing. But the bus is going to the mall. I have some shopping to do."

Taylor retrieved a card from his pocket. "Here's my phone number. He scribbled his name above Palmer's. "If you need anything, anything at all, call me."

"I will," she said. There was a quick knock, and the door opened.

"Ooh whooo," someone called out from the foyer. "I've got a little present for you. Had a helluva time getting this through without getting caught."

A brown paper bag preceded her in the living room. When she saw Taylor, the woman, who was dressed in the nursing home's uniform, tucked it in the folds of her skirt.

Mrs. Allen's eyes were bugged out. That vacant look was gone, replaced by fear.

"Afternoon," Taylor said.

"Thanks, dear, for getting me the bottled water. I don't like the city water," she said to Taylor.

"I understand," Taylor said. "Neither do I." He nudged the bag from the nursing home attendant, who looked questioningly from Taylor to Mrs. Allen. "I'll handle this." Taylor opened the paper bag to find a bottle of expensive Scotch. For the first time, Taylor closed the distance between himself and Mrs. Allen. The smell of liquor filled the air. The odor was in her clothing and on her skin. *She must spend her days drinking*, he thought.

"That explains where your jewelry has gone. You're trading it for alcohol."

"Don't be a tattle and get the woman in trouble."

"I may need to look into other accommodations."

"When you're paying the kind of money I'm paying, one place is the same as the next. Don't waste your time. If I want booze, I'm going to get it no matter where I am. I'm a grown woman. I can do what I want to do, and that includes drink."

Sadness swept over Taylor. He wondered if his grandfather would feel that way one day. That he had nothing left to live for. That he was living on borrowed time. That no one cared.

It was sad, really, when the old were tucked away out of sight. Mrs. Allen's life was withering away with little left but hours that stretched like weeks. And her son was only concerned about the jewelry. Not once had he inquired about his mother's well-being.

"You rarely leave your room, do you?"

"The room's fine."

"Do you participate in activities they arrange here? They have lots of things for you to do."

Mrs. Allen shrugged. "I don't make friends easily. So I keep to myself."

"I'm going to get someone to work with you. Pick out some activities you used to enjoy or always thought you'd do once you retired. You're still a healthy woman. There's plenty you can do. I understand you used to work on many committees through the years, the PTA, RSVP, school tutors. I'm sure they can use your skills here."

"I'm going to be late for the shuttle," she said.

Taylor walked her to the shuttle; then he talked to the

nursing home administrator about the alcohol, concerned that it might conflict with her medication. He asked the administrator if there was an AA program at the nursing home and she informed him that there was. He also asked her to work with Mrs. Allen in finding something that interested her. Maybe even encourage her to head a committee. The administrator promised she would get her more involved.

Taylor assured her he would make weekly visits until he was sure Mrs. Allen was improving.

Audie passed Lisa's accessory store in the small shopping center on the ground floor of a high-rise office complex on his way to a meeting on the top floor. There was also a gym, a couple of clothing stores, shoe stores, a drug store, a barber, a shoe shine stand, and numerous restaurants and fast food establishments, all located on the first floor.

He was an accountant. He loved his work, and he was good at it. At least he was good at something, he thought. But his dream wasn't to push numbers for the rest of his life. He wanted to be a businessman much like his mother. She was so good at it, unlike him.

After he left the meeting, he stopped at Lisa's store. She was demonstrating various ways a woman could tie a scarf around her head. Lisa captivated his attention. She was a talented woman. She belonged in sales. She was patient, observant. He'd noticed that from the very beginning. She was also a beautiful woman, with a dark brown complexion, and her movements had an underlying grace and sexiness. The play of her fingers, the lovely curves of her body, her smile, they all aroused him. The one night they had spent together still plagued him—still kept him from sleeping months later. And it fed him erotic dreams once he did doze off. He couldn't get that woman out of his mind, nor did he want to.

Too bad his mother couldn't stand her. Too bad his mother was set on him marrying Melia. He couldn't drum up the sexy images of Melia that came naturally with Lisa. If only Lisa liked him just a little. The truth was, she couldn't stand the sight of him. So why had she gone to bed with him in the first place?

Audie gave a cursory look at the other shops. He didn't usually shop in that mall. Lisa's little store was about the size of one of the dollar stores, but if she had the right support she could go even further. He was surprised she got as much business as she did, tucked away in a corner the way she was. When he'd come by earlier, the place was packed. Now one late lunch customer was still there. He waited for her to leave.

"Well, well, well. What brings you to this side of town?" Lisa said when the woman left. The scarf tied around her head hid her hair, but at the same time it highlighted the fine shape of her face. Every time he saw her, he admired her beauty.

"Just passing through. Didn't know you worked here." He glanced around, deciding to goad her. "The boss taking a lunch break?" he asked.

"You're looking at her."

He sniffed and then checked out the place again. "It's okay."

"Did you stop by just to aggravate me?"

He crowded her space. "Stop pretending. You know you're glad to see me."

"You think far too much of yourself, probably the only one who does."

"So do you, baby."

"You better use that line on Melia. She's the only one naïve enough to believe it."

"She doesn't believe it, and you know it. That's because she doesn't like me the way you do."

"You are so full of yourself. Get out of here."

Instead of leaving, Audie pulled her close and kissed her lightly on the lips. He expected her to resist just on principle, so he didn't allow her time to debate slapping him.

"Catch you later, sugar. By the way, you've got the sweetest lips I've ever tasted." He saw her pick up something, what he didn't know, and aim it at him, but he dashed down the hallway, chuckling before she let loose.

Taylor had been so kind lately, Melia wanted to repay him. It was a real stretch, but she prepared lunch in a picnic basket and took it by his office on the off chance that he was in. She arrived a few minutes before eleven-thirty.

"Good morning," she said to his assistant, a petite woman who wore slacks and a colorful, dressy top. Her hair was braided into five thick braids, and the long strands were coiled on the back of her head. The style suited her small face.

"Is Taylor in?" Melia asked. The name tag on the desk identified the woman as Nadine Jones.

"He just called. He'll be back in five minutes."

"I'm Melia Lucas, his neighbor."

"I recognized you the moment you walked in. You look just like you do on TV, only thinner. I watch your cooking show all the time." She rounded the desk and pumped Melia's hand. "You saved my marriage. My husband and I were eating fast food every night, and he was complaining. But I didn't have the energy to cook after working all day and going to night school. You know how men can be when they're used to mama's home cooking and are too vain and helpless to do for themselves."

"I can imagine."

"Well, I cook at least three meals a week now, and he thinks the sun shines on me."

"I'm happy for you. I brought lunch. Is it possible for me to set it up in Taylor's office as a surprise?"

"I don't see why not. Follow me."

They entered a stately office with mahogany furniture. At least half of the desk was clear. "He's neater than most lawyers. You can use that space. If you touch anything, he'll kill both of us. Lawyers are funny about where they put their papers."

"I won't touch a thing, promise," Melia said as she circled the desk.

"You know, Palmer was always worried about you."

"Yeah?" Melia glanced up from her picnic basket. "Why?"

Nadine shrugged. "I guess he was worried about you being all alone and . . . but you're doing great. People are always talking about your cooking show."

Melia nodded.

"He mentioned your name just before he died."

That was odd, Melia thought. Especially so long after her parents died. Perhaps he mentioned her name when he uncovered the insurance papers.

The phone rang, jarring her out of her introspection.

"Be right back. Enjoy your lunch."

Melia set the picnic basket on the chair and began removing Taylor's lunch. She wondered why he hadn't hit on her yet. She just about fainted every time he came near. And he barely saw her as anyone more than a neighbor. The day was warm, and she hoped the sundress she wore was enough to turn up his temperature.

She unpacked the ice bucket and chilled a bottle of sparkling grape juice, thinking that serving wine for his lunch might be a little forward, especially if he had afternoon court appearances or meetings with clients.

She took out linen napkins and silverware.

Damn. She'd set the ice bucket too close to a file. The condensation was spreading to one of his folders. She picked it up to wipe the water off with a linen napkin. Papers slipped out and fell to the floor.

"Oh, my God." She was trying to do a good deed, and Taylor was going to kick her out. She bent to shove the papers back into the folder, hoping he would be none the wiser, when her name popped out at her.

"What in the world?" Thinking it was the file on her found money, she took a cursory look. Then she saw questions about her parents' deaths. There was a list of investors in Leticia's real estate investment group. She read the names of the investors. Written in pencil was "murder/suicide or murders."

What did he mean by that? She'd already talked to him about it. But why did he make a folder on her?

The papers were in her hand when Taylor walked in the office.

"What's going on?" she asked.

"I see you were going through my files."

"Actually, no. I was wiping the moisture off this ice bucket, and some pages slipped out. What is this about?"

Taylor sighed, then closed the door. "Why don't we sit down?"

"I'd rather take the bad news standing up."

He approached her, took the file out of her hands, and put them on the desk. Then he gathered her hand and led her to the couch.

"If you don't need a seat, I do."

"Has everything been about this? Are you investigating me?"

"Not really. I'm investigating my grandfather's partner, and your name keeps popping up, or at least your family's name."

"How? And why?"

"First of all, Palmer tried to murder my grandfather. Granddad found some complaints from some of his clients. When he approached Palmer, he tried to kill him."

"Oh, my—"

"In the meantime, I'm trying to make some headway through the papers."

"What's this murder/suicide information about my parents?"

"I found several notes from Palmer stating your parents wouldn't sell their land. Then suddenly, a couple of days before their deaths, Palmer does paperwork on the sale."

Melia focused on her hands. "I never believed it happened the way everyone said."

"It's questionable, at the very least."

"Why didn't you just come right out and talk to me about

this? At least I would have known someone besides me questioned what was going on. Why did you pretend you were just another person moving into the building?"

"I didn't know you then."

"You had plenty of time to talk to me after you got to know me."

"I was going to when the time was right."

"So what is the next step in this investigation?"

"I want a document with your parents' original signatures so that I can compare them against the signatures on the deed of sale."

"You think they're forged?"

"I just want an expert to check it out. Once that's done, either it will exonerate Palmer or I'll know to dig deeper."

"I have their signatures on papers at home."

He glanced at the desk. "Thanks for bringing lunch."

Melia stood. "Enjoy it. I've lost my appetite."

He grabbed her hand. "Don't go."

Melia stood by the door a second. "I'm glad for some direction with my parents' murders. I'm glad that I'm not fighting this battle blindly. But I wish you'd had the honesty to come to me and tell me the truth."

"I wish I had, too. But I'm accustomed to working out the details alone before I reveal anything. It's just the way I am."

Melia nodded. She'd begun to develop feelings for him. She'd hoped he felt the same way about her. Obviously, he was only using her. Well, she could live with that.

"Drop the picnic basket off at my house. I'll have the papers ready."

"Why can't you have lunch with me?"

"I promised Blair I'd pick up his groceries."

"He can call a delivery service once in a while. Or let Audie and his mother take turns. You shouldn't have to shop for him every week."

Melia sighed. "What does it matter?"

"I want to have lunch with you."

"I don't want to have lunch with you. The truth is, I'm angry and I'm hurt."

"I'm sorry. I'm not used to . . ."

"What?"

"Sharing. It's true I moved next door to you to gather information. I needed to know how you fit in the puzzle. But . . . I don't know. I stopped being objective. And that shouldn't have happened." He approached her. "I know I'm no woman's prize. My last girlfriend walked out saying she was tired of being alone, feeling alone, because I worked twenty-four/seven, that when I was at home I never actually left work. My sisters call me the Lone Ranger. They said if I didn't stop by to see them and their children, they were going to dump all the nieces and nephews on me for a week."

In spite of her anger, Melia laughed.

Taylor moved closer. "And my mother's threatening to disown me if I don't give her grandkids. I'm used to fighting. I fight for my clients. I fought for my sisters when we were younger. Now I'm fighting for my grandfather. I don't know how to be any other way."

"All of life isn't a battle. Sometimes you can just enjoy it instead of looking for windmills to tilt at."

"There's always another fire to put out."

"Did you ever think fires find you because you're looking for them?"

He shrugged, and his shoulder muscles rippled. "I don't know. I don't consciously go looking for them, but they seem to find me, anyway."

"You're lucky you have so many people who love you."

"Sometimes it seems like a curse. But I know I'm lucky." He grasped her hand in his. "I started out trying to find out about the kind of person you were and your connection to Palmer. But I grew to like and respect you. Have lunch with me."

His voice was so low and seductive, Melia was hypnotized. The subtle scent of his cologne enticed her, and before she knew what hit her, she found herself giving in.

His hands caressed her arms, causing goose bumps to scatter over her skin and ruining her concentration. Warm hands turned her slowly as he bent to kiss her neck.

Standing by the door, he took her in his arms and kissed her again. Shock waves exploded through her. It was as electric as the first time he'd kissed her. She'd never felt emotions this volatile this quickly before. Sometimes when she was with him, she wondered what was happening to her.

She also didn't like the way he'd handled the whole situation about her parents and Palmer, but Melia turned in his arms and gave herself up to what she was feeling, anyway.

She'd deal with the repercussions later.

She was driving him crazy, Taylor thought. He had no intentions of kissing her this way, but he found himself sucked in by her sweetness. She even tasted sweet, and her soft skin was as supple as fine cotton.

He was grateful she forgave him so quickly. She needed a protector. She looked out for everyone else, but who looked out for her? But, he told himself, he couldn't stay. As soon as he found his answers, he was leaving.

"I can't stay," he said, not realizing he'd spoken the words out loud.

"Who asked you to?"

"You entice me like fine wine. As much as I can't afford to get involved, I can't let you go. You're a forever kind of woman, and I can't give you more than right now."

"I'm not asking for anything. Maybe I have my motives, too. If Leticia sees me with you, she'll leave Audie alone to find someone he really loves."

She was giving him what he wanted on a silver platter, yet suddenly he didn't like the feeling of being used. But he wasn't ready to let her go, either.

"For now," he said and pressed his lips to hers.

Chapter 6

Taylor had many more files on Melia and her parents than was warranted by the small amount of business they conducted with Palmer. He gazed at an unfamiliar name scribbled along the side of one file.

"Peter Bowman." He'd seen that name some place before but couldn't remember where. He scribbled it on a pad.

Nadine, his assistant, came in with the mail, and Taylor rifled through the junk, the bills, and everything else until he found a letter addressed to Palmer.

He slid the letter opener through the envelope and opened a letter written in squiggly handwriting, as if the person were arthritic.

Dear Mr. Wainright,

I was told there is a shopping center and condo complex built on the property I own. I haven't given anyone permission to build on my property. Those buildings had better come down and my home had better be restored, as I plan to get out of this place and return there shortly.

If my demands aren't met in a timely manner, I will go to the authorities.

Sincerely,
Emerline Miles

Taylor chuckled. This was the third letter he had received from Mrs. Miles. He'd visit her again soon, hopefully on one of her more lucid days. Judging from the letter, Mrs. Emerline Miles didn't mince words. He was looking forward to seeing her. He liked women with grit. She'd be a character, he thought as he scanned her home address and froze. The street name was indelibly etched in his mind. He'd been staring at it for weeks now. The street was located on the parcel of land that included the acreage that had belonged to Melia's parents.

"We haven't spoken in like forever," Lisa said to Melia as they met at a downtown restaurant for dinner. "How is it going with Taylor?"

"He's just a neighbor," Melia said.

"And what a gorgeous neighbor. What are you doing tonight after dinner?"

Melia glanced up from her menu. "Not much."

Lisa groaned. "Since you have no plans, why don't we go to the movies after dinner."

"Can't."

"What about on Friday, right after work? I have to be home around six, but you get off early on Fridays."

"I promised to do Blair's weekly shopping. He has a date with Christina Friday night. Isn't it wonderful?"

Lisa rolled her eyes. "I suppose you're going to fix dinner for them, too?"

"Of course."

"And you're going to the first floor to coax Christina up the elevator."

Puzzled at Lisa's attitude, Melia frowned. "What is this third degree about? You know how she is about elevators."

Lisa dropped her fork onto her plate. The clatter sounded too loud in their space. "I can't believe you. Let him fix his own dinner. And let the doorman coax Christina up the elevator. That's what they get paid for."

"He isn't going to be patient with her. It's a real ordeal for her to ride the elevator at all. Look at Blair. He still can't go outside. She also needs someone who's kind and patient."

Lisa tossed the menu onto the table. "You're a piece of work, you know that? Get a life, Melia. And let them live theirs."

"Having a life doesn't mean I can't show compassion to others. Besides, I have a life—a wonderful one at that."

"Buying Blair's groceries is the highlight of your day? Get real."

"Why are you always pushing?" Melia asked, laying her own menu aside. "It's okay if I'm helping you, but I can't help my other friends?"

"I don't impose on your time unless I really need help, and you know it. I don't monopolize your life."

"Buying Blair's groceries takes an hour once a week. This is the first time he's asked me to prepare a dinner for him. This date is important. And a move forward."

"I could strangle you. You don't even get it. Even the monthly party at your place is too much. Everybody should bring a dish. You can still experiment with one or two dishes. You shouldn't have to do all the work, Melia."

"Look—"

"The main reason you started it in the first place was so you could bring the entertainment to Blair. He won't go out for it, so he gets his once-a-month fix at your place."

"Is that so bad?" Melia didn't understand why Lisa was so angry.

"Yes. Because he has one more excuse to stay hidden in his apartment. He's not forced out of his safety zone."

"You're strong, a fighter. People like you don't understand

people who don't look for battles around every corner." Melia seethed with anger. "Look, his phobia is serious. It shouldn't keep him from having some kind of life. I don't ask you to put yourself out, so why do you care, anyway?"

"Because I care about you," Lisa said softly, deflating Melia's anger. "You need a life, not one in which you're filling up your schedule just to do something. Start to think about what you want, what you need. You are so busy with incidentals, you don't have the time right now. Besides, Blair isn't weak."

"Let's order dinner. You're preaching, and I don't want to argue."

"Maybe a good fight is what you need."

Melia perused the specials. "The salmon looks good."

"Arggggg."

"I wonder what the catch of the day is?"

The waitress took their orders, and Melia watched Lisa. "Since you want to talk about relationships, why aren't you doing something about Audie? He loves you, yet you let him play this . . . this game with me."

"What game?"

"Don't act dumb. You care for him, too."

"He drives me crazy with his annoying mother always trying to run his life. I can't live with a man who won't stand up for himself."

"Give him a reason to stand up for you. I've seen him do it."

Lisa lapsed into silence.

"Lisa, you keep dating these men you could care less about. They don't care about you, either."

"I don't know. Sometimes dealing with a man's family is more trouble than it's worth."

"Coward."

"There's nothing like a mama who only sees your bank account. I can't compete with that."

"Audie could care less about my money. He has his own."

"Bet you can't say that about Leticia."

"She has money of her own. She's self-made. I've never seen anyone work harder to make it. Trust me, she doesn't need mine."

"Some people never get enough, no matter how much they have."

"Leticia really cares about the people around her. She treats me like a daughter."

"If you say so."

"What now?"

"Leticia doesn't have to lift a finger to help her son when she has her 'daughter' to do everything for him."

"She cares."

"Humph."

"She visits him every week. Because of her animosity toward you, you aren't willing to accept that she does things for him."

"But who shops for him? Who scouted out doctors who would make house calls? It wasn't Leticia."

"Come on, Lisa. You know she helped with finding doctors. She even found a new therapist. Getting Blair to accept him is the problem. You're trying to paint her as an evil villain."

"Not evil, just controlling. I think you're paying a price for her love. And deep down you know it. Maybe one day you'll wake up and see her for who she really is."

Taylor had his briefcase in his hand and was on his way out the door when Nadine beeped him about a phone call from Leticia.

"Afternoon," Taylor said.

"I'm glad I caught you. First, I'd like to know if someone is taking over Palmer's practice."

"My grandfather is in the process of selecting someone. In the meantime, I'm handling everything."

"How long will you be in Seattle?" she asked with an interest Taylor couldn't miss, even over the phone.

He smiled. She was still trying to get Audie and Melia married. It was none of his business, but he didn't like the idea of that at all. "As long as it takes to finish the active cases."

"I see. Well, Palmer has been the attorney for Northwest Coastal Real Estate Investors for the last few years. The partners have asked me to find out if you would handle the next venture for us. It's been delayed somewhat because of Palmer's untimely death."

Taylor already knew that they were interested in Melia's land. Also he was investigating them on behalf of his grandfather, who was his client. He would have a conflict of interest if he were to handle the real estate group.

"I'm sorry. This would be a new case, and I'm not taking on any new cases at this time. I would be happy to recommend someone to you," he said.

"No, no. Someone *will* eventually take over this firm, won't they?"

"It's still up in the air."

"Palmer did such a wonderful job; I hate the hassle of breaking in someone new."

"I understand."

"Well, when your grandfather makes a decision, please inform me."

"I will." Taylor slowly hung up the phone, hoping Melia didn't cave in to Leticia's wishes. Although Melia assured him she was keeping the land, when Leticia started in on her, she could be coerced into changing her mind.

Nadine buzzed him again. "Traffic is crazy out there. If you don't get moving, you're going to be late."

Taylor snagged his briefcase. "I'm on my way."

Every morning that week Melia filmed a cooking show. They were now wrapping up the last one. It had been a tough session. Nothing went right. She had to do more than the normal retakes.

"You've got dark circles around your eyes," Andrea, the make-up artist, said as she put her supplies away. "Didn't sleep well?"

"Unfortunately." Melia had tossed and turned with thoughts of Leticia and her conversation with Lisa.

"You still look a little washed out," Jessica said. "What's with you? You usually sleep like a log."

"I know. Couldn't last night."

Melia had already taken the thick make-up off.

"Girl, you can't go out like that," Andrea said. "Let me at least do a little touch-up for day wear. I'll take care of the circles under your eyes." She planted Melia in a seat. "You're our local celebrity."

The truth was, people often walked up to her in stores. But they weren't intrusive.

"Did you hear about the accident last night?" Jessica asked. "I saw it in the paper this morning."

"Which accident?" asked Melia.

"Parker," Jessica said. "He works with the no holds barred environmentalists who fight just about everything big companies want to do around here. He was in our shop a couple of weeks ago."

"What happened?" Andrea asked.

"They said he was found in the Cascades. He fell a couple of hundred feet."

"How awful."

"The article mentioned that his poor brother found him."

"That's hard to take," said Andrea.

"Sometimes I wonder if seeing my parents dead is what caused Blair's phobia," Melia added.

"You mean he wasn't always like that?" asked Andrea.

"No. He found my parents. Thought I was coming home. He got the weekends confused. He saw the cars outside and the lights on. But no one answered the door. When he went in, he found them."

"My word," Andrea said. "That's a horrible thing to witness."

She applied loose powder to Melia's face. "There. You look like the celebrity you are."

"Girl, please. I'm not even on the Food Network."

"Their loss. You're something else in the kitchen." Andrea grabbed her bag. "Got another show to do. See you later." And she was gone, her long skirt flowing gracefully after her.

"I always wondered why you did so much for Blair. You feel responsible, that you owe him something," Jessica said, dusting powder off the counter.

"That's not the reason. I'd do it for anyone in his condition."

"I know you're giving, but you can't bring the world to him. You should talk him into getting professional help."

"I've tried. Leticia has tried. Nothing's worked. A psychologist wanted to give him anti-anxiety pills, but he hates medication."

"We all have to go there some day." Jessica had a faraway expression on her face as if she'd escaped to her own world.

"You seem despondent today. Is anything wrong?"

"Not really." Jessica studied her hand and bit down on her bottom lip to keep it from trembling.

"Come on." Melia pushed her into a seat. "Talk to me."

Jessica lifted her gaze to Melia before she focused on the far corner of the room. "Mark and I had a fight last night."

"Want to talk about it?"

"It's like he wants to control me. But he wants all his freedom. I can't ask where he goes for long stretches of time. How he spends his days is a puzzle, since he doesn't arrive here until closing."

"Well, ask him. Be up front with him."

"He's drawn the boundaries, and I can't cross them."

"Why do you put up with it? You deserve so much more. You're your own woman."

Jessica shrugged. "I know. Things were great in the beginning. It's just now he seems to be changing. He was so loving and giving. He still is to a certain extent. But, he wants me to move in with him, and I'm not ready for that, especially knowing he will never marry me."

"He told you that?"

Jessica nodded. Melia heard the raw pain in her voice when she spoke next. "No marriage, no children. Ever."

"Can you live with that?" Melia asked. "You aren't still thinking of forever with this man, especially after he's been up front with you, are you?"

"You know, at first it sounded okay. I've dated so many men who put me through hell until I'd given up on marriage and children, anyway. And then the man who's every woman's dream came along, and I was floored."

All this was news to Melia. She'd thought that other than the minor problems Jessica and Mark encountered, that their relationship was pretty good. Not perfect, because she didn't believe in perfect any longer. "What changed?"

"I don't know if . . ."

"Just because he doesn't want marriage doesn't make him bad," Melia said softly. "It may be that you need someone on the same wavelength as you."

"I know I'm not ready to make a home with a man who won't be there."

"Then don't. Living together is a serious step. One you should think about carefully."

Jessica's misery was like a steel weight. "That's why he's so angry with me."

Typical, Melia thought. "Don't give in just because he's angry." Melia understood how men used silence to punish women when they couldn't get what they wanted.

"God, I hate myself for being insecure, but what if he loses interest? I don't want to lose him."

"If he'll go to another woman for that reason, moving in should be the last thing you do. Because he'll eventually leave, anyway. Girl, don't let him manipulate you with anger." She regarded Jessica closely. "You do see it as manipulation, don't you?"

"I suppose so." Her face clouded with unease. "When I told him we needed space, he told me I didn't trust him or love him enough."

"Tell him you've heard that old line. They know how to wring us dry with that one. If he loved you, he wouldn't give you ultimatums."

"I'm sticking to my decision for now."

"Think long and hard before you act."

"But there are so many good things about him. Like he's so concerned for our safety. Every night he comes at closing time to make sure we get safely to our cars. When he's with me, I feel like I'm the only woman alive. Most of the time he's so patient. Don't you agree?"

"Yes. But what a man is to his employees and even to his friends isn't necessarily what he is to a lover. The same man who is a saint to friends could also be a lover's nightmare."

Melia's stomach roiled. It was always easier to see someone else's problem.

Melia hadn't been home ten minutes when Julia Jacobs, a member of Leticia Sims's real estate investment group, called.

"I'll get right to the point," she said. "Ordinarily Leticia would make the offer, but because of your relationship, the responsibility has fallen on me. Leticia won't get involved any longer."

"What is this about?" Melia asked as if she didn't know.

"It's no surprise Northwest Coastal is interested in your Bainbridge Island land for our next investment. We are prepared to make a formal offer for both your land and house." She named a figure that was very fair if Melia was in the market to sell.

"Your offer is generous, Julia, but my land isn't for sale."

"Now don't be rash, dear. Why don't you at least take a couple of weeks to consider the proposal first?"

"The time won't—"

"Two weeks, Melia. I'll call you again for your answer."

"Julia—"

"Take care. That land will do a lot of good for many people."

Melia moaned. Julia always could outtalk a parrot, she thought as she hung the phone up. But she wouldn't change her mind. Her family had invested too much in the land for her to let it go for another upscale development. There were plenty of them out there.

Taylor thought about Melia throughout the day. Instead of being an outsider and feeling the whole world was operating on a different wavelength, with Melia he felt included. But then, with her personality, he imagined she put most people at ease. He wasn't immune to her charms.

As much as Taylor wanted to keep some distance between them, before he knew it, he found himself dialing her number. "What are you doing?" he asked when she answered the phone in her smoky voice.

"Just finishing a shoot. What about you?"

"Knee-deep in paperwork. Did the shoot go well?" he asked, twirling a paperweight on his desk.

"It's been a bear of a day. I'm glad it's finally over. We had to do so many retakes, I was embarrassed."

"You can't be perfect all the time, although you come pretty close to it. Do you know I'm watching your cooking program now and I don't even cook?"

"Everybody needs to know how to cook."

"I didn't say I don't know how, just that I don't." He leaned back in his chair.

"Well, perhaps you'll cook for me one night."

He laughed at the thought of her eating his amateur cuisine. "I didn't say I was a great cook. Steak and potatoes are my specialty."

"Everybody has that one dish that they're great at."

"I don't know about that. I'd rather take you out. How about tonight?" he asked.

"Why don't I cook something?" she said. "I can whip up dinner in no time. If you're good, I'll even let you help." The sultry pitch of her voice was warm and soothing.

"Actually, I'm extending an invitation from my mother and grandfather."

"I'd love to meet them. What time?"

"I'll pick you up at six." Taylor hung up and dialed his mother.

"How's Granddad?" he asked.

"Resting comfortably. He's improved a lot since he came home."

"Great. Can I bring a guest over for dinner?"

"Sure. When?" she asked.

"At six."

He hung up before his mother could emit a full scream. That'd teach her to keep nagging him about finding a woman.

When Melia opened the door to Taylor, he said. "I made an egregious error."

"What?" she asked, looking up at him.

"I shouldn't have told my mother I'd bring you to dinner. With you looking so gorgeous and smelling so delicious, I just want to back you into your apartment and spend the night."

"Your mother would kill you if she's spent hours in the kitchen."

He chuckled. "You don't know the half of it. But if we must."

"Just one moment." Melia retrieved a basket from the foyer table.

"What's this?" Taylor asked as they walked to the elevator.

"A little gift for your mother."

"How did you do this at the last minute?"

"I have my ways."

"She doesn't expect a gift, you know." The elevator arrived.

They were the only ones in it. Taylor pulled her into his arms and pressed his lips to hers. "I've missed you," he said, and Melia felt the whisper of his breath against her mouth.

"I've missed you, too," she said.

He kissed her again. The basket she held kept her from circling her arms around his neck. She rubbed the hard contours of his chest with her hand.

"You don't want dinner, do you?"

"I certainly do," she whispered. "This is just an appetizer."

When the elevator slowed, Taylor groaned and pulled back from her. "Just hold that thought because I'm looking forward to dessert."

Taylor's father had come to Seattle for the weekend, and Melia decided Taylor was a younger version of the older man. His father was slim, yet built. His hair was cut short, with attractive salt and pepper sprinkled around the edges. Melia got a glimpse of how handsome Taylor would be at that age.

"May I get you a drink?" Edward Harrison asked Melia.

"Club soda, please."

Taylor's mother smiled. "I'm pleased to meet you, Melia. We've heard so much about you."

"Likewise. May I help you with anything?"

"Thank you, but no. Everything's almost ready." She stole a look at her son, who smiled when he thought Melia wasn't looking. Melia wondered at the message. "We've had our two minutes of rain today so I thought we'd eat outside."

"It's lovely. And the yard is spectacular. My father would have loved it," Melia said.

"My father retired a few years ago and gardening is his pastime," Taylor's mother murmured.

"He and my father would have become fast friends." There was a time when just the thought of Melia's parents plunged her into grief. As much as she still loved them, she could once again talk about them and remember the good times they shared.

Mrs. Harrison nodded. "Well, I've been watching your show. You look even more beautiful in person."

"Every time that show comes on, she's glued to the TV," Taylor said.

"You watch it, too," Taylor's mother teased. "You told me the other day you were going to get your housekeeper to prepare one of her recipes."

They laughed as they walked toward the patio. The flowers around it were an artist's paradise. Watching the older man straighten as he rose to great them took Melia back to her father, who often pruned bushes and culled plants. "There is always something to do," he'd say, and she felt her eyes going misty.

"Melia, meet my grandfather. Ralph Johnson. Granddad, you shouldn't be in your garden."

Mr. Johnson peered at Melia, breaking out a bright smile. With halting steps, he approached her. She met him halfway.

"I know my body," he said in a gruff voice. "I needed to get out of that hospital and into my normal surroundings." He captured Melia's hand in his. "It's a pleasure to meet you, my dear."

"The pleasure is mine. How are you?"

"Much, much better, now that I'm home. There's nothing like having your own things around you."

Chapter 7

It was just his luck, Audie thought, to drop by Blair's place when his mother was there. If he'd seen her car, he would have kept on driving. Most Seattleites dressed casually. Not his mother. She wore a stunning royal blue pantsuit with pearls. His dad, who was there also, wore a comfortable polo shirt and black slacks. Audie wore jeans. His mom hated jeans.

"Earl, why don't you get Christina and escort her up. Audie will walk me to the elevator in a few minutes." His mom and dad had arrived within fifteen minutes of each other in separate cars.

"Will you, Dad?" Blair asked. He was as eager as a geek with a new, top-of-the-line computer.

Audie's mouth curved into an unconscious smile. Christina was good for Blair. She got him off his computer and out of his office. Anyone who could accomplish that was okay in Audie's book.

"Be happy to, son."

When Earl left, Blair called Christina then disappeared into the bedroom suite, while Audie stared into space.

The handbag distributor had walked away with half his merchandise and all the money he'd made selling it. Audie wasn't going to have enough money to reinvest. Just another business deal gone bad. It was true, he was wealthy, but his grandfather had fixed the trust so that he received only small increments until his thirty-fifth birthday. He had the added burden of finding a trustworthy distributor to sell the remaining handbags until they were able to work out a deal with a larger chain.

"Audie?" his mother called from her lofty perch on the sofa.

He focused on her. "Yes?"

"You seem troubled. Can I help somehow?"

He shrugged. "Not troubled. Just tired," he said when Blair returned to the living room, smiling.

"Where's Melia tonight? She wasn't in when I stopped by," Leticia said.

"She went to dinner with Taylor." Blair looked at himself in the mirror that hung above the foyer table. "He's introducing her to his parents and grandfather."

Leticia pursed her lips. "He's not letting any grass grow under *his* feet, even if you are, Audie."

Audie's gut tightened into a knot. "I'm not in the mood tonight, Mom."

She observed him closely. "Aren't you feeling well?"

"I'm fine." He pushed himself to a standing position and thrust his hands deep into his pockets. "I'll walk you to the car."

On their way, Audie lapsed into silence once again.

"We're ready to begin a new development project. I'll get the paperwork to you so you can start a cost analysis." Leticia pushed the elevator button.

"I'll get on it right away." One thing about his mother was that everything she touched was successful. After his paternal grandfather disowned his father for marrying her, she'd flaunted her success in his face. She must have been disappointed that he was such a failure, Audie thought. And why would Lisa want to hook up with a failure?

"One encouraging thing about Taylor is that he'll be gone soon. And as far as I'm concerned, the quicker the better."

"Unfortunately for Melia. She's falling for him."

"Goodness, I hope not. I just don't want her to be his temporary pleasure while he's here."

"Melia's old enough to know what she's doing."

His mother sighed. "I don't know if any of you young people know what you're doing anymore."

Melia was one more worry for Audie. She had trusted him with her money, too. And he'd blown it. He'd known the distributor for three years. It wasn't as if he'd handed his lot over to someone he'd met an hour ago. The guy had worked in sales, flying back and forth between New York and California. Six months ago he'd quit his job to set out on his own. Since he knew the territory, Audie thought he'd throw some business his way.

Goes to show you, you can't trust friends in business, thought Audie.

After leaving his grandfather's, Taylor and Melia went to her place. She made hot toddies, and they relaxed in the den. Melia took off her shoes and curled her legs up under her.

Taylor felt relaxed in the warm and cozy room. He couldn't put his finger on why. His place felt more like a hotel room, but Melia's was definitely homey. He tried to pinpoint the reason. Could be the pictures, or the many pillows, or perhaps the color of the walls or the comfortable oversized couch with its deep cushions. Or the wall of tall white shelves filled with books. Tall white columns braced each side. Piles of books also sat neatly on the cocktail table in front of them. A bookmark peeked out from a cookbook on top of one of the piles. Everything worked. He was hiring a decorator to spruce up his place as soon as he returned to Portland.

"I enjoyed meeting your family," Melia said and sipped her toddy. Her hands were wrapped around the glass cup, warming her fingers.

Taylor set his cup on the cocktail table. "They can be a piece of work. Wait until you meet my sisters and their families. There are a lot of us."

"Not too many. Three sisters. Do they tease you about being the youngest?"

"All the time. I keep telling them our parents kept trying until they got it right."

"Oh, please. You certainly don't have a small ego. It's a wonder you survived."

"Funny. They say the same thing. But all my nieces and nephews stand up for me. I've got an army on my side."

He stretched his arm across the back of the couch.

"So what did you want to talk about?"

Talking was really the last thing on his mind right now. He wanted to leave business in the office. But he had responsibilities.

"A letter arrived from one of the estates that Palmer handled," he said. "It's from an older woman with dementia, which she's had for years. They say she has good days and bad. It seems the only family she has left is a grandson fighting in Iraq."

"Poor thing."

"It's a sad situation. Her daughter and husband fell out when the daughter was a teenager. The girl ran away and never returned. The woman had been trying to find her for years and couldn't. Finally, a year ago, after years of searching, a PI located her grandson. He's sent the boy an e-mail, but he isn't due back to the States for months. You know how it is once they get over there."

"Not enough soldiers so they have to do extended tours of duty. We all know. Parents are frightened they'll start up the draft again. Let's just hope she gets the opportunity to meet him."

"You might know her. Her name is Mrs. Emerline Miles."

"Mrs. Emerline! She lived next door to my parents. I know her very well." Melia chuckled. "Everybody in the neighborhood knew that woman. She was a terror."

"In her letter she accused Palmer of selling her land without her permission. Actually, she accused that group of outright stealing her land and home."

"She was always very vocal about her wishes. Downright tyrannical whether she was right or wrong. I don't think anyone escaped a tongue-lashing from her, except maybe my father, and that was because he was always fixing things for her. He was about the only person the old hag tolerated." Melia shook her head. "But I can't see her selling. Her family has owned that house since the 1800s. There weren't many blacks here back then."

"So you believe the transaction was illegal."

"She was always accusing somebody of stealing something from her. But she loved her home. And if she was keeping it in hopes that her daughter would return one day, why would she sell it? Why would she move?"

"That's what I've been thinking all week. I'm going to talk to her on Sunday. I hope it's one of her lucid days. When I visited her before, she was out of it." He stroked Melia's arm. "Would you like to go with me?"

"To get chewed out? That woman never had anything good to say about anyone. The kids used to play tricks on her."

"I was intrigued by her letter. A little grit doesn't bother me."

"It wouldn't," she said with an attitude so unlike her.

"Come on. I'm sure she'd love to see someone familiar. I'm sure no one visits her. With that golden heart of yours, I know you won't disappoint her. Besides, maybe it will smooth my way." Taylor didn't understand his current thought processes. He didn't need Melia to smooth the way. He could deal with Mrs. Miles on his own.

His gaze roved lazily over Melia. He wanted to be with her.

"All right. Where is she, and when are you leaving?"

"The nursing home is about an hour's drive away, so I thought we'd leave a little before noon. Give her a chance to pull herself together and eat lunch."

"That will work fine for me."

"Speaking of food," Taylor said. "I didn't get dessert." He

lowered his head and pressed his lips to hers. She tasted sweet like the toddy.

Melia smiled a mysterious smile.

"You've driven me crazy all evening," Taylor said.

"I'm glad something moved you."

Was she challenging him? The light of battle flared in his eyes. "Oh, you move me all right." He looked her over seductively, pulling her into his arms. "In all the right places." Her perfume intoxicated him. She was the opposite of the women he usually dated, and he couldn't understand this sharp desire. Damn it, he couldn't envision having a good fight with her, yet he was still drawn to her. He was the moth, and she was the flame. He couldn't resist her.

He lowered his head, kissed her neck, then drew an imaginary line to her lips with his own. His mouth covered hers hungrily. One hand stroked her arm; the other drew her closer until he felt the pressure of her soft breasts against his chest. He wanted this woman with a desperation that took his breath away.

Melia shivered, staggered by the aching need, the burning desire he invoked. One hand clutched the back of his head, and the other moved over the solid muscles of his shoulder and back.

He pressed her back until she was lying flat on the couch, his body covering hers, tucking her curves neatly into his contours. Blood pounded in his brain, leapt from his heart, and made his body sing.

He kissed a path down her neck to the curves of her soft rounded breasts, unbuttoning her blouse as he went.

"Umm, delicious," he said as his tongue curled around one brown peak. He caressed the soft skin of her stomach and . . .

It took a moment before he gathered his wits enough to realize the doorbell was ringing.

"Damn," he said. "Let it ring."

"I can't do that," she whispered, fighting his fingers and trying to button her blouse.

"If it's important, they'll come back." Brushing aside her collar, he ran his tongue along her collarbone.

"I hate to do this but . . ." Her moan was deep and seductive. Reluctantly, she pushed him aside and, with shaky fingers, buttoned her blouse and ran her hand through her hair as if that would fix it.

Taylor wanted to put his fist through the wall. He tried to bring himself under control, but he wasn't cooling down by any stretch of the imagination. His heart picked up a staccato beat just watching her behind as she walked from the room. Slowly, he straightened on the couch. He heard muffled voices from the door.

"Anything wrong?" he asked when she returned, hoping they could pick up where they'd left off.

"Christina is ready to go back downstairs. I have to go."

Taylor couldn't believe it. No, she didn't just say she was getting up and leaving him just like that. He caught her arm, tried to drag her back to him. "Tell her you're busy. They can wait until you're ready."

She had the nerve to blush and push at his chest. "I can't do that."

Taylor was shocked, his temper simmering. "You can't even neck without somebody in that family interfering."

"Stop acting like a kid whose toy got taken away."

"Damn it, I got a lot worse taken away than a mere toy." His body was still ready for her, and she didn't understand a damn thing.

"I have to go. I don't have time for your temper tantrum."

Just like that she was leaving, without giving a thought to his needs—their needs.

"As long as Blair, Audie, Leticia, or Earl needs you, you'll never have time for yourself," he said with contempt. "Can't you see that they're using you?"

"This will be a forgotten blip on your radar when you move on in another month or so. So don't worry about it."

Her angry retort hardened his features. He glowered at her

and followed her out of the apartment. His temper drove him to his own place. He marched down the hall, slamming the door after him. It gave him only a small bit of satisfaction. He leaned against the surface of the door, inhaling deeply until the anger slowly subsided and reason instead of blood rushed to his brain.

She was right. What right did he have making demands when he'd be gone soon? Long after he left, the Sims were still going to be there. Her life would carry on as usual. But he'd be in Oregon and on to the next woman, the next multimillion-dollar real estate development deal. Even if he didn't like the idea of her moving on to the next man, he was going to do something about other people monopolizing her time as if it were their due, whether Melia liked it or not.

Melia closed her eyes tightly after Taylor slammed his door so hard. It was a wonder it didn't pop him in the back-side. As much as she wanted to take their attraction to another level, she dared not. Already, she was feeling too much, too deeply, too quickly. Her emotions were too complicated for a casual encounter. She needed to pull back and put some distance between them, put the brakes on the attraction that was building, and decide how far she was willing to go when the future was predetermined. And she would, as soon as she visited Mrs. Emerline on Sunday.

In a sense, she was looking forward to seeing the old woman again. Had Mrs. Miles been younger, Taylor would have met his match. She had grit, Melia thought, feeling inadequate. She lifted her chin. She wasn't going to let Taylor destroy her self-confidence. She had enough on her plate.

This was good, Melia thought as she rang Blair's doorbell. If she didn't pull back, she'd be in Taylor's bed. But she had a nagging suspicion that that wouldn't be such a bad thing.

* * *

Melia didn't sleep well the previous night. Not at all, she thought, as she emptied chicken stock into the industrial-size pot at the food shelter and stirred it. Once a month she and Jessica helped to prepare meals. Modern Gourmet donated supplies, a tradition that had begun when Vaughan Graham, the original owner, had owned the shop.

Many meals were packaged and trucked to seniors and shut-ins. The homeless weren't the only people who could use food. Medical services and prescriptions were so costly that many seniors were forced to make a decision about which medications they would do without. Without the food program, many would be reduced to eating cat food or would nearly starve.

Jessica carried in a huge pan of diced celery and carrots and stirred them into the pot.

"You're down in the dumps this morning," Jessica said.

"Restless night."

"Hummm. I've had my share of those lately."

"Let's eat lunch at Mel's when we leave here."

"Sure." Mel's was one of Melia's favorite restaurants. Located in the Central District, it even had its own brewery.

She and Jessica worked another couple of hours before relief arrived and they left for the restaurant.

Of all places, Melia didn't expect to see Taylor sitting at a table eating ribs with Mel Cummings himself. When Mel saw her, he beckoned her over. The last place she wanted to be was around Taylor, but she couldn't deny the older man. Several folders of papers were on the table.

Mel stood and gave Melia a hug. "How's my favorite girl?"

"Can't wait to sink my teeth into your barbecued chicken and ribs."

"I've got plenty for you. Let me introduce you ladies to Taylor Harrison."

Taylor stood. "Melia and I live next door to each other," Taylor said.

Mel raised an eyebrow. "Have you met Jessica Bell?"

Taylor extended a hand. "It's a pleasure."

"Likewise," Jessica said.

Melia and Jessica soon went to their own table and ordered lunch. Melia was seated so that she had a view of Taylor. As much as Melia was looking forward to the lunch, it might as well have been paste for all she tasted. She had most of it packed up to carry home.

Taylor and Mel finished their business at the same time Jessica and Melia completed their meal.

"I never get tired of this place," Jessica said.

"Neither do I."

The two women had driven in separate cars, and once outside, they parted. Before Melia could drive away, Taylor knocked on her window.

She lowered it with trepidation.

"Sorry about last night," Taylor said.

Melia nodded.

"I acted like an ass."

"Look, I understand how you felt. But I think we need time to regroup, to think about what we are doing. I'm not accustomed to having sex just to ease a need," she said.

"I already know that. But you've been driving me crazy with wanting you, lady. But that's my problem." He caressed the side of her face.

Melia closed her eyes and sighed deeply.

"Still going with me tomorrow?" Taylor asked.

"Sure."

Taylor bent and kissed her briefly, as if he couldn't help himself, before he backed away from her car.

Melia started the motor and backed out of the parking space. He focused on her as she drove away.

Farther down the street, Taylor glimpsed the boarded-up, unoccupied buildings that mingled with the neighborhood's thriving businesses. He wondered about the number of people who drove in from other areas only during the day because they wouldn't be caught dead there at night.

* * *

On Sunday morning, Melia called Leticia to tell her she wouldn't make it to Sunday brunch.

"Why not, honey. Are you ill? Should I come over? You always attend church and have brunch with us afterwards."

"I'm going out of town. A last-minute decision."

"You should have told me. What if something happened with you out there all alone?"

"I'm going with a friend. I know you're late for church. I just wanted to tell you I wouldn't be there. I'll call you tomorrow."

"Well . . . okay, dear."

Beautiful green shrubs and colorful flowers graced the grounds of the home for seniors. It was situated in a beautiful pastoral setting on the banks of the Columbia River. Some of the residents were sitting on benches under the trees or in wheelchairs, visiting with each other or with family who came to see them for the day.

Melia was shocked at the sight of Mrs. Miles. She remembered the feisty woman who walked with her cane, more to point at folks than anything else. Now, she was a feeble, drugged-up version of her former self.

"Who's there?" Emerline Miles asked. If nothing else, her voice still resembled that of a drill sergeant.

"Mrs. Miles, you have visitors," an aide said.

The older woman opened one eye. "Who's there?"

"Do you remember Melia Lucas, who used to be your neighbor? And this is Taylor Harrison. They drove all the way from Seattle to visit you. Isn't that wonderful?"

The woman cracked her other eye open and peered long and hard at Melia. "You married, girl?"

"I'm still single, Mrs. Miles."

She peered at Melia again before she spoke. "I guess I'll sit with them a little while," she said.

"You just have a nice visit," the aide said. "You can push her out to the pier. She loves to sit by the water."

Taylor pushed the wheelchair down the floral pathway. The woman was slumped over, and Melia thought she was sleeping until she saw the sharp eyes peering at her. Eyes as sharp as they had been fifteen year earlier when kids had played pranks. The aide was gone, and Mrs. Miles looked as if she was about to get into mischief.

"Is it going to take you all day to get there?" she snapped at Taylor.

Taylor almost jumped at the sharp bark coming from what he'd perceived to be a feeble, kind woman. "No, ma'am."

"Well, hurry up, will you? We've got the place to ourselves right now. But if you don't hurry up, Willy will be over here trying to slip his hands up my skirt. That decrepit old fool. If only I had my cane, I'd teach him a lesson."

"Still the old bat," Melia said under her breath, not realizing she'd spoken out loud.

"My hearing's good," Mrs. Miles said.

Melia darkened with embarrassment. "If you can hear, why was the nurse screaming at you?"

"Because I pretend. Not a thing goes on that I don't know about."

"Never did," Melia said under her breath.

"Heard that, too. Never listened to those devil boom boxes, so I still can hear better than the average teenager."

They arrived at the area beside the water. The sharp volcanic peaks of the Cascade Mountains rising in the distance made for a magnificent view. Taylor and Melia sat on one of the benches, facing Mrs. Miles.

"Why are you here?" Mrs. Miles asked.

"I received the letter you mailed to Palmer Wainwright," Taylor said.

"Figures. If he'd gotten it, he would have ignored it just like all the others I mailed him."

"How many have you mailed?" Taylor asked.

"Don't remember. But there have been plenty. Why do you read his mail?"

"He died, and I'm handling the practice until a replacement takes over."

"How did he die?"

"There was an accident."

"He was up to no good," she said, shaking a wrinkled but straight finger at Taylor. "Maybe he finally tricked the wrong person."

"How did he trick you?" Melia asked.

"Sold my house right out from under me. Tried to convince people I was crazy, but I'm as sane as you." She leaned over so far in her wheelchair, Taylor thought she was going to topple over. "I never signed any papers. If he said I did, he's lying."

"It clearly has your signature on it."

She impaled Taylor with her wizened brown eyes. "I. Never. Sold. My. House! I was leaving it for my grandson. I hadn't found him then, but I was looking. Recently, I discovered he's fighting in Iraq, and I wanted to leave something for him. He didn't even know he had family." Then she looked at Melia. "This wouldn't have happened if your daddy was still living. They got rid of him, too. Him and your mama, God bless their souls."

"Are you saying they killed my father?" Melia asked. Knowing someone else believed what she'd known all along made her feel better.

"As sure as I'm breathing. And he didn't kill your mama. What a bunch of bull. How could you believe such a thing, girl?" she said, narrowing her eyes.

"I don't. Never did. I even hired a PI to investigate when I couldn't get justice from the police. But he couldn't find anything."

"Incompetents, the lot of them. Your father wouldn't have

sold the land his grandfather bought any more than I'd sell mine. And he'd never kill your mother. That Palmer was as crooked as one of my fingers."

Melia glanced at the woman's fingers. Never let it be said she didn't have a sense of humor.

"Your PI wasn't worth the ground he stood on if he couldn't find anything on that crooked group. Why'd you choose him, anyway?"

"Leticia recommended him. I was so devastated right after. It was all I could do to go through the motions," Melia said.

Mrs. Miles patted Melia's hand. Her voice softened when she said, "Sure you were. But you've dealt with your grief. Now it's time for action. Hire someone else or do the search yourself." She impaled Taylor again with her stare. "I want my house and my land back. You should have yours to pass on to your young ones," she said to Melia.

"We'll look into it, Mrs. Miles," Taylor said. "Then we'll get back to you. But first, I'd like to have a sample of your signature so that a professional can compare it against the signature on the deed to your property. We have to prove the signature on the deed isn't yours." He pulled a pad and pen out of his pocket, and Mrs. Miles scribbled her signature in a squiggly line.

"What happened to the signature I gave you?" Melia asked.

"The analyst is out of town, but he'll return on Monday. I'll get both copies to him. I'm told he's the best."

"That's what we want. The best," Melia said.

"Which is the reason I waited for him," Taylor murmured.

"I know people thought my mind was going. But the nursing home staff had a pharmacist check our medications because they realized that wrong combinations were causing problems for some of the patients. They discovered my dementia was from the medications. They've changed them, and I've stopped having the episodes." She glanced at the buildings. "I'll be out of this wheelchair soon. I hurt my ankle. I don't plan on staying here much longer. But I have to find a place to live now that my home is gone." The sorrow on her face was heartrending as she looked across the river as if she were set adrift on a wobbly raft. "You have no idea how upset and angry I am that my home is gone. I thought I would die there. These people should be punished for what they did." She looked at Melia and Taylor in turn. "I'm counting on you to get to the bottom of this. Don't disappoint me," Mrs. Miles said.

Taylor smiled. "I wouldn't dare." If they stole property, murdered people, they would be punished. He'd see that they were.

"Are they treating you all right here?" Melia asked.

"Sure. Sure. As good a place as any to be locked up in, I guess." Then she mumbled in disgust. "Here he comes. Didn't I tell you that you had to talk fast?"

Melia twisted in her seat. An older gentleman was stepping toward them briskly, barely using his cane for balance. She wondered if the cane was for show. He certainly looked as if he didn't need it.

"Always following me," Mrs. Miles said.

Taylor stood. "I'll take you back to the building."

Mrs. Miles waved a hand. "No need. Willie will wheel me back. I'm motorized. I might outrun him."

"Afternoon. Afternoon." The older man was thin and tall with a thick salt-and-pepper beard and a bald head. "You're looking sprightly today, Emerline. I see you have visitors." He raised his bushy eyebrows and nodded toward Melia and Taylor.

Mrs. Miles introduced Melia and Taylor to Willy. Then Melia asked, "May I bring you anything when we return?"

"Got everything I need. Except maybe chocolate-covered peanuts. That's my favorite."

"I'll bring you a box."

Taylor remembered passing a B&B on their way to the nursing home. "It's getting late," he said. "Why don't we spend the night here?"

"We can still return to the city before it gets dark," Melia said.

"What time do you have to be at work tomorrow?"

"I have tomorrow off."

"Then do you really have to return to town tonight?"

"If you're implying what I think you are, I'm—"

"I'm not asking for sex. I just want to spend time with you." Away from the Sims, he left unsaid.

Melia was quiet for a moment. "What if *I* wanted sex?" she said so quietly that Taylor had to strain to hear. And when he heard it, his heart almost leaped out of his chest.

His whole being seemed to be filled with waiting as his astonished gaze met hers. "Don't play games if you don't mean it."

"Who's playing games?" Melia merely stared back at him.

The prolonged anticipation was almost unbearable. He lifted her hand and kissed the back of it. "As much as I want you, I can't promise you tomorrow."

"I'm not asking for more than you can give. I'm attracted to you. And when it's over, I'll deal with it."

"You're so sweet. I'll feel like an ass if I hurt you. Besides, you've got a slew of friends who'll be ready to take my head off."

"This is between you and me. That's all."

He wasn't really afraid. He wanted to give her the opportunity to change her mind before his hopes skyrocketed. He stroked her arm, giving her time. Every time his gaze met hers all warm and sweet, his heart turned over. He stared at her for several seconds before he could speak. His voice was unrecognizably husky when he said, "I can't turn down what you're offering. Especially when I want you so damn much and have for so long. Seems like a lifetime."

Facing forward, Taylor started the motor. A sense of urgency drove him.

Chapter 8

On their way to the bed and breakfast, they stopped in a quaint little town to shop for a change of clothing. With the Cascades as a picturesque backdrop, the area never had a shortage of tourists, and they ended up at stores that catered to visitors.

With their purchases in the backseat, it wasn't long before Taylor parked in front of a beautiful Victorian house, tan with green gingerbread trim.

"It's not too late to change your mind," he said, noticing Melia's apprehension.

"Don't worry. I'm not going to change my mind." Her feelings for this man were growing by the microsecond, and this was all she was going to get. She'd live with that when the time came. Her eyes were wide open. She knew their friendship was destined to be short-lived. She wouldn't let the fear keep her from enjoying intimacy.

She glanced at Taylor, who hustled around the car, his eyes sparkling with anticipation. Her life had been full even before he arrived on the scene. But he called her sweet. She wondered if after tonight he'd call her "cold and unfeeling beneath the surface—the ice queen."

Gallantly, he opened her car door, and they went inside together. The check-in desk was a Queen Anne table, and a young woman was working there.

"You're lucky," she said. "A couple checked out a day ahead of schedule. Would you like to see the room?"

Before Taylor could open his mouth, Melia said, "Yes, please."

Melia was pleased with the large room. The king-size bed was covered with a rose-and-white bedspread. There was luxurious rose carpeting, a Queen Anne sofa reproduction, a writing desk, and thick, fluffy rose-colored towels in the bathroom.

"You'll have your own bathroom," the clerk said. "I think you'll love it."

"I'm sure we will," Taylor said.

As they trooped downstairs to complete the paperwork, a knot tightened in Melia's stomach.

There was nothing wrong with the room, but spending the night with Taylor was an enormous step. Melia knew she'd reached that point. It had been a very long time since she felt close enough to a man to let herself relax enough to spend the night.

"Why don't we get ready for dinner?" Taylor said.

Melia was ready to get out of her clothes. It was a good thing the place was informal. Many of the patrons wore jeans.

Melia gathered the bag with her new clothes and headed to the bathroom. While she showered, Taylor checked his answering machine for messages. There was one from his boss. It must be urgent if the man had left it on the weekend.

Taylor dialed his number and listened to the sound of the shower, wishing he could get in there with Melia. He imagined her naked body and the spray pulsing on her smooth brown skin. He was well into his musings when he heard a response on the other end.

"Taylor here," he barked into the phone.

"Glad you called," Warren Carmichael's pleased voice came over the wire. "How are things going up on your end?"

"They're progressing," Taylor said.

"Got some good news. The Mason Group wants you to be the lead attorney on their next development project." Taylor had just finalized their previous project. "It's going to be their biggest yet," he continued. He went on to describe two huge projects. One concerned some waterfront property in Philadelphia that had been a poor neighborhood for generations and now was slated for gentrification. Everyone wanted waterfront property. The other project was in Portland. More and more people who lived in Portland's suburbs were moving closer to the city. Gas prices were high, and the convenience of being in the city made for comfortable living.

At one time Taylor would have jumped at the opportunity, but how many similar projects could he do before it became old, or his conscience kicked in about what happens to the people who already lived there? Every job didn't pay six figures. Moderately priced housing was needed, too.

"When do they want to begin?" Taylor asked.

"In a couple of months. Plenty of time for you to finish up whatever you're doing in Seattle and get back into the swing of things here."

Taylor hung up. Money was money, and his goal was to keep pushing forward to make as much as he possibly could to secure his future. These hundred-million-dollar real estate deals paid handsomely. He wasn't hurting financially—not by a long shot. So why didn't he feel the usual anticipation and renewed energy that came with beginning a new project?

After Taylor dressed, he expected to take Melia to dinner immediately and warm her up for the intimacy to come. But when he came out of the bathroom in his jeans and set eyes on her sexy image, all his plans flew out the window. His feet moved before his mind had time to come up with a reason, and she was in his arms.

He'd planned to be gentle, to touch her body leisurely, to take his time, but he'd waited weeks, and he wanted her with a desperation that astonished him. He pulled at her clothes.

She tugged his off. Her hands seared a path down his chest, then shoulders, moving him closer to her. She didn't want leisure any more than he did.

"I hadn't planned on this," he said and kissed her with all the pent-up longing he'd held in check. He pressed subtle kisses to her neck and warm, sweet-smelling shoulders and suckled gently on her nipples, teasing her until she cried out in pleasure.

She caressed his nipples with her tongue and blew a whispery breath over the dampness.

His moan was deep and rasping. "You're killing me here." His hand seared a path down her abdomen and charted a course up and down her thighs, lingering at her pleasure points.

A hot ache grew in her throat, and she gasped in delight.

He captured her hand in his and guided her to his penis. She wrapped her fingers around him, stroking him gently while she sheathed his member.

And then his body covered hers, and it was flesh against flesh. He entered her as a moan of ecstasy slipped through her lips.

"Oh, baby," his anguished moan tore through the silence. And they were moving together like practiced performers. Together, they found the tempo that bound their bodies together. They soared higher, higher, until the pleasure was pure and explosive. She cried out as waves of sensation pulsated through her body, and he felt as if he were melting and merging into something greater than themselves. The sensation was so unlike anything he'd felt before that it alarmed him.

Much later they showered together and dressed for dinner, hoping it wasn't too late.

Surprisingly, the restaurant was full, not with overnight guests, but with locals. *A sign of good food*, Melia thought as she opened the menu. There wasn't a huge selection, just four entrees actually—beef, chicken, fish, and a vegetarian dish. Melia chose fish and Taylor beef.

"A bottle of wine to go with our meal?" Taylor asked.

"Sure."

"This is going to be difficult. Red wine goes with steak and white with fish. Which will it be, or would you like two?"

"One is more than enough. I like chardonnay. It should go with both," Melia offered.

"Chardonnay it is."

"It was good seeing Mrs. Emerline again," Melia said after they placed their orders. "She hasn't changed much."

"She's quite a character." Dressed in a sports shirt and jeans, Taylor himself was a striking character sitting across from her.

"Do you think we have enough to go to the police?" Melia asked.

"Unfortunately, no. With Mrs. Miles's reaction to the medication for so many years, they'll think she was under the influence when she signed the papers. We have to obtain concrete information. If both your parents' and her signatures turn out to be forgeries, we'll have someplace to start." Taylor sipped his water. "But I have another concern. Was Palmer working alone, or with someone or a group?"

"I don't know. If he was, who was it?"

"I'm going to begin gathering information on the real estate investment group—all the members. See if they've ever been in any kind of trouble before. The corporation's names will be in the title documents. Then we have to get the principals from the state corporations office."

The waitress returned to let Taylor approve the wine. She filled their glasses and left the bottle in an ice bucket.

"The group met at Leticia's when I was living there," Melia said, picking up where their conversation left off. She sipped her wine. It was good. "You know Leticia and Palmer. No one has taken his place so far. Mark is new. He's been here a little over two years. He took Vaughan Graham's place. When

Vaughan's mother became ill, he sold his business interests and moved back East. Leticia used to work with two of the members, Zachary and Julia. One member has been her best friend since elementary school."

"Seems most of them met at work, or they at least knew each other."

"Except Palmer and Mark. Leticia had heard of your grandfather's reputation and hired Palmer as their lawyer because of it. When they approached him, he decided to invest with them. They started by purchasing a small office complex and gradually grew. They're making hundred-million-dollar deals now."

"Who introduced Mark to the group?"

"I don't know. I'll have to ask Leticia." Melia pulled a pad and pen out of her purse to make a note.

"Their phone numbers and addresses will help. As soon as I get them, we'll get these names to the PI I use and see what he can come up with. He'll check real estate transactions through the county courthouse and the city's property tax Web site. He can get additional information through his sources."

"How much of it can we do?"

"We'll just get the names and let Elliot do the rest. He's good at gathering information. Plus, he has the resources. We don't." Taylor scanned the room. The lights were low, the atmosphere intimate. "We're in a romantic setting, and we're ruining the atmosphere by talking business," he said. "I'd like to see you during one of your filming sessions."

"That can be arranged," Melia said as the waitress brought their entrées. "Be forewarned. We do retake after retake. You'll soon get tired of the repetition."

"Never." His voice was low and husky. "I'll never get bored watching you."

Melia blushed as she gathered a forkful of fish. "We have just a few sessions left until we start filming for the fall season." A sly smile flirted across her face. With that mischievous expression, she looked even more beautiful. "The next session will be cooking with kids."

"I see." He wasn't interested in being around a bunch of kids. He loved his nieces and nephews, but his tolerance ended there.

"I'm sure you'll enjoy it. I'll let you know when we'll film."

He wouldn't chicken out. "Do that," he said, leaning back in his seat.

Anticipation hung between them as they chatted. Before they knew it, they were on their way up the stairs. Their door had barely closed when Taylor snagged Melia in his arms and kissed her. He slowly peeled layer upon layer of clothing from her body, revealing her beautiful curves. When she was naked in the middle of the huge four-poster bed, he could only sigh with pleasure as her hands reached out to undress him.

"I wanted you the first time I saw you. Did you know that?" Taylor said. His stare was bold. Slowly and seductively, his gaze slid down her body. He eased the lacy cup of her bra aside. His hands moved down to skim her hips and thighs.

Melia moaned as he lowered his head and moved his hot tongue over her breast, searing her skin and stoking a glowing fire.

Her hand explored the sinewy contours of his shoulders and back.

Gently, he laid her across the bed. Their first time had been hurried. This time, he'd take the time to leisurely explore her body.

He stroked her body softly, using feathery motions that awakened her nerve endings. Melia felt sublime, like a dream come true.

She caressed his sinewy strength like a gentle breeze, keeping him on the edge.

When the heat from Taylor's hands seared her body, she didn't think about the "ice maiden." She didn't feel alone. In the back of her mind, she knew this was temporary. But, dear fate, let her have this for a short time if that was all she'd ever have.

They teased and excited each other until he slid a condom

on and entered her. They moved as one. And when it ended, it felt as if the earth shook.

His grandfather walked more easily, Taylor thought. The older man's eyes lit up when he saw Melia with him.

"A pleasure to see you again, my dear," Ralph said.

"How are you feeling today?" Melia asked.

"Improving by the day," he responded.

When they were seated in the living room with cups of hot tea, Taylor updated Ralph on their visit with Mrs. Miles.

"Mrs. Miles and your parents were Palmer's clients." The older man patted Melia's hand. "I'm so sorry my firm brought you so much heartache," Ralph said.

"He hid his crimes well," Melia said. "After all, he tried to kill you once you began to ask questions." She reached out and gathered his hand in hers. "I'm so glad you survived. Too many people have died already. You know Palmer better than anyone. Do you think he killed my parents?"

"I don't know. But he might have engineered it."

"You know the real estate group the Sims are involved in really wants my land on Bainbridge? Leticia hasn't pressured me lately, but I know it's coming. I believe someone else must be pressuring her."

"Count on it," Taylor said.

"The same thing may have happened with your parents. Be careful, dear," Ralph said.

Ralph seemed so worried, Melia worked to ease his concerns. "The real estate group couldn't have done it without Palmer."

"That slippery weasel," Taylor said. He addressed Melia. "I know you think Leticia's honest, but do you think he could have worked with her?"

"She may have been pulled into this without realizing Palmer's duplicity."

"Then you'll have to check both of them out. These people

are dangerous. Be careful. Maybe you should hire an investigator," Ralph added.

"The one the firm usually uses will be here tomorrow. He has licenses in both Washington and Oregon," Taylor said. "We'll do a little digging in the meantime."

"I don't like this. It's dangerous," Ralph repeated with a worried frown.

Taylor stood. "We'll be okay, Granddad."

As they left, Ralph said, "Above all else, be careful."

The next morning, Taylor delivered the papers with the signatures to the handwriting specialist. He'd already faxed the names of the members of Leticia's real estate investment group to Elliot Carver, the PI. As soon as he did the background research on the names, Elliot would come to Seattle to do the legwork. After returning to his office from the handwriting specialist, Taylor continued to plow through papers until his sister Veronica called.

"We're coming up on the weekend. The entire family."

"Grandpa will be glad to see you," he said.

"We'll see him, but we're also going to check out your latest."

"What are you talking about?"

"Mama was ready to kill her youngest son when you gave her just two hours to prepare dinner for your guest. But both she and dad were impressed. Now Melia has to get our approval."

"Don't even think about it. She's just a friend." They'd crossed the friendship line, but it was none of Veronica's business.

"We're checking out your friend then. The kids are looking forward to seeing her, so plan on a family invasion Friday night."

"I'm going out of town."

"Do and die. Take care. I've got to get to work."

Taylor hung up. He couldn't leave Melia unprepared for his

brood. In resignation, he dialed her number, but she wasn't at the shop. He tried her at home.

"I needed to prepare you for my family. They're all coming down Friday night."

"The nieces and nephews, too?"

"The entire brood."

"How old are they?"

"From two to twelve."

"If they can get here early that morning, the ones six and over can participate in the Cooking With Kids show. We're taping Friday morning. Because of the children, we expect it to take longer than usual. But they might enjoy it."

"When I leave here, my family is going to disown me and adopt you. I'll tell them. And thanks, Melia. You're too kind."

"I need to know today."

"I'll get back to you. What are you doing later on?"

"I have a lunchtime cooking class. Actually, I have two classes this week. That's the only thing on my schedule, other than to finish planning for Friday's show."

"Well, I better go so you can get to work."

Melia left the apartment and headed for work. One of the things she loved about working downtown was its closeness to her condo. Within fifteen minutes she arrived at work.

"Oh, you're here." Jessica observed her critically. "Looks like you're gaining a couple of pounds. Don't worry. It won't show unless it gets to ten."

"I'm jogging tomorrow," Melia said, "I've really gotten out of my routine lately."

"Wish I could join you, but I'm opening."

"I always jog alone with my iPod." Melia started for the kitchen.

"By the way, we've started on the prep already."

"We have a full class today," Melia noted.

"Eventually, you may have to schedule more classes, even though Mark objects. He isn't going to have a choice unless he wants the competition to take away our business. We had to turn away too many people today."

"I'd love to schedule more, but Mark turns me down every time. Students are willing to do more after work, too, but he won't allow evening classes more than once a week."

"I know, which is why you started the lunchtime classes in the first place. That was really a brainstorm you had," Jessica said.

"Turned out better than I thought it would. Well, let me get to the kitchen."

"You know, sometimes I don't understand him."

"You aren't the only one," Melia mumbled.

"Anyway, everything has been washed. You can check and make sure everything is there."

Someone grabbed Jessica's attention, and Melia left for the kitchen.

She had a full kitchen with three stoves. The shows were filmed there, and classes were taught there. Her students usually worked in groups, although each person got hands-on experience. The recipes she taught could generally be completed in under an hour, less time than it usually took to run to the store for something. They were certainly healthier and tastier than takeout.

For a long time she'd been puzzled by Mark's attitude. The classes were definitely a money-maker. Not only did the students pay the high cost of the classes, but they also spent a considerable amount of money in the store. Many stopped in on their way home from work. Melia also tried to convince him to stock more of the supplies she used, maybe add more refrigeration so they could stock additional items. They certainly had the space.

But Mark was very cautious about making improvements. Too cautious if you asked her. She'd approached him about it once, but he just said he had other investments that made more money than the gourmet shop and with less work. If he increased his investment in the store, he'd have to put in more time than he wanted to. But truthfully, Jessica and Melia could run the shop without him. The only thing Mark concerned himself with was the money, as if they'd steal it if he wasn't there. Everyone else saw his coming by as a courtesy, a sign that he cared about his employees. But Melia wasn't so sure anymore.

If Mark didn't trust anyone else, she still didn't understand why Jessica couldn't make the drop, why *he* had to physically do it. After all, he wanted Jessica to move in with him. Why would he have a woman in his home whom he didn't trust completely? Or was this just another method of control?

Melia checked her watch. An hour before class.

Taylor had to jerk the phone away from his ear when he told his sister Veronica that the kids could be on a television cooking show.

"I only need to hear out of one ear," he said, but he couldn't suppress a smile. "What do I need two for?"

"I know I'll be there early. We'll come out Thursday night. I'm calling the rest of them right now. If they can't come Thursday, I'll bring their kids with me."

"Women."

Fifteen minutes later Veronica called back to tell him everyone was coming. Then each of the other sisters called him in turn, wasting a good hour. After he hung up with the last sister, he called Melia.

"You asked for it," he said. "They're all coming."

"How many children?" Melia asked.

"Five in that age group. But I really called to tell you I'm going to be late tonight. I'll be in around eight."

"Don't eat. I'll have dinner prepared by the time you arrive."

"Sounds wonderful."

* * *

Around eleven-thirty on Wednesday morning, students started to arrive. The lunchtime crowd was browsing, and business was good.

Along with all the women, Duncan Ford arrived early with his redheaded niece. After looking around for a few moments, they went to the class. Jessica pointed the way, then approached Melia.

"Duncan's back. He really is a cutie. Give him to me."

"Here we go again. Did you forget Mark?"

"I'll take attendance today. Leave you more time to prepare for the class."

"I'm already prepared."

"I'm the boss, and I'm pulling rank on you."

"That might work if you *were* my boss, but since you aren't—"

Jessica snapped her finger. "I knew I was missing something."

Melia passed her a clipboard with a computer printout of the students' names attached and an armful of aprons. "Have fun."

"I will. I will." Running her fingers through her hair, she glanced at Melia. "Do I look okay?"

"Fabulous."

"Excuse me." A woman about Melia's age patted her on her arm.

"May I help you?" Melia asked.

"Yes. I saw the dish you prepared for dinner last weekend, and it really looked good."

"You can pull the recipe from my Web site."

"I did, but some of the ingredients I can't find in a regular store."

"We carry most of the specialty items. What were you unable to find?"

The woman named three ingredients. But Modern Gourmet carried only two of them, so Melia suggested stores where the woman might find the last item.

"I saw a sign about a cooking class at lunch."

"Many people take the classes on their lunch breaks. There's always enough left over to take home. Most of them like cooking at lunchtime so they won't have to at dinnertime, but that depends on the size of your family."

"My mother-in-law is a wonderful cook. I'm not. I wish now that I'd learned more of my mother's recipes. My husband told me he was tired of spaghetti and hamburgers."

The woman was so young, Melia wondered what her husband had to complain about and wished he was more sensitive to his young wife's feelings. Usually men were more interested in sex than food at that age.

"I have a lunchtime cooking class for beginners coming up next week. We have fewer classes during the summer than the rest of the year, but we do have two more weeks of them."

"I think I'll sign up for a couple at least."

"Hopefully, your husband will be singing your praises before you know it," Melia assured her. She glanced at her watch. It was almost time for class. Indeed, Jessica had already taken attendance and was deep in conversation with Duncan.

After the class was over, Melia watched Duncan slip a card to Jessica.

"Somebody told me you were checking out someone else last night and Mark saw you," Melia said to Jessica after Duncan left.

"I've already told Mark I think we need some distance."

"We already know he doesn't want that," Melia said.

"His answer to a commitment was to ask me to move in with him. There's no sense in continuing to let him think that he's the only fish in the pond. If he sees other men are interested in me, he might just come up with a proposal."

"But do you really want that if he doesn't want marriage?"

"I'm ready to settle down. I'm ready for babies. I'm not serious about anyone else, but I'm leaving the door open in case someone else comes along. In the meantime, I have nice conversations with Duncan and his niece."

"It doesn't hurt that he's handsome."

Jessica raised an eyebrow. "His niece is spending the summer with her grandparents, and he's promised to spend time with her. They think he'll get the urge to settle down, so their first venture together is the cooking class. Her idea."

"He told you all that?"

"The niece told me most of it. She's a talker."

"I bet he just loved that. Poor thing. He must have been embarrassed," Melia said.

"It's cute seeing a man blush. I just loved teasing him about those rosy cheeks, and his niece was fair game."

"You're the devil, girl."

"Have you noticed we're getting more and more men in our classes?"

"Even confirmed bachelors have to eat."

"Thank God."

The sales clerks were closing their cash registers when Mark arrived. Jessica and Melia had cleaned everything up in the kitchen. There wasn't very much to do since the students did most of the cleaning before they left.

"Hey, Mark, Melia was just commenting that we're getting more and more men in our classes," Jessica called out.

"You just love playing with fire, don't you?" Melia whispered.

Jessica shrugged as Mark approached them.

"How did the class go?" he asked Melia.

"We turned students away."

"Seems to be a popular class. I pulled up just as some of them were leaving."

"We'll have to give this class again."

Mark nodded. "Are you ready for me to walk you to your car?"

Melia didn't miss the look Mark threw Jessica. This was not a safe man to play games with, and Melia would have to tell Jessica that. Using other men to get Mark to propose wasn't a good idea.

Chapter 9

On Saturday Leticia was the last person Melia wanted to see so early in the morning.

"Cleaning, dear? I thought you'd hired a service," Leticia said. She wore an elegant emerald green short-sleeved pantsuit. Pearls dangled around her neck.

"No. Jogging," Melia replied. "May I get you tea or coffee?"

"Don't bother. I stopped by Blair's. Even brought Dr. Beatty with me. Since he lives in this building, I thought if I could only get him into Blair's apartment, Blair would at least talk to the man."

"What happened?"

"Blair was very unresponsive. I'm at my wit's end. I don't know what to do about him. He can't stay holed up in this building for the rest of his life."

"Leticia, have you ever wondered how this started? I think it's related to my parents' deaths."

"He should be over that by now. But I'm aware problems like this don't always work themselves out. My grandfather ended up that way as he aged. I wonder if it's hereditary?"

"Whatever the reason, if Blair would just talk to someone, it would help."

"I agree. He listens to you. Will you talk to him?"

"Of course, not that it will help. He wouldn't listen to me the last time, any more than he listens to you."

"I thought if the doctor came to him, it would make it easier," Leticia said.

"I'll talk to Christina. She might be able to help."

Leticia walked over to the window and looked out at the panoramic view. "Anything. I'm willing to do anything to help him. I look at the outside world and it hurts my heart to know he's cooped up in his little apartment."

"I know it does."

"Thank you, Melia, for at least trying to bring the world to him. Those monthly gatherings mean the world to him. If not for them, he'd turn into a hermit."

"You're family," Melia said and felt it in her heart.

"Earl wants all of us to get together next weekend—not the one coming up but the weekend after—go away and do something. Do you think you can come? We would both be pleased."

"Where are you going?"

"I haven't decided yet. We could drive to Vancouver. Earl has a long weekend coming up, and we haven't gotten away in a while. I think he's looking for peace and quiet."

"Why not Bainbridge?" Melia offered. If Leticia went there, she'd actually see what the home meant to Melia, why she couldn't sell it. Leticia wasn't completely insensitive.

"I'll talk to Audie. I hope he can get away."

Leticia seemed troubled about more than Blair's refusal to see the psychologist, Melia thought. The older woman seemed distracted, sad, actually, a mere shadow of her vivacious, overpowering self. Perhaps she needed another woman to talk to. As sweet as Earl was, sometimes his mind was on his practice rather than on Leticia.

Melia left her perch on a chair and joined Leticia at the window. "Is everything okay?"

Leticia linked her arm with Melia's and presented her with a sad smile. "Just feeling my age, I guess."

"You can't be serious. You're always full of life." This

woman encouraged everyone. Melia fervently believed her survival had been ensured by Leticia. After her parents died, through Leticia's care, constant optimism, and encouragement, little by little, Melia had begun to get out of her depression.

"What happened?" Melia asked.

"So many people seem to be dying. Young people."

"Who died?" If it was one of the family's close friends, she would have heard about it. No one had mentioned going to a funeral, other than Palmer's.

"Michael, one of Earl's poker buddies, died in his sleep. His cousin found him last night. Someone called him to say he'd missed work three days in a row. Michael doesn't miss work."

"It took three days for someone to report it?"

"He had a lot of leave accumulated. They thought he was taking some. Someone finally called his cousin, who went to the house. When he went in . . ." Leticia shook her head.

"Was he sick?"

"His cousin said he seemed healthy. But a couple of years ago, his brother died of a heart attack in the middle of the night. They think . . . well, the autopsy should tell."

"I'm so sorry, Leticia."

"I'm going to visit his family tonight to offer my condolences and see if there's anything I can do."

"If I can help in any way . . ."

"Just listening is enough." Leticia shook her head. "He was part of the Friday night poker game with Earl, Palmer, and their buddies. Those men. They have a little group going."

"Seems odd that he and Palmer died so close together."

"It's not only Palmer. Another played died a couple of weeks before. His name was Gregory Lumas."

"Did Vaughan Graham play with them?"

"I think so. I don't know all the members, and according to Earl, all of them don't play all the time. There's a core group that plays every two weeks. Some are diehards who would have to be in the hospital to miss a game, but some of the rest only drop by every two or three months, like Earl."

"Do you know all the members?" Melia asked.

"Not all, but some. Why?"

"Just curious." Actually it was more than that. For some reason Melia felt uneasy. Palmer might have set something in motion.

"I can get the names if it's important. I'm not without my resources, you know." This was the first smile from Leticia since she'd arrived, and Melia was glad for it.

"I would like a list. Thanks."

Leticia was at her best on a mission, Melia thought.

"Is Mark in that group?" Leticia asked.

"I believe so."

If someone was going around knocking off members of the card group, perhaps Mark's life was in danger. She should mention it to Jessica or to Mark himself. But if people suddenly stopped showing up, Mark already knew he might be in danger. She'd talk to Jessica, but first she and Taylor needed to research this possible tie-in to Palmer.

Melia went jogging at the Washington Park Arboretum at least three mornings a week since the arboretum was close to her condo. Enjoying the outdoors was preferable to lifting weights in the exercise room in her building.

At the arboretum, she encountered the regular joggers and walkers. She didn't know any of them personally but recognized them because this was the usual time she jogged. Melia inserted the earplugs to her iPod and began a fast walk to a peppy beat. Once on Arboretum Drive, she left the worry of traffic behind her and relaxed, breathing in the scent of the trees and plants, mixed with a hint of the lake. There was everything from native conifers to specially grown plants from around the world. A few were in bloom, adding perfume to the air.

Taylor had spent the night at her place. Dinner was fabulous and the sex even better. She was feeling on top of the world and began to think of the children's menu for the taping. She thought she'd add sugar cookies. After the taping, the children get to eat whatever they cooked. She was eager to meet Taylor's family, eager to soak in the camaraderie.

Time passed quickly, and before Melia knew it, she was crossing the street to her condo. Suddenly, someone grabbed her and hauled her back to the curb. She felt the rush of air from a passing motorcycle, which barely missed her and was traveling full speed before she heard someone yell after the uncaring driver, "Hey, people are walking here! Ever hear of a stop sign?"

Melia's heart tripped as someone threw the finger at the driver's back. The cyclist was pressed forward, hunched over his handlebars, dodging between cars. A woman shook her fist at him.

Melia had narrowly escaped being run down. She'd crossed with the light, hadn't she? At least she thought she had.

"The SOB ran the light and would have run you down," said her rescuer, a man with a head full of shocking white hair. "You need to turn the iPod off when you're jogging, especially on the streets. Everyone was screaming at you, but you couldn't hear," he continued. "Are you okay?"

Melia nodded. Her heart was still caught in her throat.

"Anybody get the license plate?" her rescuer asked. By silent consensus he had taken the lead.

"Covered with mud. He was out of here like a shot. Inconsiderate ass."

"You need help getting home?" her rescuer asked.

"No, thanks," Melia said. "I live close by."

He tapped her earphones, which were now hanging limply around her neck. "Turn the thing off when you're out of the park so you can hear."

Melia nodded and started for her condo across the street, extra cautious about looking both ways.

A delayed reaction kicked in. Suddenly, her legs felt so shaky she thought she was going to sink into a puddle right there on the street. Putting one leg in front of another, she finally made it to her building, up the elevator, and into her condo. She hoped she didn't pass anyone she knew, because she was incapable of speech, much less a cordial conversation. Seconds after she closed the apartment door, she collapsed on the sofa.

She thought again about Leticia's suspicions that members of Palmer's card group were systematically being killed. Melia had nothing in common with them. Maybe it was just an accident, but she was still worried.

Melia was on her way out the door when the phone rang.

"Thought you were already at work," Taylor said.

"You almost missed me," Melia said and curled up on the couch. "More news. Leticia stopped by today."

Taylor groaned. "She bugged you about your property again?"

"Surprisingly, no. Did you know Palmer was part of a poker group? Three of the cardplayers in the group died recently. Doesn't that seem strange to you?"

"It does. But it doesn't necessarily mean anything. Although it could be the reason Palmer needed to steal money from the kitty, especially if these men play for high stakes. Who's in the group?"

"Leticia's getting names for me."

"And she didn't mention the land once?"

"Not once. The deaths shook her, one right after the other."

Audie tried not to let apprehension deter him from his goal. Night after night, week after week, he tossed and turned, wrinkling his sheets in knots, wishing Lisa was beside him. He knew it would take work to win her heart back, that is *if* he'd won her heart in the first place. He was willing to make the effort.

Hopefully, his mother was finished with this nonsense of his marrying Melia. He had the unrelenting hots for the cantankerous Lisa. He was on his way to Blair's, hoping to stop by Melia's for some leftovers. She always kept something sumptuous on hand. Suddenly another thought emerged. Before he could stop himself, he made a U-turn at the traffic light, ignoring the honk of angry horns, and drove toward Lisa's house, with a quick stop for Chinese takeout. He arrived just as rain began to pour down. Hoping that wasn't a bad omen, he ran for the door. By the time he made it, the rain had stopped. *That's Seattle for you*, he thought as he rang the doorbell. Lisa answered wearing a slinky pink robe that revealed the outline of her curves.

The disdain on her face would have frightened a lesser man, but Audie had pulled out all the stops, even in the face of her disinterest. He could win her over, he was sure. She hadn't been an easy woman to tempt in the first place. He stood only half a snow-balls chance in hell this time.

"What are you doing here?" she asked, tightening her robe around her curves.

He held out the bag of Chinese takeout, from which delicious aromas emerged. He was starving. Should have eaten hours ago. He'd skipped lunch, trying to track down his distributor, and he'd been hopping with work all week with barely a spare moment.

"Delivery," he said, hoping Lisa would see the humor.

"Wrong house," she said and slammed the door.

If she thought that was going to deter him, she had another thought coming. He pressed the doorbell a couple of times. She ignored him. *Well*, he thought and leaned on the doorbell until the door popped open again. Slowly straightening, he said, "Are you going to let me in, or do I have to ring your bell all night?"

"Oh, come on in before you break my doorbell. I don't know why you're making a nuisance of yourself, anyway."

"Such a gracious hostess," he said, handing the brown paper bag to her as he crossed the threshold.

"Why aren't you courting your intended?" she asked.

"I am."

"Does your mama know?" The snide way she asked him was a clear indication his feelings weren't one-sided. She was attracted to him, too, and for the first time that evening, he relaxed.

Ignoring her comment, Audie followed her to the kitchen. Lisa disappeared, bringing back a towel before she left the room again. He swiped the soft towel across his face and arms.

In three minutes she returned wearing shorts and a green top. Taking plates out of the cabinet, she put them on the table, then poured wine for both of them.

"I don't know what your game is," Lisa said. "But I'm glad you came with food. I was just debating what to fix for dinner."

"I know you hate to cook."

Obviously wondering if he were criticizing her, she said, "We aren't all perfect little homemakers like Melia."

He brushed the hair from her face. "You don't have to be jealous of Melia, you know. You're you. And that's good enough for me." He approached her cautiously and linked an arm around her shoulder. "I think you're a sexy little package whether you can cook or not. Besides, you have other attributes."

"I'm not jealous."

"You have no reason to be."

Lisa focused on her plate, putting some distance between them. "So is the dinner a prelude to sex? Then, tomorrow, you'll be convincing Melia to marry you again?"

Audie couldn't help but smile. Slowly, he shook his head from side to side. "A prelude to a movie. Not sex." He retrieved a DVD from his jacket pocket and handed it to her. Then he pulled his chair closer to hers. He wasn't going to sit halfway across the room.

When the meal was finished, he helped her clean up, and

then they sat on the overstuffed couch to watch the movie. With the lights turned low, Audie glanced over at Lisa. There was enough space between them for two people to sit. He shook his head in resignation. Courting her wasn't going to be easy.

Although the food had been delicious, Lisa couldn't recite one thing on the menu. When Audie stopped by her shop a few days before, she was just getting over him. What game was he playing? She wasn't going to let him break her heart again. She knew that Melia and he didn't have romantic feelings for each other, but that meddling mother of his would never leave them alone. Audie wasn't strong enough to stand up to Leticia, and Lisa didn't want a mama's boy.

But he could be so kind. That's what she missed about him. His thoughtfulness. She'd felt less alone when he was courting her.

"Audie . . ."

He slid down the couch closer to her and pressed his finger to her lips. "Shush . . ." he said. "Stop trying to analyze. Just enjoy the movie."

"And then what?"

"We'll play it by ear. Nothing intense about dinner and a movie."

"I can't—"

"Stop, Lisa. We don't have to fight. I'm not going to marry Melia. Period. You already know that." He slid a hand across her shoulder. "Although I kind of like you when you're jealous. It's kind of cute."

"In your dreams."

He checked the miniature grandfather clock. Seven-thirty. They had a long night ahead if it was going to be spent fighting.

"You want to turn the DVD player on?" he asked.

Melia was still rattled from the near brush with the motorcycle when she started on dinner. Cooking was relaxing for her.

When the roast was in the oven, she pulled out hurricane candles for the balcony table. As she wiped down the table, she looked out at the lights twinkling over the city. *What a soothing view*, she thought, pausing for a moment as she smoothed on a tablecloth. Then she put two candles on either side of a small bouquet of flowers. She'd light them at eight-thirty.

Melia found herself singing as she continued to prepare the meal. Then she stopped. Her mother used to sing when she was happy. "Singing happy songs," her mother would say. But more than likely her mother would sing spirituals.

At quarter to eight she took a quick shower and put on a dab of mascara and lipstick. After smoothing perfumed lotion over her body, she donned a long, sleeveless turquoise dress, which revealed half her back. After donning gold hoops and a necklace, she finger combed her hair.

Back in the kitchen, she tied on an apron and put the finishing touches on dinner. Then she lit the candles on the balcony. It's a good thing mosquitoes didn't fly that high. There was a tremendous difference between dinners on the patio on the island and much higher above sea level.

Taylor rang the doorbell five minutes later. Melia hurriedly untied her apron and put it on the kitchen counter. Taylor came through the door, barely letting it close behind him before he pulled her into his arms and kissed her.

"Who needs dinner," he asked against her lips, "when I have you for an appetizer?" Smiling, she glanced up at him. Her calm was shattered by the hunger of his kiss.

His smell, everything about him, was pleasing and familiar. For a fleeting moment, Melia wondered for how long she would be able to share this experience with him. Or how she would react once he left. But for now she tried to put the inevitable out of her mind so she could enjoy the moment.

She cleared her throat. "Are you hungry?"

"Ravenous." His breath whispered over her neck, and her heart pounded in an erratic rhythm. "You look fabulous," he said. Dipping his head, he continued to explore her mouth with his kiss. "Much too pretty to be tucked away alone with me."

Melia's smile was shaky. His kiss left her breathless. A Miles Davis CD was playing in the background, adding to the intimate mood.

As much as Melia enjoyed his kisses, she pulled back. "We're missing the surprise I've prepared." She grasped his tie, leading him to the balcony. Pushing him into a chair, she said, "Just sit back and relax. I've got a treat for you." Kissing his cheek, she stroked his solid chest before she left his side.

He caught her hand. "What a woman. After a full day, you prepared a feast. I couldn't get any better at a five-star restaurant."

Melia cocked her head to the side. "Enjoy it while you can."

Taylor chuckled. "Trust me. I am."

Smiling, Melia left for the kitchen, her heart tingling. She poured a glass of wine for him. Then she placed the roast and some sautéed vegetables on a platter and took it to the deck. Usually she served hors d'oeuvres first, but it was so late. And as Taylor was famous for saying, they could have each other for dessert. A warm shiver spread over her body. She couldn't get enough of him. She forced herself not to think about the future. Portland was less than three hours away. They could still see each other, although it wouldn't be the same.

Taylor took the first forkful of the roast and swallowed with a sigh. He wondered if her mother prepared meals like this. Had she learned her cooking skills from her?

"Tell me about your parents," he said. "Unless it's too painful for you."

"I can talk about them. It's ironic because I was thinking about my mother when I prepared dinner. She used to sing spirituals when she was happy."

Taylor captured Melia's hand in his. "Are you happy?" he asked. She nodded.

"Did you learn to cook from her? Did she prepare the same types of food and enjoy cooking as much as you do?"

"Actually, no. She cooked because she had to. But she worked outside the home, and often she brought food home. We ate a lot of MacDonald's and Wendy's, but she always cooked a huge Sunday dinner. That started when I was in high school. My grandmother, my paternal grandmother, was the cook in the family. When she was alive, she'd cook huge Sunday dinners, and we ate at her house. She'd always send food home with us. My mom and I cooked together when we were on the island."

"And your father?"

"My father loved the land. As I told your grandfather, we had the most beautiful yard around. One of his goals was to build a maze, using shrubs. He'd started on it before . . . well. He'd planned to spend his retirement gardening. We lived on three acres of land. It was the largest plot in the area." Suddenly, it was as if she were in a world of her own. "They were very happy together. It's more than most people experience in marriage."

"Perhaps most people's expectations are too high."

"Perhaps." Silence hung in the air for several seconds. "Are your parents still here?" Melia asked.

"My grandfather's much better. My parents returned to Portland Sunday. I stop by Granddad's every day to make sure he's okay and to check to see if he needs anything."

"Family is irreplaceable."

"I don't know. I don't think some people feel that way, especially if they have a black sheep in the family. And most families do."

"Who's the black sheep in your family?"

"I suppose it's me, although I don't feel that way. As long as I'm clueless, I guess I'm okay."

"You can remain blissful in your clueless state."

He raised his wineglass. "I'm all for the clueless."

Melia and Taylor were in the bedroom. Taylor tugged at her clothing as if he couldn't wait to get her in bed, and truthfully, she couldn't wait to be there. In a few seconds her mind was going to be mush.

"I have those addresses and phone numbers for you. Is that enough?"

"Plenty. I'll send an e-mail to the PI tomorrow. But right now, I don't want to think about work."

Taylor couldn't wait to feel her skin against his. He slid her dress up her legs, up her torso, and over her head, tossing it aside. Then he touched her soft skin with delicate strokes. He gazed at her delectable body. She was soft and beautiful, all womanly curves. She seemed surreal somehow, yet very warm, very womanly.

Her hands were gliding up his body. She unbuttoned his shirt and tugged it from his shoulders. Running her soft hands over his chest elicited a deep, primal sigh from him.

He thought again about how she was working her way into his system like an addictive drug. How was he going to let her go when he was through here?

Taylor knocked on Melia's door the next day, just as she returned home and before she could slide her feet out of her shoes.

Instead of pleasantries, he asked, "Do you have any papers of your parents' real estate transaction?"

Melia nodded. "I kept all the paperwork."

"Is it here?"

"Copies. The originals are in a safe-deposit box."

"Let me see them. We should have the signatures authenticated."

Melia went to one of the spare bedrooms she used as an office and gathered the papers from a file drawer. She copied the forms she knew her parents had signed and the real estate papers for comparison, and slipped them into an envelope. She handed the envelope to Taylor.

"It's hard to believe the Sims could have done such a thing. They have been so good to me."

"Perhaps that's why they've been supportive."

"Blair and Audie?"

"Are they involved in their parents' transactions?"

"No. They're independently wealthy. Earl's father disowned him when he married Leticia. Blair said he absolutely hated her. He left his money to Blair and Audie. Audie is always trying some scheme or other, but he's already quite wealthy. I guess he hasn't found that one thing to make him happy."

"Better than sitting around on his butt playing Nintendo." Taylor gathered her in his arms and kissed her. "Back to work for me."

"And I have to try out some recipes."

"Does that mean I don't have to pick up takeout for dinner?"

"If you're willing to be my guinea pig."

Taylor put his hand to his chest. "It's a hard cross to bear, but I'll endure."

Melia hit him, and he quickly ducked out of the apartment, laughing.

Taylor was supposed to be thinking of work, but he was thinking instead of the night spent in Melia's bed. He kept scanning the document before him, aware he was missing something, but he couldn't focus enough for it to register. He examined Palmer's documents again. After several seconds he realized what puzzled him. It was the name "Peter Bowman." He'd seen it on another form in regards to the Lucases.

He pressed the intercom.

"Yes?" Nadine, his assistant, responded.

"Could you step in here a moment, please?"

In seconds Nadine entered his office.

"Have you heard of a Peter Bowman? It might have something to do with the Lucases."

"That name doesn't seem . . ." She thought for several seconds. "I know. Palmer went to high school with him. I remember him visiting the office several years ago. I remember because he had the most unnerving eyes I've ever seen. I'll never forget them."

"Why was he here? I can't find a file on him."

"He was just visiting the area and dropped in. I remember Palmer using that name again just before he died. I didn't think much of it at the time. Only I really wished I'd been out of the office when he arrived. He looked at me as if I were a piece of steak." She shivered slightly. "I was supposed to be out to lunch when he visited, but I came back to the office early. He was already in the office talking to Palmer when I came in."

"Do you have a phone number or address on him?"

"No. Palmer didn't give me any information other than they grew up together. That's it."

"Thanks."

Why would Palmer make references to this Peter Bowman on the Lucases' files if this man was simply a high school friend? What did he have to do with the Lucases? To be fair, Palmer could have been doodling.

Taylor picked up the phone and dialed Elliot Carver, the PI, to give him Bowman's name to investigate.

"In the meantime," he told Elliot, "I'm going to try to get my hands on Palmer's high school yearbook and see what I can find in there."

Chapter 10

Leticia called Melia to make sure she would attend the Sunday picnic. Every year Leticia pulled out all the stops for the catered affair. Business associates and friends alike would be in attendance, in a crowd large enough to get lost in.

"Is it okay for me to bring a friend?" Melia asked.

"Of course, but why don't you let Audie drive you and your friend. Parking is scarce, you know."

"Not possible. I'm not coming directly there."

"You know, I'd love to stand in for your family and plan your wedding. I think a fall wedding would be absolutely beautiful."

Give it a rest, woman. Some people didn't know when to quit. "I don't have any plans on marrying in the near future," Melia said, remembering what Lisa had said about her. That she didn't stand up for what she wanted. Melia wasn't a doormat, and she resented that Lisa thought that. There was a difference between a doormat and kindness.

"Maybe soon then. I'll see you at the picnic."

Melia hung up. Just because Leticia was overprotective of her sons, it was a far stretch from being a murderer. Taylor got ticked off every time she defended the Sims—even with Blair and Audie. She thought he was pissed off in general with her because she wasn't assertive like him, and she didn't want to be. Taylor and Lisa would make a great pair.

Right now, however, she and Taylor had to concentrate on Palmer. But there were so many other things to worry about. Jessica was courting trouble with Mark. Women had been killed for less. Jessica really didn't know that much about Mark's background before he arrived in Seattle. She'd have a heart-to-heart talk with her friend.

The signatures were forged. The question was, Taylor thought, did the Sims know, or was this something Palmer engineered? Or perhaps they worked together. Melia's parents would have had to come to the office to sign the papers. And Palmer presided over that. Also, if Leticia was part of the real estate investment group, her friend would have talked to her about it. So Leticia must have known as well. Was the entire group involved in the fraud? Taylor was interested to hear what Elliot had to say about these people.

Taylor couldn't believe it. Melia was going shopping for Blair. Since he wanted to be with her, he trooped along. But he didn't like Blair cutting in on his time with her.

"You know there are a million other things we could be doing beside shopping for Blair," he said as she smelled a pineapple. *Blair can smell his own fruit*, he thought.

"You didn't have to come. I'll be finished soon." Obviously, the pineapple wasn't ripe enough, because she put it back and picked up another one.

"You've got half a shopping cart of stuff. How much can one guy eat?" he asked. When he went shopping, he just picked up what he needed. It didn't take him a whole hour.

"Enough, Taylor. You've already stated your opinion. You don't want me to go grocery shopping for Blair. I know that. Stop getting on my nerves. You could have stayed at your office or something." Her nerves were rattled, and she was disgusted with what she'd put in the shopping cart. All things she liked but Blair didn't. It was as if she were stocking up for a person who cooked instead of someone who considered the microwave the only way to cook.

"I wanted to talk to you."

"Then talk." She pushed the cart down another aisle, with Taylor dogging her steps.

"I got the handwriting analysis back."

"And?" She stopped in the middle of the aisle, waiting.

"The signatures are forged."

"I'm not surprised. My parents would never sign their land away." Then she stopped and looked at him. "You know what that means, don't you?"

"What?"

"That my father definitely didn't kill my mother and himself."

"Well, I believed you."

"So where do we go from here?"

"I'm waiting for information."

"We should take this to the police."

"We really don't have enough evidence to make them reopen the case. We still need to know who was working with Palmer. And without more concrete information, they aren't going to take you seriously."

He was right. "But you're sure he was involved?"

"Of course. He handled their legal affairs. We always knew he was involved somehow. The question is, what did he engineer? How deep did his hands reach? Were the other members in the real estate investment group involved?"

"You still believe Leticia is involved."

He shrugged. "I'm not ready to say she isn't."

They drove separate cars back to the apartment. Melia started to put Blair's groceries away, like she always did, when she remembered Taylor and Lisa's warnings.

Yes, Blair needed someone to shop for him, but he didn't

need her to put his groceries away. He wasn't afraid to walk around in his own kitchen.

The telephone was beeping on the kitchen counter. There were twelve messages. He must have turned his ringer off. Melia decided to search for him.

Blair was in his office, working on some computer program. Melia stood in the doorway. The office looked so cluttered, she was scared something would jump out at her. How could he live like that? Thank goodness the maid was due tomorrow. Sometimes when he was deep into a project, he wouldn't let the woman in the office.

"Blair, I'm going to let you put your groceries away."

"Hummm," he said, unaware of a word she'd said.

"I said—" She stopped in mid-sentence. His hair was in disarray from dragging his hands through it. He'd thrown on a T-shirt that morning, along with a ragged pair of jeans.

"Are you listening to me?" Melia asked. "Do you need to replenish your wardrobe? Is that the best you could find to wear?"

"Nag, nag, nag," he finally said, dragging a hand over his face and looking at her for the first time. His eyes were bloodshot.

"What's wrong with you?" Melia asked.

"I was up all night. This started going well, and I just couldn't stop. Oh, Melia, this program is the bomb."

"I just bet. Have you eaten today?"

"Humm." He thought a few seconds and shrugged. "Don't think so. I must have forgotten." Looking around his desk, he saw the wrappers that had fallen to the floor. "I may have eaten a doughnut or crackers. Can't remember."

"That's ridiculous," Melia scoffed. "I'll be right back with some leftovers." She didn't care what Taylor said. She couldn't let the closest person to her starve. *Men*.

"Thanks, Melia. Anything you fix will be great."

"You need to stop working for a few minutes and put your groceries away. I'm leaving."

He looked at her with a puzzled expression. "You always put them away."

"I know, but I have some things to do." He was so sweet, like a clueless teddy bear, that she couldn't tell him he was a big boy and needed to do some things for himself.

"Oh. Okay."

"If you're not finished by the time I return, I'll help you. But you need a break from your work. Your eyes certainly do. And maybe you should get a nap after you eat."

It took Melia ten minutes to put a light lunch together. When she returned and saw what Blair had done with his groceries, she was ready to knock him upside the head.

He had put everything in the wrong place. "The mayonnaise goes in the cupboard," she told him, "until you open it."

"Oh."

When he started to put the lettuce on the top shelf of the refrigerator, she told him, "Put the lettuce in the produce bin. You know that's where you usually find it."

What would he do without her? "Blair, don't you notice where I put things every week? You don't seem to have a problem finding things. At least you've never complained about it."

"If I don't know where something is, I search until I find it. Much like I have to do when debugging computer programs."

"How in the world do you jump from debugging programs to putting groceries away?" When he opened his mouth to answer, Melia said, "Never mind." When they finally finished, Audie walked in, clearly in a foul mood.

"What's wrong?" she asked.

"Keith, the distributor, disappeared with the money from our sales. That was half the stock I was responsible for. Half my damn stock! I've searched all over for him, and he's gone. Without a trace," he lamented.

If poor Audie didn't have bad luck, he wouldn't have any luck at all.

"Are you sure he disappeared? Maybe he's taking the day off," Melia said in her usually optimistic way.

"He's gone. He's given up his apartment. Cell phone's disconnected. And the Kiosk is an empty shell. He was only renting it." Audie plopped down on the sofa and rubbed at his face. "Now I have to find a way to unload the rest of my shipment. It's sitting in a storage room, costing me money each month."

"You have one customer here. I'll take a handbag in each color."

He waved her offer away. "I'll give you some."

"You can't give your merchandise away. I'm a paying customer."

"Who carries Gucci, Coach, and every other name brand?"

"I don't use them every day. Just bring me the handbags. Besides, you have plenty of contacts. You'll sell them someplace."

"I'll drop some off. The question is how am I going to sell the other eight hundred?"

She tapped his hand. "One at a time. You can do it, Audie. You're resourceful."

"That's not true," he said with a very un-Audie-like gesture. "I've failed at everything I've started."

"Now who's lying to himself? You're a great accountant. You don't even fit the green eye shade profile. Besides, who always gives me sound advice about my taxes? Who files my taxes and makes sure they get done on time?"

"That's true, Audie," Blair said as he joined them. He looked a little more human.

"You see? I'm not the only one who believes in you."

"You two are family. Of course, you'd say that."

Family. As sorry as she felt for Audie, the fact that he really thought of her as family warmed her heart. And she hugged him. "You'll find a way. Like I said, you're resourceful. Just give yourself a little time to think about it. You don't have to solve the problem overnight."

"Thanks, Sis."

Audie screwed up because he had too much money. For him, nothing was really at stake. Most people would have checked out the distributor more thoroughly. Melia knew she would have.

Jessica looked pale, Melia thought, when she opened the shop the next morning. Melia didn't usually go in so early, but with the taping of the children's cooking show the next morning, she wanted to make sure everything was in place and all the prep work was done.

Melia stood to the side and watched Jessica, but she wasn't even aware Melia was there. "Are you okay?" Melia asked.

Jessica jumped.

"Jessica, what's wrong?" Melia asked, really concerned now.

Jessica's mouth worked a couple of seconds before she burst into tears.

"Come on. We have time before the store opens. Besides, a salesclerk will be on duty so you don't have to work at the cash register for a while."

She led Jessica to the classroom. "Can I get you some coffee?" she asked.

Jessica shook her head. "I can't swallow a thing."

"What happened? Is it Mark?"

"Melia, remember the guy I was flirting with a couple of weeks ago when Mark arrived, not Duncan?"

"Yes."

"He was killed yesterday. They don't know who did it. I saw it in the morning paper."

"Oh, my God!" There were too many deaths all at once for her to dismiss it.

"A hit-and-run. They don't know who hit him."

"A hit-and . . ." Melia felt faint. "That's different from the other murders." But it was similar to what had almost happened to her. Was there some kind of thrill killer out there? And why would he want to kill her? Or was she just the unlucky one standing there when the urge came over him? *Was* she being targeted?

"Do you think . . . I feel horrible for even thinking this, but do you think Mark could have killed him?"

"Come on. You don't think Mark killed a guy just because he was talking to you. You work in a store. You have to be friendly to customers. That's part of your job."

"It was more than talking. We were flirting."

"I know he seems a little possessive, but do you really think he murdered that guy? That's a stretch from just being jealous. He'd have to be crazy."

"Of course, I don't believe Mark did it." Jessica rubbed her forehead with the palm of her hand. "Forget I said anything." She chuckled. "Can you image geeky Mark killing anyone?"

"Not really." *But someone killed that man.*

"What am I saying? It threw me, that's all." She dried her eyes with the tissue Melia handed her. "I was thinking all kinds of crazy things. That poor man," Jessica said, shaking her head. "His life taken just like that. It goes to show, you shouldn't wait on things in life. If you want it, you should just go after it. None of us knows how long we have here. Life is precarious."

"We can't go around thinking about when we're going to die, Jessica, or we'll drive ourselves crazy. But you're right. Whether you're thinking of life or death, you should do the things you want. Live your own life, and . . ."

"And?" Jessica cocked her head to the side, waiting.

"I was just going to say, try not to live your life according to others' wishes, but only your own." With a wry smile, Melia said, "And I should take my own advice."

"You're a sweet person, Melia. I'm grateful to have you as a friend. Don't change."

"That's exactly what everyone wants to do. Change me, that is."

"Don't listen to them. You're okay just the way you are. We can't all be type A personalities. There has to be some B's out there. The world wouldn't work if everyone were the boss."

"There is that. The key is not to let the A's take over."

"True enough. I've got to stand up for what I want with Mark. And if he doesn't want what I want, then I need to be strong enough to let him go, once and for all."

"Follow your heart."

Jessica smiled. "I'm okay now. Let me go back to the front and open up. I'm still trying to get that fool to change his mind. Mark can be so gentle. I don't know why I thought he could kill anyone."

After her conversation with Jessica, Melia thought about how many times women had tried to mold men into who they wanted them to be, and how many times it had backfired. She was doing the same thing as Jessica. She realized she'd hoped Taylor would stay, or at least want a lasting relationship with her. And yet when his search was over, Taylor was moving back to Oregon and on to another woman.

What they shared was only temporary, and that didn't sit well with her, especially when she knew very well she was falling for him in a way she never expected to. God, if she felt this way now, what would she feel by the time he left? Would her heart lay in pieces at his feet? She had to do something about that. It was time to pull back before it was too late—if it wasn't too late already.

Melia sat in front of the TV, glued to the news. The hit-and-run was the top story. The police department's public relations representative announced that there were no known suspects in the killing. Melia trembled all over. Goose bumps covered her arms, and she couldn't get warm. What was going on?

Her balcony door was open. She got up and closed it. Then she checked her front door to make sure it was locked and nearly jumped out of her skin when the doorbell rang while she was still in the foyer.

Peeking through the peephole, she exhaled a long breath. It was Taylor.

"Hi, sweetie," he said, pulling her into his arms. Then he held her away from him. "You're tense. Anything wrong?"

"I don't know."

He set down his briefcase near the foyer table. "Come on," he said, linking an arm around her shoulder and leading her to a seat.

"Now tell me what's wrong," he said as they settled on the seat.

Melia rubbed her hands up and down her arms. "Someone on a motorcycle almost hit me yesterday after I left the arboretum. I thought it was an accident until . . . the hit-and-run. Are these incidents linked to Palmer, just like I'm linked to him? Maybe it wasn't—"

"Wait a minute. Someone almost hit you? We're investigating murders, and you didn't say a damn thing about it? Just went on your merry way?"

"I thought it was an accident."

"We're uncovering lots of 'accidents'," he said. "Baby, you should have said something."

"I'm okay now. I'm used to taking care of myself."

"You don't have to with me here."

"For now, anyway," she said, the meaning circling the space between them.

Taylor merely gathered her into his arms and held her close. "Melia, don't go out alone until we find out what's going on."

"Now who's being ridiculous? I have a job. I have a million things to do."

"You also have to stay healthy and whole."

Melia sucked in a deep breath. "It seems all we talk about lately is death. I need a rest."

Taylor rubbed the side of her face. "You aren't sleeping well."

"Who can sleep with all this going on? I'm going to look like hell tomorrow."

"Why don't you take a nap now. In my arms."

"I have to fix dinner."

"For once we can order in, after you wake up."

"But—"

"If you're going to say something about preparing Blair's dinner, I'm going to strangle him. Then he can't eat."

"You're mean."

"And don't you forget it."

Saying wasn't doing, and so Melia thought about Jessica and her friend's death. Every time she closed her eyes, she felt the rush of the motorcycle just before the good Samaritan yanked her back.

Taylor knew Melia wasn't resting. Even in his arms, she was shifting uneasily. He stroked her arms. Someone had tried to run her down. The investigation was heating up, and he needed to call Elliot. Somebody was going to pay for frightening Melia. He'd see to it.

It seemed that half an hour had passed before Melia actually fell asleep. Taylor dozed off himself, but only for a little while. When he awakened, Melia was breathing easily beside him. He felt the steady beat of her heart against his chest. He wanted to stroke her, to feel her naked warmth against his own, but her rest was more important now. He couldn't resist kissing the top of her head, which rested beneath his chin, and holding her closely before he eased out from under her, gently laying her head on a pillow. For a moment he watched her to make sure she continued sleeping. Then he retrieved his briefcase and escaped into her den to made a phone call.

"Hate to call you so late, buddy, but we need to step up the investigation." He filled Elliot in on the attacks and a possible link.

They considered a thrill killer. It didn't seem to be a serial killer, especially since the police hadn't considered a connection between the crimes. There was enough there to confuse. They talked another five minutes before Taylor hung up.

Stretching, Taylor rose from the chair and stared out the window. While he would readily agree Leticia couldn't be the killer, and that she obviously didn't try to mow Melia down, he fervently believed she could be conspiring with someone from her real estate investment group. Copycat crimes constituted an easy solution to their dilemma. And Melia presented a serious dilemma for Northwest Coastal.

Stepping away from the window, he settled at Melia's desk. It was neat, with just one stack of papers piled in a corner. Taylor glanced at the sheet atop the stack. It was the menu for the next day's filming. The kids were really going to enjoy the cookies and ice cream. She'd chosen every child's favorite food as well.

Melia was a trooper, Taylor thought. No matter what catastrophe hit her, she kept chugging along. He admired her for that. A lot of people would be floored by half the hammers that hit her, but not Melia.

A man would be proud to have a woman like that by his side. A fist tightened in Taylor's chest. If a man was ready to settle down, he amended.

Taylor brought his family by the gourmet shop early the next morning. All of the prep work was done. The kids looked cute in their fresh summer outfits. His sisters had enough sense to dress them casually.

"Melia, this is the rest of my family," said Taylor. He pointed to a woman who wore slacks and a sleeveless blouse. "This is Selina, the oldest, and her two children. Meet Pauline and her two, and Veronica and her son. Her other child is only four. A little too young for the show."

"Pleasure to meet you, and so kind of you to let your children participate in the show."

"Oh, the pleasure is ours. Thank you for inviting them," Selina said.

Melia saw the family resemblance. Taylor favored his older sister. She was thin and seemed delicate, until Melia felt the firm grip of her handshake.

One of the little boys tugged at Melia's sleeve. "Are we really going to be on TV? Can we turn on our TV and see ourselves?"

"Yes, you will. Not only that, I'll give you a videotape, and you can show it to all your friends."

"Oh, wow."

"I've never been on TV before," the little boy said. "Do we have to cook? Can't we build something? I want to build something."

His mother tried to shush him. "All your friends will be envious," she assured him.

"I'll let you build the brownies," Melia said. "You can go back and tell your friends you had the best brownies at the ice cream party."

"I get to eat them, too?" he asked.

"Definitely," Melia assured him. "A good cook always samples his food."

"Wow!"

"Let's get to work. I hope you don't mind if they get dirty."

"For once they won't get in trouble for playing with food," Taylor teased.

"Don't you have work to do?" Selina asked.

"I wouldn't miss this for the world." Taylor whacked his sister playfully. Melia left them to their bantering and joined the children.

Families, she thought with a stab of nostalgia as they rehearsed. *How precious*. Then she glanced at Jessica, whose sister had flown into town with her two nieces. Melia greeted the girls and introduced them to the other children. The make-up artists applied make-up to their faces, which thrilled the girls and appalled the boys. No one watching them on TV would know they wore make-up, she assured them.

Watching the longing on Jessica's face was enough to break Melia's heart. She interacted so well with children and wanted them so badly. At one point when Melia glanced up, she noticed Mark was in the room and was watching Jessica. Unfortunately, he didn't seem moved by her maternal instincts.

Melia glanced at Taylor. When he smiled at her, his mother, who was sitting beside him nodding approval, smiled also. The poor woman was going to be disappointed again if she expected her son to settle down. But in his family's warm embrace, she forgot that she was thinking of breaking up with him to save her heart.

She closed her eyes briefly. It was already to late for that.

Finally, it was time for filming. The kids were in place. The people in the studio grew quiet. Melia forgot all about the family she wanted so desperately.

Chapter 11

"Your mama is going to have a hissy fit," Lisa said as Audie parked his BMW on the driveway of the Simses' estate. There was a huge difference between this affluent section of town and the modest homes in the area where Lisa lived.

As they walked slowly toward the house, he gathered her hand in his, brought it to his lips, and kissed the back of it. "It's time she realizes I'm serious about you. What better way than to bring you to one of her functions? You're going to be part of my life."

"This marriage she is trying to arrange between you and Melia is her match made in heaven. She considers Melia a socialite, born with a pedigree. I'm just plain old me."

He stared with longing at her. "Plain old you is what I want, woman. Who believes in that nonsense anymore, anyway? Old money dies out. When you have too many rich people coming together, sometimes they turn into ne'er-do-wells. The drive and energy for life dissipate over time. I can see it in my father. Although he's a good man, he's just skating through life on his family pedigree."

"Your father is a wonderful and well-respected physician."

"That's true, but something is missing. He doesn't have the drive my mother has."

"What a blessing."

"She isn't all bad, Lisa."

"Your father doesn't have to be like Leticia. If he were, you and Blair would be nervous wrecks. You need that calming influence, and your father is definitely it."

"I don't know. I want that drive you have, for me and for my kids." Suddenly sadness overwhelmed Audie. Just because he wanted more didn't mean he'd get it. Case in point, his failed handbag venture. Already he'd have to take a hit for that.

"It's one of the things I lo . . . like about you. You're never willing to settle. I don't care how many mistakes you make."

Audie was so steeped in his own misery, he missed the slip. "Don't be too sure of that. I've made my share of mistakes and more."

"So have I."

Audie glanced at Lisa from the corner of his eye. "Oh yeah? I thought you were just about as perfect as they come." At least to him, she was.

Lisa snorted. "Not by a long shot. I tried an ice cream shop that bombed. Then it was perfume. But I knew that I wanted something of my own. I must have gone through four or five businesses before I finally settled on my accessory shop. It felt right for the first time."

Audie thought about her helping a customer the day he stopped by her store. "It's you," he said. "Very feminine. Tasteful. I like it."

Lisa blushed. "If only I had a talent for accounting. I can sell. But I'm terrible at balance sheets and taxes."

"Balance sheets are my forte."

"Oh yeah?"

"I have a degree in accounting."

Lisa turned to face him as they neared the Simses' house. "I didn't know that."

"There's a lot you don't know about me," he said.

"See. I took you for a rich boy who is always running

around dabbling in one thing or another. Well, I guess I'll have to take the time to get to know the real you."

"Hold that thought."

"I asked you to do one thing, and you couldn't do it. Why are you here with that—" Leticia raged.

"Don't say it, Mama," Audie warned. Using some lame excuse, Leticia had dragged him up to her bedroom and had slammed the door behind them. Poor Lisa was outside somewhere alone. Just before the kitchen door closed, he had noticed his father walking toward her, thank goodness. Dad didn't care whom he dated, as long as she treated him okay and she wasn't on drugs.

"I have tried to impress upon you how important it is for you to court Melia."

"It's time you accept that Melia and I will never be a couple."

"Of course not. She won't give you the time of day as long as you're courting Lisa."

"I know I've said this a million times. Melia's in love with Taylor. You can see they love each other. Even if I weren't dating Lisa, she'd still see Taylor. Get used to it, and get used to Lisa and me."

"That's ridiculous. Melia just started seeing him. If you did like I told you and dated her, she wouldn't have had time for that man. He's from out of town. He won't stay here. I don't think you have much to worry about as far as he's concerned. He has to return to Portland eventually."

"He's got an apartment here. I wouldn't be surprised if he moved here permanently."

"Don't count on it."

"How many times do I have to tell you, Melia's like family. I can't go to bed with her."

"Not by blood, she's not. And, son, don't pull that crap on me. You've gone to bed with a lot worse."

Audie turned and paced to the window with angry steps. He couldn't see Lisa from where he was standing. "This conversation is going in a direction I don't want to go."

"Have you gotten Lisa pregnant? Has she trapped you already?"

"Lisa doesn't need to trap me. Give it a rest, Mom. I'm a grown man. You don't like Lisa any more than Granddad liked you, so you should understand."

His mother turned her back to him and crossed her arms. "That's different."

"No, it's not. Dad loved you and married you, despite Granddad's threats. I feel the same way about Lisa. You of all people should understand."

"So you're going to leave Melia, who you profess brotherly feelings for, to sink on her own. There's talk that the people in Palmer's circle conspired to have him murdered. Taylor might be part of the conspiracy."

"Then we need to tell Melia and help her."

"Do you think she'll believe us when she's so smitten with that boy?"

"What makes you think he was involved? He was in Oregon at the time. His own grandfather was almost killed in an accident."

"I'm sure they're still investigating."

"We need to warn Melia if you feel she's in danger."

"She'll go straight to Taylor and endanger her own life. Let your father and me handle it."

Audie didn't think Melia was in trouble. This was just another of his mother's tactic to get him to date Melia. And it wasn't going to work.

"Get used to Lisa. I don't want the kind of estrangement you had with Granddad. It was so unnecessary."

Melia and Taylor arrived at the picnic late. Leticia and Audie were walking out of the house, and both of them appeared angry. Leticia smiled at a group of people and soon was caught up in conversation. Audie grabbed a glass of champagne and approached Lisa.

"Somebody was raked over the coals," Melia whispered to Taylor.

"Glad it wasn't me."

Audie made his way to Lisa. Melia and Taylor approached the couple just as Audie was summoned away by his father.

"Thank goodness friends have finally arrived. I thought I'd have to hole up in enemy camp all evening," Lisa said with heartfelt warmth to Melia and Taylor.

"You aren't the only one," Taylor said when he noticed Leticia eyeing him.

"You two, stop it," Melia said.

"Easy for you to say." Lisa sipped her drink. "I better not eat anything. If she had her way, she'd poison my food first. Girl, that handbag is new, isn't it?"

"Sure is. Like it?" Melia held it out to Lisa.

"It's gorgeous, girl. Where did you buy it? I want one like it."

"From Audie."

"You're kidding. This is from his shipment?"

Melia nodded. "To tell you the truth, I expected them to be some cheap-looking crap."

"So did I."

"I told him I wanted to buy one in every color. He dropped off six yesterday. Shocked me, girl. I actually got something I could use instead of one more thing to hide in the back of my closet."

"His merchandise must be keeping that Kiosk busy."

Melia shook her head. "Actually, the distributor ran off with the profits from half the shipment. Audie's looking for another seller."

"You're kidding. I wonder why he didn't tell me?" Lisa took the handbag out of Melia's hand and examined it. She even opened it up to check the inside.

"I think he was embarrassed."

"But why? The quality of the leather is fantastic. The workmanship is excellent. In a few years, the value is going to really increase. I really like this. It's something I could sell at Lisa's."

"Would you? He was so depressed. But don't tell him I told you."

"I won't. Trust me. I understand men and their egos. You know what? You're a local celebrity. Why don't we come out with Melia's bag? You can advertise it on television."

"I don't know if my name will carry any clout, but these handbags certainly are for a good cause. They've helped the women in Haiti. You know the woman who manages that factory offers the workers a free lunch every day. So the employees get at least one good meal if nothing else. The money they earn supports their families."

"If you could get on that national cable network, your name could carry this message across the country instead of just a local celebrity endorsement."

"I'm not a celebrity."

"Girl, please. There aren't many people in Seattle who don't know you. And women who can't cook adore you. One small step at a time."

"Speaking of steps, look who's coming."

Melia glanced around to see Leticia approaching them. She noticed Taylor had disappeared.

"Hello, Lisa, Melia. I hope you two are enjoying yourselves." Leticia greeted them with a hostess smile, except it turned warm when she spoke to Melia.

"We are. Your parties are always fabulous," Melia said. "I'm glad Lisa could join us this year."

"Indeed. I hope all is well with you, Lisa. Is there anything I can get you? Perhaps refresh your drink?"

"I'm fine, thank you," Lisa said.

"Great."

Audie came rushing over as if afraid Leticia would frighten Lisa away. "So," he said, "how's it going?"

Leticia rolled her eyes. "The big bad wolf hasn't eaten her yet. Why don't you take Lisa to get a plate? There's a veritable feast on the banquet table."

"I will. Should have thought of it before. Hope you're hungry," he said and cupped Lisa's elbow.

Leticia dug into her pocket and took out an index card, handing it to Melia. "These are the names of the members of Palmer's Friday night card group. I don't know if the list is complete, but it's as many as I could get."

Knowing Leticia, it was complete. The woman was dogged about gathering information. "Thanks," Melia said, scanning the names.

"I'm curious about why you want them."

"Just concerned about so many people dying."

"Let me know what you come up with. My mother and father have finally arrived. I'll talk to you later, dear." Leticia headed off in the direction of her parents, and Taylor joined Melia.

"Did she rake you over the coals?"

"She gave me the names of the members of the card group."

"Great. I've been digging through the newspapers for information about all the men who were murdered. We can work on similarities."

"Let's eat. I'm tired of thinking about death."

"This has to be tough for you," Taylor said as they approached the banquet table.

Upon leaving the picnic, Lisa and Audie drove to an area in the Capital District that was unfamiliar to Lisa. "Who lives here?" she asked. "Or are we taking in the sights?"

Audie could barely see her in the dimness of the car. "Wait and see." He rubbed a hand up her thigh.

Lisa shifted in her seat, trying to get a good look. "I wish it were daytime so I could really see the view. The houses look like old, old money."

"They are." They glimpsed stately mansions and lawns as they twisted along narrow roads and ribbons of steep hills.

Finally, Audie slowed and pulled into a long drive. Slowly, he drove toward what could be termed a mansion.

"You have some wealthy friends," Lisa said as he exited the car and escorted her to the front door. Instead of ringing the doorbell, he used a key to open it. Lisa was silent as she walked into the impressive and opulent old-world foyer.

"Welcome to my home," Audie said.

"Your home?"

"Mine and Blair's. Our grandfather left it to us."

"I knew you could be extravagant at times, but I never knew you were . . ." She couldn't take it all in. And she was going to offer to sell his handbags in her shop. Get real. He didn't need her little piddling shop to sell his goods. She sucked in a breath. She'd known he came from money but never envisioned it included a home like this.

Audie wrapped his arms around her, comforting her, warming her. "It's just a house," he said, nuzzling her neck.

"You've got everything, Audie. Why do you want me? You don't need me."

"Without you, I don't have everything."

"But you can get any woman you want."

"Hey, you weren't born yesterday. You know very well I'm not attracted to just anyone. It's you I want, so nothing else matters."

With his arm looped around her, they walked to the kitchen. Lisa took in the cherry cabinets, old gas stove, and spacious pantry.

"I want you to meet my grandparents," Audie said, taking something out of the fridge, but Lisa was busy taking in the view.

"I thought they were dead?" she said absently.

"My father's parents are. I'm talking about my mother's parents."

"If they're anything like your mother, I'll pass."

"They're the kindest people you could ever meet. They want to meet you, too. I've told them all about you. How sassy you are. How badly you treat me."

"You didn't," she said in horror, noticing for the first time the bottle of wine in his hand.

"Not yet. If you're not good to me, I might." He approached her, kissed her neck. "You taste sweet. You smell sweet."

She turned in his arms, and he enveloped her, bringing her close, kissing her sweetly on the lips.

"I've missed this," he said when he came up for a breath.

"What took you so long? I was beginning to think you were thinking of me like a sister, too."

He ran his hands along her curves. "You can forget that. I never, ever, thought of you like a sister. That first time was pretty quick. I wanted us to spend some time together, get to know each other. I already know about the desserts you offer."

"Dessert, hum."

"Better than banana pudding."

"How romantic." She wasn't sure she liked being compared to banana pudding.

"You don't know how much I love banana pudding," he said as he ran a tongue along the sleek lines of her neck. "Vanilla wafers," he said.

Lisa laughed. "You're crazy. You know that?" She finally relaxed. Her Audie. Whatever his surroundings, he was the same unpretentious, loveable man.

"Yeah. You're too serious," he said, working kisses along her collarbone. He handed her the bottle and two wineglasses before he suddenly picked her up and carried her up the elaborate spiral staircase. They stopped in a huge room. She could fit the entire upstairs of her home in that one room. Her two bedrooms and bath, and still there was room left. What must the closet look like?

"Your eyes are only supposed to be for me."

With an impish grin, she said, "You pale in comparison."

"Thanks a lot. At least you have your priorities straight," he said tongue-in-cheek.

She said, "I think so," just before his mouth covered hers hungrily. She forgot about the house, the size of it. Audie filled her mind completely. As he continued the slow, drugging kisses, her insides jangled with excitement.

His lips left hers, spilling kisses along her cheek, her neck, and then trailing their sweetness down her body until he stopped at her breasts. Using his hands to peel her clothing away, he kissed the skin that was revealed.

Slipping beneath his clothing, Lisa's hands moved gently down the slope of his back.

"All these clothes are in the way," he said, and Lisa quickly undressed him, reveling in the sleekness of his hard body.

They had wasted so much time, she thought as they explored each other's bodies until he finally entered her after sheathing himself. They danced to a tune that was as old as time. When they both exploded in complete satisfaction, she was a glowing image of fire, passion, and love.

After leaving Leticia's, Taylor stopped by his place to pick up the newspaper clippings on the killers and then joined Melia at her place. They settled down at the dining room table and spread the clippings out.

"Seven people have been killed so far."

"Three were members of Palmer's card group," Taylor said.

"And one came to our store. Jessica was talking to him, and she was concerned that Mark had taken exception to it and killed him."

"Does Mark strike you as the violent type?" Taylor asked.

Melia laughed. "Are you kidding? Jessica would have to protect *him*. He's so clueless, it's ridiculous. We have to tell him everything to do in the store. I don't know why he bought it in the first place. He doesn't know a thing about business."

Taylor mulled that over for a moment. "What do you know about him?"

"Only that he came from back East I think. Not much more."

"Maybe we need to add his name to the list."

"You're being silly. You might as well add my name or Jessica's."

"Adding Jessica might not be a bad idea."

"Stop it. Before long you'll have everyone I know on that list, even Blair."

"Hum. We both know Blair's not leaving his apartment. It's a big deal for him to come over here."

"I never knew being an agoraphobic could save him from people like you."

"Hey. Your life's on the line. I'm cautious. Sue me."

Melia released a long sigh and shook her head. She was making light of it, but the situation was serious. She might be on somebody's hit list, and she didn't have a clue as to why.

"At first, I thought they were after you because of the land, but all these people don't own large blocks of land, do they?" Taylor asked.

She shook her head. "I only know two of those people, and they don't own land. Any that the real estate investment group could want, anyway."

"Let's check and make sure. I'll give these to Elliot and see what he gathers."

"What about the police?"

"I think it's time to give them some info, too. I'll call them first thing tomorrow."

Suddenly, chills shook Melia. She rubbed her hands up and down her arms.

"Come on. We're going to get to the bottom of this."

"It seems the more we find out, the less we know."

"But we're making progress. Enough of this." He pulled

Melia out of her chair and onto his lap. "Let's talk about something else."

"Like what?" she asked, linking her arms around his neck.

"I don't know. Talking isn't exactly what I had in mind." He pulled her head to his, and his sweet kiss sent fluttering butterflies into the pit of her stomach.

"You have a one-track mind," she said moments later against his lips.

"Yeah," he said and nuzzled her neck. "And you love it."

"Maybe."

"Maybe?" He tickled her side. She was very ticklish and fell into peals of laughter.

"Take that back."

"I'm not."

He tickled her again. She nearly fell off him, she laughed so hard.

"Okay, okay. But I can't get too used to this."

He gazed at her. She wondered what was going through his mind. "I'm here now," he finally said.

She didn't respond. She shouldn't have said anything, because the levity of the moment had vanished. But her skin tingled as he pulled her close once more and pressed his lips to hers. It was obvious he wanted her every bit as much as she wanted him. What they shared was so unexpected. So confusing.

Melia awoke slowly the next morning and pulled the covers to her chin. She and the Sims were going to Bainbridge for the weekend, and she had forgotten to tell Taylor about it. Everyone was going except Blair, as usual. The Sims often went on family vacations—without Blair. She'd spoken to him before about seeing a psychologist, but he was adamant about not seeing one.

She thought of one particular summer when Leticia had left the boys with her mother and her on the island because she had to return home for business. In those days, Jessica had spent many nights at her home. The two of them would think up mischievous things to do to the boys, and they'd retaliated. Those were some fun times. Her mother would just shake her head. She wasn't as uptight as Leticia. Leticia always made sure the boys toed the line when she was on the island, but her mother let them run free. And they took every advantage.

Those were good times, Melia thought. Often her mother would ride her bike with them. Mrs. Sieverson, Melia's grandmother, and her mother would teach Melia and Jessica how to can food. Lord knows, apples were so plentiful that they'd can jars of jams, and they made pickles, too. Melia's grandmother would teach them how to prepare fish, using recipes from "the old country," she would often say. Of course, Jessica never liked picking vegetables from the gardens and canning and freezing, but Melia lapped up everything. She used some of the very same recipes she learned during those long ago summers on her cooking shows.

Melia laughed. Often her grandmother would try to rope Blair and Audie into learning to cook, but her grandfather would save them by taking the boys fishing or boating. One good thing though, the women never had to clean fish. She also remembered the first time her grandfather took the boys hunting. Poor Blair threw up. He was sick as a dog. Audie, Melia's grandfather, her dad, and Mr. Sieverson were left to prepare the animal.

Hunting was a thing of the past for most families. But her grandfather always said you never knew what the future held. It was best to know that you knew how to survive.

Melia rose from the bed and headed to the bathroom. Blair had always been a gentle soul, and he had many good qualities. He and Christina made a good couple. They would be respectful of each other's shortcomings. Neither would have to pretend to be what they weren't. After all, they knew each other's fears and weaknesses.

Blair had to be convinced to accept help so that he could live his life to the fullest. He'd enjoyed those summers spent on Bainbridge. It wouldn't be the same without him. This trip would be their first to the island as a group since her parents died. Melia knew she'd be okay. She'd spent a week there alone already. The Sieversons had made it easier. They'd brought back fond memories.

The Sieversons would visit again, Melia was sure. She was looking forward to seeing them. But first, she thought as she headed to the shower, she had to have another talk with Blair. She had to convince him to seek help for his agoraphobia.

Taylor got copies of all four years of Palmer's high school yearbooks from Palmer's sister. Then he went to Melia's place to go through them. They sat side by side on the couch and slowly looked at the yearbooks. This Peter Bowman person wasn't necessarily in the same grade as Palmer. They wanted to cover all the bases.

Taylor flipped a page. He felt guilty because he was stuffed from Melia's good cooking. If he wasn't careful, he was going to end up with a gut. "Maybe we should go jogging tomorrow or walking or something. I'm enjoying your food too much."

"Sounds good. I've cut back on walking and biking since you moved next door."

"Do you bike? I shouldn't be surprised. You look pretty fit. Even on TV."

"Seattle is the city of the fitness conscious. I'm sure even your grandfather walks on a regular basis."

"I guess so." He flipped a page in the yearbook. "I got the preliminary results from Elliot today."

"What did he say?" Melia asked.

"There was nothing in the files that implicated any of Leticia's investment group. You already know Mark arrived on the scene years after your parents died. He lived in New York then. So he's really not a suspect."

"Who is?"

"Truthfully, Palmer is it. Everyone else turned up clean, even

Leticia, who I suspected. But Elliot is going to continue to search. As I said, Mark wasn't in his preliminary search because we thought this reached back to your parents' murders. But now he's going to include him."

"I wish we could hurry this up."

"Everything takes time."

"Look." She pointed at a picture on one of the pages of the yearbook. "I found Peter Bowman. He wears glasses."

"So he does. Does he look familiar to you?"

Melia studied the picture closely. The boy was in the tenth grade. He'd be larger now. Thicker than the skin and bones high school kid. And, of course, much older. Maybe even bald.

"I wonder if he has a beard or if he's clean shaven now," she mused.

"Who knows?"

"I don't remember ever seeing him. He certainly wasn't part of Leticia's group. The question is, how does he fit into the equation?" Melia said.

"I guess we have to consult Elliot."

"I found Peter in this yearbook, too. He and Palmer were in the same class. They were on the debate team, which means they were more than likely good public speakers. Palmer certainly was."

Taylor closed the book and took it out of Melia's hands. "That's it for tonight. We can't do anything else until Elliot gets back with his results."

"When are we going to give the handwriting analysis to the detective in charge of my parents' case and get him to reopen it?"

"After we gather all the information. I don't want to give him dribs and drabs."

"If the police had done a complete investigation in the first place, they would have gotten this information. I told them then that my parents wouldn't sell the land and were killed for it, but they treated me like a distraught daughter."

"Which you were."

"Of course, I was."

Taylor put his arm around Melia and held her close. "We'll get to the bottom of this. Trust me."

"I do. I enjoyed meeting your family the other day. They're wonderful. You're so blessed."

"I know. My family fell in love with you, too. Believe me. They've already picked out the wedding day, the church, the reception hall and all."

"I know you hated that. If only they knew. You're a confirmed bachelor. They should have gotten the message by now."

"You would think, but people believe what they want to believe."

"You don't have to worry about that with me. Both my feet are planted in reality."

He leaned back to take a good, long look at her. "I don't know about that."

"I do."

"Well, let me see if I can get you to enjoy another bit of reality."

Melia glanced up at him. "And what would that be?" she asked.

"Spending the night"—he nipped her ear—"in bed with you."

"And what kind of reality is that?"

"Some things can't be talked about. They have to be experienced."

"Do tell. By the way, what are your plans for the weekend?" Melia asked.

"Jogging ten miles."

"Do you have to stay here to do it?"

"No, why?"

"Leticia wants the family to spend the weekend on Bainbridge. I could jog with you there."

"I'm not about to let you go alone. I'm definitely going." His sigh was long and labored. "Another weekend with that family."

Chapter 12

Blair stared out of his office window at the beautiful star-filled evening and wished he could walk out on his balcony. City lights kept the view of stars to a minimum, but just to feel the breeze, to look down on the sparkling waters and the boats cruising by would be sheer pleasure. Audie didn't know how lucky he was to be free. Even if Mama worried him half to death.

Everybody was going to Bainbridge. He'd spent many fun-filled summers there. His mom would take him and Audie there for at least a couple of weeks. Jessica spent the summer on the island with her grandparents. The four of them—Audie, Melia, Jessica, and he—would explore the area and go fishing, biking, and boating. He missed those times. If only he wasn't so afraid.

He ventured to the balcony door, unlocked it, and began to open it wide. He felt faint with fear. He thought he was going to collapse to the floor. He shut the door tightly and clicked the lock in place. As he backed away from the door, defeat overwhelmed him. He'd never be able to go outside again. Never. What was wrong with him? Why couldn't he just snap out of it?

Blair backed into a side table and knocked over a lamp and

papers. He bent to retrieve them. The lamp wasn't broken, at least. He put it on the table and gathered up the papers, stacking them in a pile. Then he saw a business card a few feet away. Picking it up, he read the name on the card. It was the therapist, Dr. Beatty, his mother had brought by.

Melia had cooked breakfast and brought it over to eat with him earlier. Halfway through, the conversation had turned to the therapist.

"Blair, I'm going to miss you this weekend. Now that I can go back to the house, I want you there with us. It will almost be like old times."

"Not quite," he said.

"It will never be the same. But at least I can go back now. And I want to make new memories with all of us. You had some great times there, didn't you? I thought you loved going there, especially after Granddad and Mr. Sieverson quit insisting you go hunting."

Blair nodded around the lump in his stomach. "I loved the island. You know that. Especially after your folks got the computer."

"You spent hours on the computer. The rest of us had to drag you away."

"I remember. I . . ."

Melia cocked her head to the side in a familiar gesture. "What?" she asked.

Blair glanced at his plate. He'd barely touched his omelet and fruit. "I'm going to miss you. Miss going."

Melia reached across the table and clasped his hand, which was balled into a fist. "Call the doctor, Blair. Please. What do you have to lose?"

He shrugged.

"Pick up the phone. Call him."

Blair looked down at his plate. "Okay," he finally said.

"Right now."

"Today. I promise."

They resumed eating. Blair had a hard time. The thought

of dealing with another therapist made the food roil in his stomach. But he'd try it. He wasn't going to do anything he didn't want to. Not this time. But he'd give the guy a try, he vowed. One try.

An hour later, Blair was surprised to hear the doorbell ring. Only his family visited, and they all had keys. They'd walk right in. Unless it was a delivery. No deliveries were due. And Melia had left already, saying she was going to do his weekly grocery shopping.

He got up, strolled across the carpeted floor in his bare feet, and looked through the peephole. He was shocked to see Christina standing there dancing around in the hallway. He snatched the door open.

"How did you get here?" he asked, looking around for Melia or the doorman or someone.

"My therapist's doing. My current assignment was to go up the elevator alone." She spread her arms. "I'm here. And I need a seat," she said, inhaling deeply and pushing him aside. She looked sick. "My heart's about to beat out of my chest," she said as she fell into a chair.

Blair thought she was the bravest woman alive for conquering her fear. Brave and beautiful, even though at that moment she resembled a wilted flower. Now she was even more appealing for her courage. Unlike him. Now that she'd conquered her fear, how long would he be able to please her? How long before she decided she wanted to spend her time with someone who could take her to a Mariners' game, or boating, or hiking, or out to a movie or dinner?

Right now he needed to concentrate on her and the huge step she'd taken. She was entitled to a celebration, not a man who was too wrapped up in his own fear to notice her progress.

Blair sat beside her, gathered her hands in his, and rubbed warmth into her cold fingers. "I'm proud of you."

"You might not feel that way when you realize you're

stuck with me a while. I don't think I can go down right away." She shrugged. "Sorry."

He put his arm around her shoulders and pulled her close. "You've got nothing to apologize for. Besides, I'm sure I can find something to entertain you with."

"The sax will do it every time."

He groaned. "I was thinking of something more . . . personal."

She ducked her head and blushed. He changed the subject. He had not been able to talk about his fears and how they started. Others didn't understand. Certainly not his mother, who feared nothing, or his father, who believed two shots an evening took care of all problems.

"Have you always been afraid of elevators?" he asked.

Christina glanced up at him. Her breath had slowed to a normal pace.

"No." She cocked her head to the side. "It was just a couple of years ago that it got really bad. I lived on the eighteenth floor in college, and although I didn't *love* elevators, I didn't have a problem with using them. It gradually got worse and worse until I couldn't take them at all." She glanced up at him again. "How about you?"

"It was sudden. I was living here. I had a horrible nightmare. Can't remember the details." He remembered them, but he wouldn't divulge them. "I got to my front door and couldn't open it. Couldn't leave the condo."

"Do you know what about the dream frightened you so?"

He shook his head.

"Maybe you should go to my therapist. She's very good, and she works with a lot of patients who are like us."

He liked the way she said "us" as if they shared something different from everyone else. They had something in common. Just the two of them.

"I've thought about it," he said. But he didn't want to live through those nightmares over and over. Pandora's box. He knew Lisa's therapist would make him come face-to-face with his demons. He was afraid he'd lose something precious if he opened up that box. Now he was taking sleeping pills to make sure he'd sleep dreamlessly through the night.

After Christina worked up the courage to ride the elevator down the next morning, Blair hovered near the phone until she called him from her apartment, telling him she'd survived her ordeal. She had to dress quickly for work.

The night he spent with Christina was the first night he'd spent with a woman in years, and it was memorable.

As soon as he hung the phone up, he quickly picked it up again and dialed therapist's Dr. Beatty's number before he lost the nerve. The man sounded sleepy.

"Sorry," Blair said. "I didn't realize how early it was. Didn't mean to wake you."

"It's okay," Dr. Beatty said. "How may I help you?"

"My name is Blair Sims. I live in your building. I believe my mom, Leticia Sims, spoke to you about me."

Late Thursday, Melia, Taylor, Lisa, and the Sims boarded the Washington State ferry to Bainbridge for their thirty-five-minute ride. They stood at the stern as the ferry pulled away from the dock.

"You're in for a treat," Melia told Taylor, who stood beside her. Lisa and Audie were on her other side.

As they drifted across Puget Sound, they took in the panoramic view of the Seattle cityscape and Mt. Ranier to the east.

It was twilight when the ferry pulled alongside the pier. Night was quickly approaching as they drove to the more remote part of the island. The magnificence of the lush greenery of the place could not be denied, even at night. Suddenly, a house came into view, and Taylor was directed to the road leading there. As they left the car, they could hear the rushing of the tide against the shore in back of the house. The breeze cooled their skin.

While the men hauled in the luggage, the women un-packed the groceries and made up the beds. Melia had called to ask the Sieversons to open the house, and when she arrived that night, it smelled fresh. Sheets had been pulled from the furniture, and the wood gleamed. A note telling them to enjoy their stay was taped to the fridge. Melia smiled. The Sieversons probably had worked tirelessly until the job was done, even though it was at the last minute.

When Taylor saw a bottle of wine chilling on the bar, he said, "It's the perfect night for the hot tub beneath the stars."

A gentle breeze had cooled the air, making it ideal. "I agree."

"Sounds perfect to me," Audie said, setting a bag on the floor. "How about you, baby?" he said to Lisa.

"I don't know if we're invited," she said, glancing from Taylor to Melia.

Taylor remained silent, but Melia said, "Of course, you are," wanting to whack Taylor on the head for being standoffish. They'd have plenty of time together over the next three days.

"You young people go on. Since Mrs. Sieverson prepared dinner for us, why don't you relax for an hour? As soon as I unpack, I'll put the food on the table and we can eat."

"I'll help," Melia and Lisa said simultaneously.

"Go, go," Leticia insisted.

They shucked their clothes, donned swimsuits, and gath-ered towels. Taylor gathered the wine and glasses on his way to the tub. Melia sank into the churning water while Taylor poured four glasses and grunted when Lisa and Audie appeared. The warm water lapped at their skin, while the cool breeze stirred. In the open, with a minimum of light, the stars were bright and clear. For the first five minutes, they en-joyed the view and each other.

Taylor sipped his wine and set it on the deck.

"Tell me," Melia said, stretching her toes and relaxing completely, "How did your family venture to Seattle?"

"My great-grandfather was a Pullman porter."

"Really?" Lisa said.

Taylor nodded. "And he loved seeing the country. He was able to work on different routes in his lifetime. He thought Seattle was the prettiest."

"So he moved here?"

"Actually he married late in life. He was forty-five and his wife was twenty-five. He met her on a trip to D.C. My grandfather was born a year later."

"It must have been frightening for your great-grandmother, coming to a new land with no family and with him away most of the time."

"It was. She was a teacher. But when she got pregnant, her mother moved in with her."

"Her mother and your great-grandfather must have been the same age."

"They were. But it was typical for that era. He wanted a chance to save up some money before he married. And he had. Granddad said he was very tight with a penny. Saved enough to put him through law school. But my grandfather had to work from a young age. His dad wanted to instill the work ethic."

"He was a little too successful at it. You're a workaholic."

Taylor winked. "Keeps me out of trouble." Feeling mellow, he sipped on his wine. "How did your family end up here?"

"My mother is a recent import. She and my father met in college. But my father's family came to Seattle after the California Gold Rush."

"He was a miner?"

"You mean *she*. You're talking about two sisters here. My great-great-grandmother was a miner. Her sister ran a boarding house, laundry, and bordello."

"One-stop service."

"Get out of here. You never told me that," Audie said.

"Family skeleton."

"We could never tell looking at you."

"You're elegant and sophisticated," Lisa said. "Just don't

tell Leticia. She'll banish you from the family if she discovers you came from the wrong side of the blanket."

"Actually, I didn't. My great-great-aunt ran the bordello. My great-great-grandmother was the miner."

"I wonder who made more money," Taylor mused.

"I've read that the water carriers at the mines made more than most miners," Audie said.

"Exactly. After making a piddling amount, my great-great-grandmother came in from the mines. Said she wasn't turning up her skirt for anyone. So she took charge of the laundry and cleaning, while her sister took care of the guests' other needs. They made a fortune."

"How did they end up in Seattle?"

"Well, after a few years, my great-great-grandmother met a strapping and handsome miner who had done rather well. But he got tired of getting jumped. And as more miners moved in, the sisters needed protection. He traded in his pan for a gun. After they made enough money, he married my great-great-grandmother, and the three of them moved to Seattle to begin 'respectable' lives."

"Sometimes I get the feeling that Leticia envies your mother," Lisa said.

"She does," Audie said. "Mom's parents were blue-collar workers at Boeing—hardworking people. I don't understand why she's never satisfied and proud of them. I am."

"Were?" Taylor asked.

"They're still around. They were at Leticia's picnic. Remember I introduced you," Melia said. "They're a warm, loving couple who dote on their grandchildren." She sipped her wine. "They're the ones who kept me going in my darkest hours."

Taylor reached out and gathered her in his arms. It wasn't a time for lovemaking but for love. He held her close to him. "You're not alone," he whispered.

Audie nudged her with his leg. "You'll never be alone. You have two brothers."

"And a best friend," Lisa reminded her.

"My parents love you," Audie said.

For now, Melia thought.

Melia was awakened early the next morning by the door-bell. *Jesus, who could be calling at quarter to seven?* she thought as she rolled out of bed, still half asleep. Grabbing a robe, she padded to the door in her bare feet.

Mrs. Sieverson stood on the other side with a bucket in one hand and a brown paper bag in the other. "Still abed I see," she said when Melia opened the door. "I brought over some geoduck and potatoes from the garden. Thought we'd make geoduck and green onion hash for breakfast and serve 'em with eggs."

Melia smothered a yawn. "Sounds delicious." Truthfully, she hadn't eaten the hash in years. Geoduck wasn't fowl, as one would think, but gigantic clams found under the sand along Puget Sound.

"I'll help you fix it. Aslin went fishing. He'll bring the catch by with some I took out of the freezer this morning. Should be thawed out soon. Maybe we can have a fish stew outside." She talked on in rapid-fire motion. "I think I saw a stew pot in the storage shed when we looked for the furniture."

"I'm going to put some clothes on," Melia said.

"Go on, go on."

"Who's there?" Earl asked, belting his robe around him.

"Mrs. Sieverson," Melia responded. "She's going to help prepare breakfast. We're making a hash."

"I'm going to start separating the meat from the shell while you dress," Mrs. Sieverson said to Melia. "Already cooked 'em. How many of you are there?"

"Six."

"Better prepare enough for eight and some for leftovers. Everybody loves the hash." The older woman headed to the kitchen with her bucket and bag. Melia and Earl looked at each other.

"You can go back to bed," Melia told Earl, who was clearly still sleepy. "I hope we didn't wake Leticia."

"She's wearing earplugs. Said my snoring disturbs her sleep."

Earl scratched his chin. "Guess I'll dress and drive to the store for a paper."

They went to their respective bathrooms. Melia dressed quickly. When she emerged from the bathroom, she smelled the blessed aroma of coffee. Following the scent to the kitchen, she immediately grabbed a cup and poured herself some. She drank half a mug before she felt human.

"Thought my coffee would get you stirring," Mrs. Sieverson said. She was still working with the clams.

"These are some tough little buggers," she said. "We're going to have to pound them before cutting them in bite-size pieces."

"I remember," Melia said and began to help. When they finished with the clams, Mrs. Sieverson started peeling the potatoes, while Melia pounded the clams and cut them into pieces.

They were halfway through when Taylor entered the kitchen. "I smelled coffee," he said, then stopped when he saw Mrs. Sieverson.

"Whole pot full on the stove," the older woman said, her hands busily peeling potatoes.

"Mrs. Sieverson, meet Taylor Harrison, a friend of mine."

"Pleased to meet you, young man."

"My pleasure, ma'am." Taylor started to extend a hand until he realized her hands were occupied.

"Help yourself to coffee."

Melia got a cup out of the cabinet and poured him a cup. "Sugar is on the table and cream in the fridge," she said. Earl returned with his paper, and Melia handed him a cup of coffee, too.

"That hit the spot," Taylor said. "Anything I can do to help?"

"We have it under control," Mrs. Sieverson assured him.

"What are you cutting up?" he asked Melia.

"Geoducks." It was pronounced "gooey-ducks." After the potatoes were peeled and the clams were cut into little pieces, they started the hash. To a sour cream and spice mixture, they added the clams, diced potatoes, minced green onions, and diced red peppers. When they added the mixture to a hot oiled skillet, the aroma brought the rest of the house to the kitchen. By the time everyone sat down to breakfast of hash and eggs, Mr. Sieverson had returned with his catch.

"I've died and gone to heaven," Audie said.

"You aren't the only one," Taylor agreed over a forkful of hash.

"I'm adding this to a breakfast cooking show on the fall schedule," Melia said. "This is incredibly fabulous. How could I have forgotten?"

Mrs. Sieverson beamed across from them and began to regale them with old tales of the island, Melia's parents and grandparents, as well as her own family. It was two hours before they left the table.

It felt like old times, Melia thought. That evening they enjoyed the seafood stew Mrs. Sieverson prepared with Mr. Sieverson's catch around the fire on the beach in back of her house. She and Taylor had driven to town and purchased loaves of French bread from the bakery to serve with the stew.

Over the next two days, they fished, biked around the island, toured the winery, explored charming boutiques, visited the museum of the Suquamish Indian tribe, picked raspberries on Melia's property, made pies and other sumptuous desserts, and invited the Sieversons to dinner again. The couple had been pleased.

The island had come to life again for Melia. It almost felt like old times with her friends. She forcefully pushed the worries of the city behind her. If they sneaked up on her, she mentally pushed them away.

Even Taylor relaxed. He didn't often wear jeans and a T-shirt, but he wore them all weekend and looked very handsome in them. He seemed to be adapting to the western Washington lifestyle.

Melia inhaled a deep breath, smelling the Sound and the fresh pine. Such peace. Such quiet. Without a doubt, Leticia must now have understood how important it was for her to keep her home. The woman wasn't heartless. The island had been a big part of Audie and Blair's childhoods as well. They could all enjoy the house, once Blair overcame his phobia. She missed him.

When Sunday afternoon arrived, Melia hated to leave. Taylor tucked an arm around her shoulders when they stood at the railing of the ferry, watching the distance spread between them and the island. The snowcapped Olympic range made a fantastic sight in the distance.

"We'll have to return later to pick blackberries and apples," Melia said.

"Umm. I think I gained five pounds this weekend." They settled into silence as they watched the breathtaking view. "The weekend was a wonderful idea," Taylor said.

Melia nodded. He'd even sneaked into her bedroom one night in the wee hours of the morning, and they'd made love quietly. Gratefully, her bedroom was separated from the others. He told her he saw Lisa sneaking up to the bedroom in the attic, where Audie was sleeping.

He massaged her shoulders and kissed her cheek before wrapping his arms around her waist. "Don't let anyone force you to sell."

One look at Jessica and Melia knew something else had happened. "What happened this time?" Melia asked. She was wrapping up the last TV show for the summer. After the tapings were done, she came into the store sporadically during the summer months for the occasional cooking class and supplies for new recipes. The rest of the time she experimented with recipes at home.

"Girl, it seems one thing after another is happening with Mark. It's driving me crazy."

"What happened this time?"

She glanced around to make sure no one was in hearing range. "I happened to look at one of his bank receipts. You know he always makes the deposits for the shop."

"Yes?"

"His deposit was for thousands more dollars than we actually take in. Why would he do that?"

"Are you sure of the day? It could have been an old slip for one of our busier days."

"I saw the date. Besides, we never took in twenty thousand in one day, even on our better days."

"Are you sure it was for the store? Or was it for some other business? He's involved in other things."

"It was for the store. He has a separate account for it. I know what I'm talking about. Why would he make a deposit for more than we take in?"

"The only thing that comes to mind is money laundering. But Mark wouldn't be involved with anything like that. He's . . ." Speechless, she shrugged.

"I'm beginning to think we don't know him at all, Melia. I thought he lived a clean life. How could he be involved in anything like that without me knowing about it?"

"Easily. You're at work most of the time. He only shows up to take the deposit and sales receipts."

"He's not the man I thought he was, is he? He and I need to have a long talk."

"Don't you dare. If he's involved in anything illegal, you could get hurt. I think you need to get more information. But be careful."

"I will." Color had seeped back into Jessica's cheeks. She looked more her usual self.

"I'm thinking you're not in love with Mark any longer, are you?"

"No. Mark's so possessive that I'm getting a little afraid.

I think I'll get a card from Duncan during the lunch class.
Maybe even some advice. It turns out he's a detective."

"Just make sure Mark doesn't catch you enjoying Duncan's
company. I'm nervous about dead bodies turning up. And he
always struck me as clueless. I thought I had troubles. Now
you're knee-deep in crap, too."

"What kind of trouble do you have?"

"I told you about the development of my parents' land in
Seattle. Well, Taylor found out their signatures were forged."

"My word."

"Taylor agrees with me. He thinks they were murdered. And
we're trying to find out who did it."

"Is there anything I can do to help?"

"Thanks, but no. We better get ready for the class. People
are arriving." She nodded toward the door. "And guess what?
Your detective is early."

Jessica blushed and turned around nervously. Sure enough,
Duncan and his niece were walking in together. This time she
was leading him.

"I saw your grandparents this weekend," Melia said. "We
had a wonderful time."

"They told me when I called. If I didn't have to work, I
would have gone, too. She told me you all had geoduck. I can't
wait to get there. She always prepares it when I visit." Jessica
glanced at the students pouring in. "Well," she said, "I have
work to do."

Taylor was at his grandfather's house when the phone rang
for him. It was Elliot.

"Man, the U.S. Marshalls just left here. They were asking
questions about Peter Bowman."

"Why?"

"They wouldn't say. I told them I'd have you contact them.
But that didn't work. They were ready to arrest me if I didn't
reveal your name. Hope you don't mind."

"I don't. I have nothing to hide," Taylor said, wondering what can of worms he'd opened up.

"In the meantime I found some pretty hot stuff on this guy. It seems he used to work for the mob. This guy was the one who arranged hits. I got that information from a PI friend who lives in New York."

"Hits as in murders?"

"Exactly. He didn't do the killing but contracted for various hit men once a crime was authorized. He went out of commission about four years ago. Something to do with the district attorney. They believe he went into the witness protection program. The US Marshalls were protecting him. Bowman testified against the mob. So they're still after him. That's all my PI friend knew."

"Jesus."

"Yeah. Your buddy hung out with a real character in that one."

"Do you have a phone number for me?"

Taylor jotted the Marshall's number down as Elliot rattled it off. As he hung up, he wondered if Palmer had hired Bowman to murder Melia's parents. He also wondered how the district attorney could put a man who arranges contract murders in the witness protection program when so many people who did far less were rotting in jail with a life sentence or on death row. That was justice for you.

"Can you get a recent picture of him?"

"I'll try. I'm sure he was in the local and national papers. Anything dealing with the mob is news. I'll call my contact and get back to you."

"Thanks, man."

The mob. Could they be responsible for the murders? But why? More importantly, was Melia in danger from them? The mob would be searching for Bowman. And what possible connection could this man have with a group of Friday night poker-playing buddies?

* * *

Melia was putting the finishing touches on a new recipe when Leticia dropped by her apartment.

"You're just in time. I want you to sample this." Melia dished a small portion into a bowl and passed it to her.

"It's fabulous. It tastes like my mother's recipe."

"It *is* your mother's recipe. Only the cooking time differs. Instead of it taking two hours, I've shortened it to forty-five minutes."

"Wonderful when you can get flavors like this. She's going to be pleased."

"Actually, she helped me streamline the cooking process."

"My mother has some wonderful family recipes. I'm not much of a cook, not like my sisters, anyway. At least the family collection is being passed on."

"True."

"I really enjoyed spending the weekend on the island."

Melia smiled. "So did I. Lisa can't stop talking about it. Audie and Taylor enjoyed themselves as well." She sent Leticia a sad smile. "Everyone except Blair."

"Good news there. Dr. Beatty called me today. Blair contacted him Thursday."

"You're kidding!"

"I can't tell you how happy that makes me."

"I know, I know. Oh, Leticia!" After so many years, Melia was speechless with joy.

"I pray the two of them connect."

"They will. If he made the first move, that means he's ready to get help. He'll be more open to it."

"But I have a specific reason for being here."

"Oh?" Melia asked.

"Northwest Coastal has asked me to get a reply from you concerning your land on the island. The weekend brought back all those old memories. I know it's a wonderful place. I believe I can work out a deal where you can keep the house and maybe three or four acres around it. But I know they will want water access. You own plenty of waterfront property. Enough even for both the group and your private needs."

Melia couldn't imagine a noisy marina so close to her house. The solitude would disappear, not only for her but for the Sieversons, too. It wouldn't be fair. Melia sighed. She'd hoped to confront Julia Jacobs, not Leticia, about this. She studied Leticia's features. Having to deal with her was much harder.

"Leticia, I'm never going to sell that land. It's the only piece left from my family, and it's my responsibility to pass it on to my children. I want Blair and Audie and their families to enjoy it just as we did when we were children."

"You still can. I'm sure Northwest Coastal will agree with your keeping the house and a small portion of the land," Leticia said hopefully. "Their offer is fair. Just take this and study it."

"Le—"

"You don't have to give us a decision immediately. I'm merely asking you to consider it." She took Melia's hand in hers. "Just take some time and think on it."

"Julia said the same thing before. I don't want to keep you hanging when it isn't going to make a difference."

"Just a week, dear." She patted Melia's hand. "Oh, by the way, I saw this beautiful lapis necklace the other day. I thought it would go beautifully with your black dress or your white one or some of the other things in your closet. I don't see lapis as much as I used to."

"You don't have to buy me gifts." The bribe was too high when Leticia expected her land in return.

"You're the daughter I never had. You're a blessing for me."

As long as I do what you want me to do, Melia thought. "I can't accept this."

"The necklace has nothing to do with the land. It gives me so much pleasure shopping for you. It's given from the heart. I love you, darling. We all do." Picking up her purse, Leticia started for the door. "I'm going to drop in on Blair before I go." She kissed Melia on the cheek. "Take care, sweetheart. I'll see you on Sunday. You've missed a couple of brunches. I hope you'll be there this weekend. And bring Taylor. Lord knows Audie will bring Lisa. I have a hard time accepting her, but . . . as a parent you do what you have to."

"I'll let you know."

Melia looked at the necklace as if it were a snake coiled in her hand. Usually when she was upset, she did busy work just to keep her mind occupied. But this time, work wasn't going to take away the pain of losing her second family. She had felt so connected this weekend. So loved. She couldn't sell her land to Northwest, even if it cost her the Sims. To her, the land was priceless, and it had nothing to do with money. She couldn't sell it at any price. Her family had worked too hard to acquire it. They had worked tirelessly to build a future for themselves and their descendents. Her own descendents would know that. She'd tell the story, just as her grandparents had told her. They needed proof of the strength of their forbearers. So much of their history was lost, like ashes scattered in the wind. But she had evidence of their lives in the land and in the recording of their history. An oak tree out back bore her grandparents' names, her parents' names, and hers. Money couldn't buy that. She was doing well where she was, thank you very much.

If the price for Leticia's love was sacrificing her heritage, then she'd have to do without the love. A pain stabbed her in the heart. Melia climbed onto one of the barstools in the kitchen. She'd have to relive losing her family all over again. Would that include Blair, Audie, and Earl? Even if it did, she couldn't, she wouldn't, change her decision.

The country had enough luxury developments without adding her land. Leticia's love came at too high a price. And her heart already belonged to Taylor.

In a short while, she was going to lose most of the people she loved. It was so much all at once. As soon as the investigation was over, Taylor would leave and go on to the next chapter of his life. She was going to lose Leticia and her family as soon as she told them her decision. She might as well put an end to all of it at once. Why drag it out? Why go through the pain twice when she could get it done in one fell swoop? And why did her losses have to be so complete? She lost her parents on one disastrous night. History was about to repeat itself.

Melia walked to the window and gazed out at Lake Washington. Just as she kept telling Jessica that you can't change a man, she couldn't change Taylor, much as she wanted to. It was time she listened to her own advice.

It was late that afternoon before the U.S. Marshalls appeared at Taylor's office.

They flashed badges and handed him business cards. After looking over the badges, Taylor offered them seats across the desk from him.

"We're here about Peter Bowman. I'm sure Mr. Carver warned you."

Taylor nodded. "Why are you searching for him?" Taylor wasn't protecting a client. He only wanted answers. Answers he wasn't going to get from the FBI, especially if they were protecting Bowman. But that wasn't going to stop him from seeking answers. He gave them information about Melia's parents and Bowman's connection to Palmer.

"I'm searching for the Lucases' murderers," Taylor said.

"The police believe it was a murder and a suicide."

"It wasn't."

"Can you prove it?"

"If I could, the police would have the information. I also want to know why Palmer tried to kill my grandfather. Do you know where Bowman is?"

"No. He left the witness protection three years ago. We've been searching for him since then."

"Why? He testified at the trial."

"There will be a retrial. New evidence, according to the defense. We need Mr. Bowman to testify at the new trial."

"I see."

The men stood in unison. "You have our cards. If you find out any information, contact us."

Taylor stood also and nodded.

"Mr. Bowman can be a dangerous man," one of the suits said.

"Then why was he still on the streets?" Taylor didn't expect an answer, and he didn't get one. As a lawyer, he already knew. There were always bigger fish.

"So, you spent the weekend on the island with Melia," Ralph Johnson said to Taylor.

He would have to pick a time when they were the only two in the elevator, Taylor thought.

"Yes, with Leticia and Earl as chaperones. Audie and Lisa were also there. Very respectable." Did his grandfather actually think he followed the old-school rules? Not even the old folks followed those rules in their younger years. If the woman got pregnant, they were usually forced to marry. But this was a new day, with plenty of protection against pregnancy, as well as AIDS. And he used it.

"How old are you?" his grandfather asked.

Taylor sighed. "Thirty-two. You know that. While you're at it, save the lecture about respect for the young woman and all that. I've heard it all before."

"Umm. You're no young stud anymore," his grandfather said.

He liked to think he was. He smiled at his grandfather. "The women think I am."

"Which women?"

"I think this is going down the wrong stream. I'll be leaving soon."

"And leaving a brokenhearted young woman behind."

"She knows I'm leaving—knew it from the beginning."

"So why did you start an affair with her if it was only temporary. Portland isn't so far away. Take a trip here a couple of times a month."

"Look, I'm not ready to settle down."

"When will you be ready and with whom?"

The elevator stopped. Three people got on, putting an end to the uncomfortable conversation.

They didn't get an opportunity to start the conversation again before they made it to Melia's apartment.

"Dear, it's wonderful to see you again." Taylor's grandfather hugged Melia as if she was already his granddaughter-in-law, and Taylor felt a stab of anger at the man's high-handedness. His great-grandfather married when he was forty-five, and while he might not wait that long, he wasn't ready now, and he wasn't going to let the old man talk him into anything he wasn't ready for. He wished he hadn't told his grandfather he was going to visit Mrs. Miles.

"I'm all ready," Melia said. "Let me get a sweater. It can get cool in the mountains."

On the drive, his grandfather didn't mention marriage or his age. He and Melia carried on a cordial conversation, while Taylor's hands gripped the steering wheel, waiting for the bomb to fall.

"Mrs. Emerline," Ralph Johnson said, "I owe you an apology."

"Why?" the no-nonsense woman asked. "You weren't running the firm then. I believe in blaming the right person. Palmer Wainwright has to take the responsibility."

"As he isn't here—"

"Well, I plan to leave here in a few weeks. I'm getting along well. I don't need to live in this place, but I'm not sure if I want a house any longer. The yard can be too much for me now that I don't have your daddy to see to things," she said to Melia.

"I'll probably look for a condo. Something convenient to grocery stores, the doctor's office, and such."

"I'll be happy to help you look if you tell me exactly what you need in a condo," Ralph said.

"That's very kind of you."

"It's the least I can do."

Was that interest he saw in his grandfather for the snappy old woman? The old man had been chasing the single neighbors away since his grandmother's passing. Taylor took a look at the snappy Mrs. Miles and thought he caught a bit of interest in her demeanor, too. Then he saw Willy, the older gentleman who was trying to court Mrs. Emerline, trotting toward them, waving his cane briskly. Would wonders ever cease?

Chapter 13

Melia had a lot to think about, and she wanted to spend the evening alone to do just that. Talking to Leticia tomorrow was going to be hell. When she asked Taylor to leave, he responded as if she were breaking off their relationship. In a sense, she was easing away from him.

"You're trying to control me. As if I didn't hear enough from my grandfather yesterday," Taylor said in frustration.

"Look, I don't know anything about your conversation with your grandfather, but I'm going to spend tonight thinking about some things—alone."

Taylor emitted a drawn out sigh. "Is there anything I can help you with?" he finally asked.

"No."

Taylor left, feeling an intense distance he'd never felt with her before. And he didn't like it. They were friends. She should feel comfortable enough to talk to him about anything.

Anger and hurt engulfed Taylor as he showered and dressed for bed. What right did he have, damn it. He'd be gone soon, as she conveniently reminded him—she was always reminding him of that fact lately. At least she wasn't the begging kind that kept hounding him about changing his mind. But women could be devious. He'd seen his sisters use their charm and

wiles on men plenty of times. Just like a woman. Get your
emotions all tangled up and then start acting weird. All this
time she'd been acting sweet. And suddenly she'd turned into
a difficult thorn in his side. Like she kept reminding him, it
was going to be over soon, anyway. So why did a fist grab his
stomach and twist it into knots?

Melia felt ice spreading through her stomach as the dull ache
of foreboding kept her twisting the sheets through the night.
Taylor had gone home peeved, accusing her of distancing herself from him as punishment. But Melia had other things on
her mind. The whole world didn't revolve around him. He
should be glad she was giving him space. That worked both
ways. If he wanted his space, he should be willing to grant her
the same.

She dressed quickly. Her heart a lead weight, she dragged
herself across town in sluggish traffic to Leticia's house. She
was unwilling to put off the inevitable any longer.

"Well, it's so good to see you, Melia. And so unexpected.
Have you decided on the land? The investment group just
called and asked if you've made a decision, so I'm glad you
stopped by." Leticia was all smiles and warm cheer. Melia did
not enter the house. If she took a chair, she'd never be able to
stand again.

"Yes, I've decided. And I'm not going to sell. The land
belonged to my family, and it's too important to cut it up for
some upscale housing."

Leticia looked shocked. "But they're offering you a small
fortune. You can buy other land."

"Are you listening to yourself? My family went through
great hardship to purchase that land at a time when it was far
from easy for black folks." Melia looked down at her hands,
then back at the older woman.

"Leticia, I know I stand a chance of losing your hospital-
ity, love, and friendship by this decision, but I can't give you

the answer you want. You've given me so much, and it cuts me up inside to say no to you. This isn't easy for me, and if you don't want anything to do with me because of it, I'll understand." Melia's voice nearly cracked. Her heart felt as if it had chipped into a thousand pieces. She felt as if she were losing her family all over again.

"Melia—"

"I know you're disappointed," Melia interrupted. "You were my mother's best friend, but I know my parents never planned to sell their home. Yet something happened, and now their home is gone forever. The land my grandparents sacrificed for is gone, bulldozed over. I can't get that back, but I'm not going to let that happen to the land on Bainbridge. You can't tear up people's heritage just to make profits you don't even need. Some things mean more than a few more dollars. If you can't understand that, then I'm sorry."

With that, Melia turned and ran away without responding to Leticia's frantic calls. She wouldn't break down and cry in front of her. She almost mowed Earl down as he came up the walkway. He moved out of her way faster than she'd ever seen him move, even tried to grab her, but missed.

"Melia?"

Tears clogged her throat. She shook her head. She couldn't speak. She opened her car door and slid into the seat. Fumbling with her keys, she started the motor and peeled out of the driveway. In the rearview mirror, she saw Leticia and Earl standing together. Earl had put his arms around the older woman, supporting her.

Soon, there would be no support for Melia. The mystery was almost solved. She didn't expect Taylor to be there more than another week or two. Then she would be totally on her own. She lifted her chin. She'd get through this. The worst that could happen already had. As much as she needed to be with someone, she wouldn't go to Taylor. For once, she had to stand alone.

* * *

"I'm spending more time at your place than my own," Lisa said to Audie the next morning as she dressed for work.

"I sleep better with you around."

"Sleep? Who sleeps around you?" Lisa asked. "I'm going to look like an old hag when I meet your grandparents. There are bags under my eyes. Cucumbers. I need cucumbers."

"What for?"

"My eyes, silly."

"Don't need them. You look fabulous. I don't know why you worry so much. Must be a woman's nature. Got to worry about something or you're not satisfied." Her shapely bottom caught his eye. He finished shaving. Then he took the towel from around his waist and swatted her backside.

She screeched. "I'm going to—"

He pulled her close. "Kiss me?" he said and pressed his lips to hers.

"You don't deserve a kiss, acting like that," she said, rubbing her behind.

"Hey, don't do that. Let me." He moved her hand aside and rubbed the soft skin. "Now do I deserve one of your sweet kisses? Tell me you don't enjoy them."

"Now why would I do that?" Lisa asked. She caressed the side of his face. He pulled her close. She felt his hardness rise to the occasion. As much as she'd like to fall into bed with him, she needed to broach the subject of the handbags. She'd known all along there was something wonderful about Audie. He usually kept it hidden beneath his humor. But he was a good man, and she wanted to help him. He deserved it. Besides, he made her world so much brighter, less serious. She needed that.

"On a different note, would you mind if I sold some of your handbags in my shop?"

He stopped caressing her and regarded her silently. "You really want to?"

"They're very well made. People will buy them or give them away as gifts."

"Thanks, but you don't have to do this just because I'm losing a mint. I don't want pity from you." He wrapped the towel back around his waist.

"Do you really think I would have anything in my store that I didn't believe I could sell? That's less than quality. I'm a businesswoman. I know what women like."

"Are you sure?" he asked. He glanced at her through her reflection in the mirror.

"Of course."

The phone rang as he pulled her into his arms once again.

"Audie, the phone—" Lisa said.

"Let the answering machine pick up. We're going back to bed."

"But . . . your grandparents—"

"We'll get there," he said, tugging her after him. When they made it to the bedroom and fell on the bed, he heard the answering machine click on. His mother's voice.

Audie, we have an emergency. It's Melia. We have to talk. The family has to stick together and deal with this. Please call me. It's urgent.

Audie groaned. His mother had done something again.

"Maybe you should call her," Lisa said.

"This is just another tactic to get me to propose to Melia. My mother doesn't know when to stop," Audie said, remembering the fabrication she'd spun at the picnic. "I wish she'd relax and let us live our own lives. I just don't understand her. She went through the same thing with my granddad. You'd think she'd be more compassionate."

"Well, we can't settle that right now, can we? She sounded stressed. If something happened to Melia, I want to know."

"I'm telling you this is another of Mom's stunts," he said. "There are some interesting things I want to do with you. We can't get it done by talking." He started to string kisses along her neck, but Lisa picked up the phone and handed it to him. With resignation he dialed.

* * *

Melia had not visited anyone that day. She needed some emotional healing. She'd turned the answering machine on so she wouldn't hear the ring. She hadn't answered her doorbell all day—hadn't even gone to see who was there. She needed to regroup, and she used the day to pamper herself, to bring some sanity to her chaotic thoughts.

When her cell phone rang, she tried to ignore it, but unable to just let it ring, she glanced at the number. It was Jessica. She picked it up

"Hey, girl. I know I keep calling you in the middle of a catastrophe, but Mark is going to leave in a few minutes for some meeting. I plan to follow him."

"Are you crazy? Don't even consider it."

"I have to know what's going on."

"If it's that important, I'll come with you. Where are you?"

"At his place. He's in the bathroom. He thinks I'm going home."

"I'll meet you at the elevator in a couple of minutes. We'll go outside before he does so he won't know we're following him."

Melia hung up and hurriedly dressed in a black shirt and jeans. Donning socks and black sneakers and grabbing her purse, she dashed from her apartment to the elevator.

"You're crazy, you know that?" she said to Jessica, who was dressed in jeans and a blue chambray shirt.

From the worried frown creasing Jessica's forehead, she understood why knowing was so necessary. If the situation were reversed, she'd want to know.

"I can't stand this secrecy any longer. He won't talk to me about this other side of his life. I want the truth, once and for all."

"You're going to feel stupid if he has some perfectly harmless explanation." They ran to Melia's car and parked it where they could observe cars leaving the garage. Scooting low in the seat so Mark wouldn't see them when he came outside, they craned their necks to peek out of the window. It was night, so he wouldn't be able to identify the car following him the way he could during the day.

They waited and waited for him to drive out of the garage. But suddenly Jessica pointed across the street. "Look, he's getting into another car." Mark was opening the passenger door to a black Ford Expedition.

Melia started her car. When the driver of the Expedition looked out of his window to pull into traffic, she got a clear look at his face.

"I've seen him before," Melia said and pulled in two cars behind the black Ford Expedition. She'd read something about detectives doing that.

"Where?"

"I can't remember. Try to copy the license plate," she said. "We could easily lose him."

"Great idea." Jessica dug into her purse for pen and paper.

The Ford Expedition traveled a long stretch on East Madison. Then the driver took the street to the waterfront. Many people were milling about there, going to various restaurants and tourist shops. Tourists were taking in the nightlife. But Melia kept her eyes glued to the vehicle in front of her.

"They probably are just going to some meeting. Or Mark might be seeing another woman. Who knows?" Jessica said nervously.

"Not with another guy in the car, he's not," Melia said.

Jessica sighed. "Maybe I'm making too much of this. I'm getting paranoid."

"You have every right to be."

Suddenly the Expedition turned down a quiet street. The driver made turn after turn until he lost Melia. Had they spotted her? But they couldn't have. She'd lagged far enough behind to remain unnoticed.

"Did you see where they went?" Melia asked.

"I've lost sight of them, too."

Melia circled the block, searching.

"There's the SUV." Jessica checked the license number. "It's the one."

Melia drove slowly by the Expedition but didn't stop. "They aren't in there. We may as well park." She found a parking space on a side street. Then she and Jessica mingled with the tourists around the shops and restaurants, scouring the area.

They walked the streets for an hour. "Maybe we should leave. We can't find them anywhere."

"Let's search a few more minutes," Melia said. "They have to be somewhere around here."

"We can't go in every restaurant and look. We could waste the entire night and still miss them."

It was a pleasant evening. Many diners were eating outside. They trooped down three more streets but still didn't find Mark and the driver. They passed many tourists wearing "I Love Seattle" T-shirts and carrying souvenir coffee mugs. They heard music that drifted from an outdoor concert taking place on one of the piers.

"Let's go," Jessica finally said, and they left. The Ford Expedition was still there. "I'm not going to sleep a wink tonight. I'm so nervous."

"He doesn't know you're on to him."

"I know."

"Come on. Let's go to one of these restaurants and have dinner. I'll get you pleasantly drunk, then take you home."

"You can stay the night at my place. I'm in the mood for tempura. A good Japanese restaurant is just a couple of blocks from my place. Then you can crash there."

"We haven't done that in a long time."

"It's time. You think Taylor would mind?"

"I don't need his permission."

"Okay. Let's go."

"Now I remember where I've seen that man with Mark," Melia said, while turning the car toward Lisa's home. "He was in the elevator the night of my last party. He's huge, and he reminded me of a longshoreman."

"What could the two be doing together?"

"Beats me."

Traffic was horrible as usual as they made their way across town to Jessica's modest two-bedroom house.

Taylor went to Mel's restaurant again. And again, the older man served him dinner. Taylor had tried to reach Melia to tell her he'd be late. But for the first time since he met her, her cell phone was turned off. He left a message, but obviously she didn't want to be contacted. So perhaps he'd been a little peeved last night, but there was no reason for her to carry it this far. How was he going to apologize if he couldn't even reach her?

The restaurant was quickly filling up. Many stopped by for carryout they'd called in earlier. Taylor debated taking something to Melia and even called to see what she'd like.

Mel returned to Taylor's table and sat down across from him. "Someone knocked out the window in the building down the street last night," he said. "We wouldn't have such problems if this area was built up. Half the houses and storefronts are empty, just what a kid needs when he's searching for trouble."

"With real estate at a premium and with this place located so close to Lake Washington, I was wondering why investors hadn't snapped it up."

"Oh, they will. Before you know it, this place will be gentrified just like inner city neighborhoods all over. They'll push the locals on out and sell these spots for a fortune."

Taylor shook his head. "What a shame."

Mel sighed. "I hate to see that happen. We need our neighborhoods. They stand for something. Not everything is bad here. If we could just clean out the bad and give our youngsters the role models they need, then we would have accomplished something."

"That's true," Taylor said. It sounded so simple, but the problem was much more complex. Everything took money. When a company could build million-dollar condo units and sell them at inflated prices, why build real estate for people who could only pay a small fraction of that?

"I tried to put a group together once to try to redevelop this area, a couple of blocks at a time, but it fell through. They were doing more fighting among themselves than anything else." The older man shook his head and looked around. "Just makes me sick to know what direction this place is going in eventually, just because we can't work together."

"The right kinds of businesses could do very well here."

"You better believe it. We get people from all over during the day, but once night hits, they scatter. It used to be pretty bad on the avenue in the U District once, too, but they pretty much got that cleaned up, and the place is now bustling at night. With a little effort, the same could happen here."

"I agree," Taylor said. "The key lies in convincing a group of investors. I've seen it happen before. Arguments result in stalemates, and when that goes on long enough, the group disbands."

"The story of our lives. Well, thanks for bringing the papers by."

"It was a sure way to get a fabulous dinner."

"You don't need an excuse to come here. How's your grandfather, by the way?"

"Coming along nicely."

"Before you leave, I have a package for you to take him. He usually stops by at least once a month, often more. The cook's fixed up his favorite."

"He'll enjoy it," Taylor said, biting off a piece of rib so tender it fell from the bone.

In the gourmet shop, Melia listened in on a conversation between mother and daughter.

"Mom, please, you cook the same thing over and over. Take one of these classes."

"You ate last night's dinner just fine," the mother said, selecting olives from the cooler.

"It was horrible."

"Didn't I put enough ketchup on it to drown out the flavor?"

"You see, if you took a class, you wouldn't have to drown out the flavor."

"Perhaps both of you can take a class. If you both sign up, you get a discount," Melia said.

"Hum. Not bad," the mother said, turning to her daughter. "Then you can cook for me. See if you appreciate the fact that someone else is cooking."

"I'd appreciate it if I didn't have to eat the same thing day after day, week after week."

"Honey, there's only so many ways you can bake a chicken. You're so health conscious you won't eat fried."

The daughter threw up her hands. "I can't win with you."

Melia handed the mother and daughter a course outline and left the battle.

"He's going out again after work," Jessica said later that day.

"We'll follow him," Melia said.

"Taylor called earlier. He wants you to call him."

"I'll call after I get home." Melia had left her cell phone charger at home. The car charger wasn't working. Now she would have to take the time to purchase a new one.

After Mark escorted them to their cars, Jessica parked her car in a nearby garage, and Melia picked her up in her car. They waited outside for Mark. It didn't take long before he turned out the lights at Modern Gourmet and made his way to his SUV.

"Looks like he's going to the same place," Jessica said as they drove along.

"I wonder if he's going to meet the man who was with him before?"

Several blocks from the pier, Mark parked his SUV in a lot.

He emerged carrying a gym bag. Melia searched for a parking space and was about to pull into one when Jessica stopped her.

"He's getting into another car."

"Is the same man driving?" Melia asked.

"No. Mark's driving and he's alone."

When Mark pulled onto another street, they were a couple of cars behind him. It was harder this time to tail him. The car didn't stand out like the SUV. A light caught them, and they lost him in Seattle's snarl of traffic.

"Let's go to the pier, anyway," Melia said. When they reached the pier, it didn't take them long to find the car Mark had been driving. They parked and walked the streets for half an hour. Suddenly someone screamed. A crowd began to gather, and they walked toward it.

"Maybe we shouldn't get too close. If something has happened, I don't want Mark to identify us."

"I want to see," Jessica insisted.

Melia sighed. "All right." They neared the crowd, elbowing their way closer to the front. Jessica made it closer than Melia. Then she stumbled back.

"Get me out of here."

"What's wrong? I told you not to get too close."

Jessica looked like she was going to faint, so Melia pulled her back and supported her.

"What's wrong?"

"It's the guy I talked to a week ago."

"Duncan, the detective?"

"No. Another one who came in looking for appetizers for a party. He talked to me for a half hour. Mark was there. My God! He's killing anyone who comes near me."

"Jessica, we have to go to the police."

"We can't even find Mark."

"Let's see if his car is still there."

They walked to the side street where Mark had parked and stopped.

The car was gone. They drove back to the lot where Mark had parked his SUV. It was gone, but the car was there.

"I'm going to be sick," Jessica said just before she opened the car door and retched.

Taylor couldn't reach Melia all that day or the day before. He couldn't even reach her cell phone. What the heck was going on? They talked every day, sometimes two and three times. He couldn't remember that many hours going by when they didn't talk. She didn't have to take this distancing to extremes.

The elevator stopped at his floor. He stopped at Melia's door and rang the doorbell. She didn't answer. Where was she? He went across the hall to Blair's and knocked on his door.

The guy was bleary-eyed as usual when he answered.

"Have you seen Melia today?"

"No. I went over there earlier. She hasn't answered her cell phone or her home phone. Christina saw her car in the garage yesterday, but not last night. Mom talked to Jessica. Seems Melia spent the night with her."

"Her car is gone now. I checked." Taylor tried to stifle his anxiety, which was quickly turning to anger. "If you see her, let me know."

Blair closed the door, and Taylor started to his own apartment. He was still thinking of Melia as he inserted his key. Before he could get the door open, the elevator opened and two pale-looking figures got off. They both appeared as if they'd looked death in the face and barely survived.

"What the hell is going on?" Taylor asked.

"I need a seat," Jessica said.

Melia fumbled with her key, then dropped it. Taylor brushed her aside and picked up the key. Her hands were shaking so badly, she could barely hold her purse, much less try to get the key into the lock. What could have happened to make those two this frightened?

Taylor opened the door and ushered them into Melia's apartment. They literally fell to the couch.

"Start talking," Taylor said, pacing in front of them.

By the time they finished, *Taylor* needed a seat.

"I could wring your necks. Do you realize how stupid that was? You could have gotten yourselves killed."

"We didn't think he was going to kill anyone. We just thought he was doing something illegal. We wanted to know what it was," Melia explained, not making a bit of sense. The look she gave him said she knew she wasn't making sense but had to talk, anyway.

"You could have gotten yourselves killed," Taylor repeated, leaning over Melia. He turned away and paced a couple of minutes, still agitated.

"I thought you went shopping or something. I never thought you'd gone on some hare-brained excursion like this. I guess that's what I get for complaining about your shopping for Blair."

"How else were we going to get answers? If we had gone to the police with our suspicions, they'd have laughed us out of the station. They'd have thought we were a couple of crazy women."

"You should have talked to me."

"Like I can bring all my problems to you to take care of."

"And why not?" He actually looked offended.

"Because you're going to be gone soon. You won't always be here to take care of me, or my problems. I have to rely on myself, like I've always done."

"I'm here now. That's no excuse."

Charged silence stretched between them.

"Maybe we should go to the police," Melia finally said. They were getting nowhere. Besides, the conversation was irrelevant since he was leaving soon and they both knew it.

"Who is this detective you met?" Taylor asked Jessica. "Do you think you can talk to him?"

Jessica nodded. She fumbled in her purse and retrieved Duncan Ford's business card, handing it over with a shaky hand.

Taking it, Taylor snatched up the phone and dialed the number. He identified himself as Jessica's friend and partially explained what had occurred. Duncan said he was coming right over. Taylor gave him Melia's address and waited with the women.

Melia's anger kept revisiting him. It was true he wasn't going to be in Seattle much longer. They both knew that. He hadn't let himself think about how soon he was leaving. From the very beginning, he'd made it clear that he was leaving and their relationship would end as soon as his questions were answered. The thought of her fending for herself didn't sit well with him. Of course, she'd fended for herself without him before he arrived in Seattle. But now he was here, and things were different. Worse, her relationship with the Sims was on shaky ground.

The thought of leaving Melia kept nagging at him like an infected tooth. While he didn't like the idea of returning to Portland without her, he wasn't ready for marriage. Besides, she was a local celebrity. He couldn't ask her to leave this. There was talk that he would soon be asked to become a managing partner in his law firm. He'd worked his butt off for that.

Thoughts of romance and forever love were all well and good, but keeping her and her friend alive was the most important step at the moment. It was time he informed the police about his own investigation, although the two didn't tie together.

Their first shock came when Duncan arrived. He came with his niece, only she wasn't really his niece. She wasn't wearing a pigtail, and she didn't look like a sixteen-year-old cheerleader any longer. Her blond hair, which had been red, was combed down to brush her shoulders in a pageboy style. He introduced her as an undercover cop.

"I really did need the cooking lessons. Only I don't chew as much gum as I did during class," the detective said.

Melia nodded.

Jessica felt betrayed. She wouldn't look at Duncan, although he watched her like a hawk. There was a real attraction there, Melia thought. Thank goodness. Knowing that Duncan was only pretending would take a toll on Jessica's self-confidence.

They discovered the detective had been suspicious of crimes Mark committed on other cases, and he had been casing the gourmet shop to keep tabs on him.

"What crime is he suspected of?" Jessica asked.

"We think he has been involved in murder and extortion. We aren't at liberty to go into detail."

"I think Jessica needs to go into hiding. It's too dangerous for her to be around Mark," Melia said.

Taylor said, "I agree."

"Right now he doesn't know that you're aware of his illegal activity. At least for a day or two, if you can go into work as if nothing is wrong, it will give us a chance to collect additional information."

"However, if you feel you're in danger at any time, call us immediately," said Duncan.

Jessica crimped her mouth. *As if he cared*, she thought. "He may be involved in money laundering."

"Do you have proof?"

"I know the money that he deposits is several times more than actual sales," she said. "And I've checked his deposits for the last week. Every night he deposits more than we take in."

After they discussed that, Melia and Taylor revealed the information they had uncovered on her parents' deaths and the attempt on Taylor's grandfather's life, although the cases didn't overlap. Before Officer Duncan left, he promised to look into it.

* * *

"Jessica, may I have a word with you?" Duncan asked.

"Follow me," she said, heading to the kitchen. She let the door close behind him.

"I know I let on that there was more going on between us than business and that you think I misled you."

"Yeah, yeah. All in the line of duty," she said. "I know."

"Not completely. I know it was unprofessional, but I do have feelings for you. When this is over, I'll pursue them. Not before."

Jessica crossed her arms and rubbed the goose bumps on her arms. "I'm cooperating, okay. You don't have to pretend things you don't feel. Besides, I don't trust you anymore."

"If I could have revealed my identity, I would have. But now that everything's out in the open, I don't have to worry about it, do I?"

He closed the distance between them and pulled her into his arms. Then he pressed his lips to hers. The sweetness of the kiss almost brought tears to Jessica's eyes. But she wasn't ready for him—or anyone right now.

"I don't like the idea of you staying alone," he said softly against her lips.

"Melia has already offered her spare bedroom, but I don't think it's such a great idea since Mark lives in this building. I've decided to visit my grandparents for a couple of days."

"Where do they live?"

"On Bainbridge Island. Their property is next to Melia's," she said.

"Does Mark know about this place?"

"He knows, but he's never been there. My folks don't like him."

"For good reason as it turns out. I'll escort you there."

"That isn't necessary. I'll be okay once I'm away from here."

"Won't Mark think it's odd that you suddenly took off from work?"

"Not really. I've done it in the past when I get fed up with the city."

He nodded. Quiet stretched between them. "The attraction isn't one-sided. Not by a long shot," he said.

"I'm so raw right now I can't even think about . . ."

"I know. But when time passes and you begin to heal, know that I'm waiting. That's all."

Jessica nodded. Just a few weeks ago, she was actively looking. And having fun. And now . . .

"If you need me, call please. Now. Do you need to go home to pack?"

"I leave clothing on the island. Everything I need is there."

"In that case, after you."

Everyone had left except Taylor. The answering machine was flashing red. She'd ignored it thus far, but then Melia put the espressos on the table and pushed the play button. She had felt that as long as she remained clueless, all was well, and that although she had lost Leticia, she hadn't lost Blair and Audie, because they hadn't confirmed it. All her troubles would miraculously go away. But they didn't. The fact that she was literally alone now was still front and center.

There were five messages from Leticia asking Melia to call. One message from Audie was recorded that day. Guess he was going to kick her to the curb, too.

Taylor and Melia settled in the den with espressos. As Melia sipped hers, Taylor set his on the cocktail table and leaned forward with his elbows on his knees. Tiredly, he glanced at Melia.

"Want to tell me what yesterday was all about?"

"I needed some time to myself," she said. It was time she put some distance between them. She knew he wasn't going to think she was fair, but what else could she do? What was wrong with it ending on her terms instead of his?

"I'm really tired."

"Oh, you're putting me out now?"

She looked at her hands, then at him, and nodded.

"Why did you turn off your cell phone?"

"The battery ran down, and my car charger broke. I wasn't home long enough to recharge. But it's charging now."

"Why the sudden distance, Melia?"

"What difference does a couple of weeks make? You're leaving soon. Whether we end it now or then doesn't make much difference."

"I thought we had more going for us than that."

"You made the rules. End of case, end of us."

"We can't remain friends?"

Melia rubbed her forehead. "Sure."

"My grandfather is taking Mrs. Miles to look at some condos next week."

"That's wonderful."

"Of course, they are condos near his home. I think he likes her."

"A budding romance."

"We'll see. I know you said Mark couldn't be involved in your parents' deaths, but since he was a friend of Palmer's, it's worth investigating."

Melia's heart skipped a beat. She'd bite at anything to prove her father hadn't murdered her mother. She glanced at Taylor. She had been willing to accept the tiny bit of himself he'd offered for a short time. She couldn't do that anymore. At some point she had to accept reality.

"I felt so guilty because I felt responsible for my parents' deaths."

"That's crazy. How could you possibly be responsible?"

"I was supposed to come home that weekend. I changed my mind at the last minute."

"That has nothing—"

"Don't you see? All these years I thought that if my parents were having problems, I could have helped in some way. If I had come home, I could have prevented their deaths."

"No." Taylor shook his head. "You couldn't have. If your father really killed your mother, you couldn't have done a thing. Just like my grandfather couldn't stop Palmer from trying to kill him."

"What are you saying?"

"That my grandfather was on his way to see Palmer when Palmer tried to kill him. And he ended up nearly dead himself."

"It was . . . an accident."

"No, it wasn't. The money Palmer paid you wasn't insurance money. It was guilty conscience payoff. For some reason, he felt you should have received that money, and just before he died, he left it to you with a letter stating that it was from an insurance account that got lost when your parents died. I tried to trace it back to an insurance company to no avail. Because it came from Palmer's personal accounts—not from any insurance company. It was his last wish, and I granted it."

"I don't understand why he would take his life over something like that. I don't need the money."

"For some reason, he thought you had been shortchanged. And he mentioned the Sims. They were involved in this some way."

"It doesn't make them murderers."

"I know someone forged your parents' signatures."

Melia glanced down at her hands. "My father had dreams of spending his hours making the grounds a showplace, even entering some the gardening shows and contests. After the property was sold, some of his plants were transferred to the Simses' estate. Leticia loved his flower gardens."

"And ended up with his flowers. Let's give this a rest and see what unfolds."

Taylor's penetrating gaze sought hers, his eyes darkening as if he were studying her.

"I missed you, you know."

"It was only one day."

"Felt like a lifetime." Slowly, he bent his head toward hers. When he looked at her like that, her brain took a holiday. Melia pushed at his chest.

"Taylor, we need to talk."

"I know." He kissed her then. His lips were warm and moist.

She was shocked at her own eager response to the touch of his lips, to the tingling that seemed to spread all over her. Again, she pushed against his chest. It was a weak gesture. When he looked at her with a question, she opened her mouth, but silence emerged. She *wanted* to be in his arms.

And then she didn't have to respond.

Chapter 14

When the doorbell rang, Melia wondered if Jessica had changed her mind about going to the island. She stood quickly, glad for the interruption. Where was her willpower when it came to Taylor? "I'll be right back," she said.

When she opened the door, she nearly fainted. Leticia, Earl, Audie, and Blair passed by her and settled in the great room. Blair had her spare key in his hand. She'd given it to him just in case she locked herself out. She was sure he would have used it had she refused to open the door.

Melia slowly entered the room. Squaring her shoulders, she approached the couch.

Leticia was nervously fingering her purse.

"I was wondering why you hadn't been by my place lately," Blair said accusingly.

Melia stared at her hands. "I've been busy."

"You were never that busy before," he said.

"I can't believe you tried to avoid us," Audie said.

Melia didn't know what to say. Why were they there, anyway?

Leticia stood, tears running down her cheeks. "I'm sorry you thought that I cared more about your land than about you. I honestly thought it harbored bad memories for you. For years you wouldn't even go there. You just paid good money for the caretakers to look after the place. I thought you'd eventually give it up."

"It's—" Melia started but was interrupted by Earl.

"You know how Leticia can be when she's on a mission," Earl said, "but she doesn't mean you any harm. She loves you just like me and the boys."

Tears gathered in Melia's eyes. She'd been so stressed out lately, she could barely think logically.

Leticia approached her and put her arms around her. "How could you think I didn't care about you? Yes, I'm aggressive, and I love making deals and money, I admit. But even I realize money doesn't buy everything. Family and love can't be replaced. You're my best friend's daughter. I couldn't hurt you."

Melia looked up to see Taylor leaning against the doorjamb.

"We were just having espresso in the den. Why don't you go in there while I prepare some for you? It's much more relaxing," Melia said.

"I'll help," Audie said. "Got any food in there?"

"It'll only take a few minutes for me to whip up some hors d'oeuvres," she said. That man ate as if a tapeworm lived inside him. "I think it's time for me to teach you how to cook if you and Lisa are going to be an item."

"I'm hiring a live-in when we get married."

Melia turned toward him. "You've popped the question?"

He held up a hand. "Not yet. But I will."

"When?"

"Soon. Give me a little time to mellow her some. Lisa isn't an easy woman. It's got to be done just right."

"Oh, Audie, I'm so happy for you."

"Hold on. She hasn't said yes yet."

"She will, she will. She'll be thrilled." Melia gave him a big hug and a kiss on the cheek.

"Hey," Taylor said from the doorway, "None of that. She's my woman."

Melia rolled her eyes and collected ingredients for Vashon

ferry coffee made with Jamaican rum, Kahlúa, and vanilla extract. It was one of the many coffees ferry boat riders drank to stay warm on stormy winter crossings. They had something to celebrate. She sliced apples and pears and juiced a lemon. She poured the juice over the fruit slices and arranged them on a platter.

"Audie, please get the sour cream out the fridge for the dip."

"That's chicken food. One little dip isn't going to fill me. What else are you fixing?"

"Baked brie topped with brown sugar, brandy, and nuts is ready to come out of the oven. That should keep you going for a while," she said, reaching for a pot holder to take it out. She set the brie and some crackers on the platter with the sliced fruit.

Leticia had started it all by wanting her parents' land, and she couldn't forgive that. By the same token, she couldn't blame Audie, Blair, and Earl for Leticia's failings. But if Leticia hadn't given Northwest Coastal the idea in the first place, Mark wouldn't have killed her parents for the land. And she fervently believed Mark killed them. He wasn't the innocent angel they thought he was.

"I'm going to have to start on the dip," Audie said. "Mom snatched me away before I could eat."

Melia handed him a plate. "Here, here. My goodness. You act as if you haven't eaten for a year."

"Feels like it."

"I know I have you for a friend as long as I have food."

"You've got that right."

On the third day when Jessica didn't show up at the store, Mark approached Melia.

"Do you know what's going on with Jessica?" he asked. "She doesn't usually take off this long."

"Last I heard, she was sick. Summer colds can be much worse than winter ones."

"Hum. Appreciate your pitching in, especially on your time off."

"Glad to help."

He finished his coffee and started to head for the sink.

"I'll take that. I'm going in back."

"Thanks."

Melia took Mark's cup, careful not to smudge his fingerprints. Once in the back room, she used a paper towel to sop up the remaining liquid in the cup and slipped it into a plastic bag. Glancing around to make sure no one was watching her, she slipped the bag into her purse, unseen.

Finally, she thought. She was beginning to think she would have to go another day without getting his fingerprints. When she left work, she carefully watched her rearview mirror to make sure she wasn't being followed and then drove directly to Taylor's office.

When she arrived there, she rushed into the building as if killer bees were on her heels. Taylor's assistant, Nadine, called him from the front office and then sent her back. Melia closed Taylor's door behind her.

"I have it," she said, leaning against his desk to catch her breath. Adrenalin was flowing wildly through her.

"Does he suspect anything?"

"Not a thing," she said, tugging the cup out of her purse and handing it to him.

"I'll call that detective, Duncan, and have him pick it up."

"I'm glad that's over."

"You're not returning to that place until it's safe."

"He asked me about Jessica today. I think he's beginning to get suspicious."

"Let's hope Duncan can get us something quickly."

Suddenly the intercom came on. "You have a call on line one," Nadine said. "A Ms. Leticia Sims."

Puzzled, Taylor picked up the phone. "Leticia."

"I know you're working, so I'll be brief. I have a family brunch each Sunday after church. I would like to invite you this Sunday. Perhaps you'd like to accompany us to church before the brunch."

"I'll be happy to join you," Taylor said, thinking to himself that the old battle-ax was finally coming around now that he was on Melia's list.

"I'm looking forward to seeing you again."

Taylor didn't really believe that.

"What did she want?" Melia asked as he hung up the phone.

"She invited me to Sunday church service and brunch afterwards."

"I gather you accepted."

"Of course. It would be rude to turn your family down."

"A few days ago, you thought she was a criminal."

He shrugged.

"I don't know why you're ingratiating yourself with her. You're leaving soon. Besides, I don't even know if I'm going over there Sunday."

"Do you have to rub the fact that I have to return to my job in my face?"

"I don't understand why you're trying to make ties here when you won't be here, that's all."

"I have made ties. There are definite ties between you and me."

Melia stood. "I have a million things to do before the weekend. Let me know what happens with the fingerprints."

"Why are you trying to create this crazy distance between us? You can't undo what has already happened."

"But I can end something that's wrong."

He snatched her close to him and kissed her. "Are the feelings we have wrong? Does this feel wrong?"

Tiredly, Melia sighed. "Does it even matter?"

"Definitely."

"Why?"

"Let's get through the next week or so without all this emotional garbage, okay? Even if you never go to bed with me again." As the words left his mouth, intense loss stabbed Taylor's insides. The thought of never entering her sweetness again was unbearable. The thought of never feeling her softness, never hearing her cries of pleasure, never waking up with her in his arms was daunting. But he didn't love her. She'd merely cast a spell on him, which would quickly dissipate once he was back in Portland.

"I have to go," she said and quickly left, leaving him in doubt and confusion.

Melia nearly ran to her car and sat behind the wheel, her heart beating rapidly. She used a few moments to gather her strength before she started the motor and pulled out of the parking space.

She loved that man. God, as hard as she had tried to deny her feelings, as hard as she'd tried to keep her feelings neutral, she had been far from successful.

She had tried to put distance between them. She couldn't, wouldn't, tell him that she couldn't be with him, because she was in love with him, and it hurt knowing their time together was brief. She wished she were a different kind of woman, that she could settle for an affair and go on without regrets, but that wasn't her. She didn't give her body freely, without intense feelings. She must have been in love with him weeks ago, when she went to bed with him for the first time, but hadn't recognized it or chose to ignore her feelings.

She wanted to save her heart if it wasn't too late.

More than anything, she wanted him gone, yet Leticia was inviting him to family dinners, forcing Melia to be in his presence even more. She wanted their good-byes over. She didn't want the dread and longing she felt when she left her apartment each day because she *might* run into him. She was tired of craving just a glimpse of him, feelings that inevitably left her angry for the very fact that she was panting after him like a helpless puppy.

She wanted her life to get back to normal. She wanted to

think up new recipes without thinking of him, or whether he would find them pleasing.

God, who was she fooling? She wanted him to love her every bit as much as she loved him.

Melia was putting together dinner when Taylor arrived at her apartment.

"Got enough for two?" he asked, watching her closely.

She didn't like the way he was scrutinizing her lately. He always seemed to be watching her. "Of course." She took out an extra plate and set it on the kitchen table.

"What, no candles on the balcony? I must really be on your shit list."

Melia raised her eyes to meet his. "I don't eat on the balcony every day."

He sat on one of the bar stools. "I heard from Duncan just before I left the office."

Melia glanced up at him. "And?"

"You might want to take a seat."

"What?"

"Do you remember Peter Bowman? Bowman attended high school with Palmer. We believe Palmer arranged a contract with him to make a hit on your parents."

Melia nearly swayed. "My God. He did this for their land."

"That's what we believe." He gathered her suddenly cold hands in his. "Melia, Mark is Peter Bowman."

"Mark . . ."

"Yes. Evidently, he was in the witness protection program. Remember when Elliot searched for information on Bowman and the U.S. Marshalls arrived on my doorstep? Well, Bowman was the key witness in their trial. Soon after the trial, someone tried to make a hit on him. He disappeared. Now, the case has been reopened. The prosecution needs him as their key witness."

"With the long arm of the mob and with the Internet, I don't understand why no one found him until now."

"He had plastic surgery. A totally new face. No one recognized him. That's why the picture Elliot found looked nothing like him."

"I've been working for my parents' murderer all this time! I just can't—"

"Don't torture yourself. You had no way of knowing."

"Has he been arrested? Is he still walking around free?"

"You better believe they're searching for him, if they haven't already found him."

"Did he kill all those people, the poker players? And why? I can understand Jessica's friends, since he's crazy. But what about the people in his poker group? That makes no sense."

"Who knows? Hopefully, they'll find out something once they arrest him."

"Lord, I hope so." She shook her head. He had taken her family from her. For at least a couple of years, she had been nearly catatonic. "This man needs to be locked up forever," she said.

"They need him as a witness. He might get life in prison, but he isn't going to get the electric chair."

"People who have committed crimes far less serious than his get the chair. Why not him?"

"The government needs him. I know it's not fair, but unfortunately, that's the way it works."

Melia rubbed her forehead. "They can't let him back on the street."

"Don't worry. After multiple murders, there's no way."

"I have to tell Jessica. She's going to be absolutely shocked. How could they let someone like that get away? Even to make a deal?"

"They were opting for the lesser of two evils."

"As far as I'm concerned, they were equal."

Melia picked up the phone and dialed Jessica's grandparents. She wasn't looking forward to being the bearer of bad news.

* * *

They arrested Mark that night just before closing at Modern Gourmet. The other employees were unaware of what was going on. As soon as Melia revealed Mark's real identity to Jessica, she took the ferry back to Seattle. She arrived at the store minutes before the arrest. When Jessica and Mark looked into each other's eyes, Mark knew she already knew the truth about him.

Mark's eyes fixed on Jessica. "You whore. You betrayed me."

"You betrayed me," she said. "How could you kill all those people?"

"You were mine. I don't give up what belongs to me."

"You don't own me."

He merely stared at her, and Jessica shivered at the coldness in his eyes.

"You killed Melia's parents, didn't you? Why? How could you do such a thing and live with yourself? What did they ever do to deserve that?" she asked, as her insides roiled. She knew he was a criminal. But she hadn't really made herself believe it until now. When she was face-to-face with him.

He didn't respond to her erratic questions. He merely stared.

The officer who had cuffed him said, "I'm sorry, ma'am, but you have to move away."

"I never knew you, did I?" she asked.

Jessica fell silent while the officer read Mark his Miranda rights. "Believe me, I already know it. I'll be back," Mark said to Jessica. Then he looked at Melia. "I'll deal with you, too. Until we meet again."

The officer pushed him ahead, and Mark stumbled; then he righted himself.

The employees were looking at Jessica for an explanation. They were baffled, but she wasn't ready to tell them about the nightmare. She sent them home and closed up. What would happen to the store? she wondered. What would happen to the employees? Although she and Melia could live without their salaries, the rest of the employees couldn't. She'd open the doors tomorrow and the day after that. Until somebody told her not to.

Brunch was a somber affair. Taylor had indeed taken Leticia up on her offer. He picked Melia up and drove them to the Simses' church, which was located in the Central District. It was one of the oldest black churches in the area, with an enormous congregation. As they passed boarded-up buildings, Taylor again wondered what could be done to lift the area. He even stopped a moment to talk about it with Mel, who was pleased to see him.

"We'll meet you at the house," Leticia said after the service. "Don't be late."

Taylor and Melia were stopped several times to talk with other parishioners on their way to the car.

They were the last to arrive at the house. Audie and Lisa were already there. But Blair was missing, as always. Melia would carry a plate back for him, Taylor thought as they settled around the table.

Leticia's cook had prepared a feast.

"It's really shocking about Mark," Leticia said. "Who would have ever guessed? He always seemed so innocent, so sweet."

"Goes to show, you never know about people," Audie said.

"I guess you're right."

"What are you going to do about his stake in Northwest Coastal?" Audie asked.

"It goes to his estate, I guess, to cover expenses, lawsuits, whatever. If anything's left over, the government will seize it."

"And what are you going to invest in?" he asked.

"Haven't given it a thought. We need to recover from this shock first and regroup."

"I was having lunch near your church a while back," Taylor interjected, "and there are so many empty storefronts, so many neglected properties in a relatively booming area. Have you or your investment group ever considered refurbishing that community in lieu of building a property from scratch?"

Leticia was shaking her head. "Actually, the thought never occurred to us."

"It might be an alternative worth considering."

"In that case, have you thought of investing in a real estate investment group?" Earl asked. "I heard that you've been the legal representative on many such projects."

"I've never invested, no," Taylor said. "Conflict of interest issues could become a problem."

"I heard you are the attorney for the Mason Group," Earl continued.

Leticia's head popped up. "But that's one of the largest groups on the West Coast," she said.

Taylor nodded.

"Who will take over your grandfather's firm?" Earl said. "Have you considered doing it? It's a shame for a firm that was so renowned in the area to get away."

"We're still looking for someone to take over," Taylor said.

"Why don't you do it?" Audie said in his normally wide-eyed manner.

"I'm sure he's doing very well at his firm in Portland, although you aren't exactly your own boss," Earl said.

"Are you a partner yet?" Leticia asked.

"Yes."

"Northwest Coastal might be more amenable to your suggestion if you were the legal representative for our group. And we don't necessarily need another investor, but the group would be open to it," she said slyly.

Taylor smiled, but the food began to curdle in his stomach. He had thought Leticia wanted him back in Portland as quickly as possible, and now she was plotting for him to stay here. "Have you heard of Mr. Mel Cummings, who owns—"

"Of course. His restaurant is very popular. The food is excellent," said Leticia.

"He suggested refurbishing the neighborhood. Perhaps he would be interested in becoming a member of your group."

"That still leaves us without legal counsel."

Taylor cleared his throat. "There are many lawyers in the city who can handle this."

"We're considering several, but . . ."

Taylor sighed. The woman was like a persistent fly. "I'll see what I can do," he said.

Taylor glanced at Melia out of the corner of his eye and wondered how she felt about him making a permanent home in Seattle. But why was he even entertaining that thought? His home was in Portland. He was the attorney for one of the largest real estate developing companies in the world. Soon he would make full partner. In Portland he had everything he ever wanted—that is, in a career.

But what about his personal life, he thought. Although his feelings for Melia were more intense than he ever imagined, he hadn't a clue about what he was going to do about them. No, he wasn't ready for forever after quite yet.

Chapter 15

Mark, aka Peter Bowman, had escaped again. Upon hearing the news, Taylor cursed under his breath, reached for his jacket, and left the office to search for Melia and Jessica. Melia wasn't home. She and Jessica had gone out to lunch, and either Melia's cell phone was off or the battery wasn't charged. They were due back in an hour a salesclerk at Modern Gourmet had said. He would meet them there.

He caught up with them just as they were about to enter the store and revealed what had happened.

"I don't think it's safe at all for you to stay here with Mark on the loose. The two of you will need to take a long vacation."

"If we visit relatives, he'll find us easily," Jessica said.

"My place in Portland would be the last location he'd suspect. I don't think he really knows me, does he?"

"No," Melia said. "Unless you mentioned Taylor's name," she said to Jessica.

"No. I just said I thought you were falling in love, but I never mentioned a name."

Falling in love, Melia thought. She wished for a black hole in the floor to swallow her whole. The last thing she wanted was Taylor to think she was wearing her heart on her sleeve for him.

"Then I'll drop both of you off, and you can pick up a few things on the way," said Taylor. "He may have already scouted out your homes."

"What about our cars?" Melia said.

"I'll take care of them after you get to safety."

They piled into Taylor's SUV and were soon driving south of Seattle.

Three hours later, they shopped for necessities before heading to an older section of Portland. There, huge Victorian houses had been renovated into modern splendor. The neighborhood had clearly been gentrified. The poor had been pushed aside and replaced with the more well-to-do, who could afford to refurbish the buildings. Once a land of plentiful, with opportunity for all, America was sending the very jobs overseas that had made it so precious.

They piled into Taylor's house. It was still somewhat early, but everybody was exhausted. Taylor ordered takeout, and after they ate, Jessica went to bed, claiming complete exhaustion.

Melia thought she would sleep in a separate bedroom, but Taylor steered her into his. He seemed to like having her in his house. But it was so hard to read someone who professed to enjoy his freedom as much as he did.

That night they made love tenderly, and Melia promised herself she wouldn't worry about tomorrow. She was going with the flow.

"What are you thinking about?" Taylor asked. His warm breath brushed her face.

"That I'm unemployed."

"Once you told me that you weren't sure about your career, that you more or less fell into it. What would you like to do if you could choose any career?"

"Funny, now that I don't have a job, I was just thinking that I really enjoy my work. Creating new recipes is challenging and rewarding. I meet so many wonderful people who thank me for making recipes simple. Most women work full time, and they don't have the energy to spend hours preparing meals," she said. "And I like taping shows. It's a good fit."

"If you owned the shop, would you change anything?"

Melia considered his question. There were many things she would change. "As far as the shows, I would do special episodes, like during berry-picking season. I'd shoot a berry farm, an apple orchard, or an edible flower farm, perhaps some of the vendors at Pike Place Market. I'd show some of the mariners so that the viewers would get a closer look at the process fishermen go through to get their catch to the market. Maybe even local restaurants."

"Sounds expensive."

"It's not something I'd do all the time, but occasionally. Makes the show different and exciting. And I would focus on the local market." Melia turned her head and kissed him lightly on the lips. "Poor you. You're supposed to settle back into your normal routine, and you're saddled with me."

He squeezed her and kissed her, lingering, savoring the sweetness. This woman had burrowed under his skin. "I can't tell you what a hardship that is. But I'll do my best to rise to the occasion." He hugged her closely, but he didn't initiate lovemaking.

"Oh, Taylor. I may not live through this. And I don't have a will."

"We *will* survive this, and you will marry and have . . . how many children do you want?"

He said we, not she. "Three or four."

"Sounds reasonable. And they will all be miniature chefs. Can't you imagine them all with chefs hats?"

Melia chuckled. "How many do you want?"

"Humm. Three or four."

"So says the confirmed bachelor."

"Yeah." He kissed her. When he released her lips, she yawned. "Think you can sleep now?"

She nodded. She felt warm and cozy and comforted.

For the last few hours, fear had dominated. Now she lay

peacefully in Taylor's arms, listening to his steady heartbeat—
a soothing rhythm—lulling her to sleep.

But Taylor wasn't asleep. He knew he had to marry this
woman. She was everything he'd ever dreamed of and more.
But he would not propose now. He wanted to make his proposal a special occasion, not linked to memories of threats.
He'd take her to dinner, or maybe on another trip to the B&B,
and would pop the question over champagne and dessert.
Otherwise, she'd ruin it by offering to cook.

They'd still have to work out the details about their long-
distance work. And the details of Mark's gourmet shop. But
those things could be managed.

"I love you, Melia," he said aloud, but she had already fallen
asleep.

The walls were closing in on Melia and Jessica. For a solid
week, they had been at Taylor's place. It was a wonderful
place, with large leaded windows and oversized rooms, but
Melia liked the freedom to come and go as she pleased. They
couldn't leave, because Mark was still a fugitive, and they knew
he was after them. You didn't betray him and live to enjoy it.

"We could be stuck here for months," Jessica said.

"Let's hope it doesn't take them that long to find him."

"It took almost three years the last time. I don't have much
faith in the authorities finding him. He could have a new face,
and then we couldn't see who was coming."

"There are so many questions I want answered. Why did
he kill his fellow card players? Did they cheat him? And
why did he kill my parents? Did Palmer ask him to?"

"You may never find your answers."

"I know."

"I wish we could go outside at least. I don't see why we can't
at least go in the backyard. Sit at the table, get some sun."

"Speak for yourself. Although that shade tree out there looks very tempting."

"Stop thinking along those lines, ladies," their bodyguard, Ronald Mayes, said. Taylor wouldn't leave them alone, and Elliot had recommended the tall, very muscular man. "Why don't you see what's on TV?"

"We're sick of TV," Melia said.

"Or read one of those books you like so much. Or you can always use me as a guinea pig. I love your cooking."

"She can't cook all the time," Jessica said. "I don't see why we can't go outside. The police are making runs by here every so often. I don't think Mark will brave that."

"A lot can happen in a half hour," the bodyguard said.

"Taylor's getting sick of our complaints. I don't think I have to worry about him proposing to me," Melia said.

"I'm not sure about that. You're feeding him so well, he's putting on a little weight. You're even packing his lunch every day. That's not going to be easy to give up."

"He's lived this long without the comforts of home; I think he can continue to survive without it. I've fallen for a committed bachelor."

The phone rang, but they didn't answer it. They weren't even allowed to answer their cell phones. They listened as the answering machine picked up.

"Jessica . . . Melia . . ." an eerie, singsong voice came over the wire, and both women stiffened with fright. "I'm coming to get you."

Melia's hand went to her throat.

"How did Mark find us?" Jessica asked. "What on earth are we going to do?"

"He's trying to frighten us."

"It's working. He could be outside watching us."

Ronald had listened, too. "I'm calling the police. And then I'm getting you out of here."

He made the phone calls at the same time he bundled them into the SUV that was parked in the garage. After carefully looking down the street, he drove away. All three of them looked around to see if they were being followed.

"Where are you taking us?"

"Taylor already had a place picked out if this happened. It's up in the mountains. I think this guy is in the city but not nearby. I haven't spotted a tail."

They drove for a couple of hours. Melia wondered if they would have been safer in the city with more police protection.

"Maybe we should have contacted the U.S. Marshalls. They want Mark. They could have set up something to trap him."

"These things don't always turn out nice and clean the way you want them to," said Ronald. "Besides, this guy is a crafty character. He's slipped the agents twice now."

Melia wondered whether Mark was so crafty that he'd lured them into a trap. She wished she could call Taylor and talk to him. Or even Leticia or Earl. Earl was quiet, but sometimes the man imparted consoling bits of wisdom.

They drove for another hour before Ronald stopped at a combination grocery store and gas station for supplies. After they made their purchases, they started of again and in another thirty minutes, they pulled onto a gravel path that led to a rustic cabin.

Taylor glanced at the picture of Melia on his desk. He picked up the phone and dialed Duncan's number.

"Have you heard anything so far?" he asked.

"Not a thing. We have found the man Melia identified as the longshoreman. Used to be a mariner, but now works for Bowman. Claims he wasn't aware of Bowman's background, but we know he was connected to the credit card scams."

"Very resourceful. Was he able to identify any of Bowman's hangouts?"

"He was as tight as a clam until I told him we were going to slap him with accessory to murder. But Bowman wasn't at any of the places he revealed."

"He's too smart for that."

"We didn't uncover a damn thing at his apartment. How are the ladies?"

"Climbing the walls with boredom."

"Could be worse."

They hung up, and Taylor grabbed his jacket and left for a luncheon meeting. He told his secretary he wouldn't return afterwards.

It was a warm day, really. Too nice for the women to be cooped up inside. Jessica had moaned about the four walls. His sisters were bringing their crew to dinner tonight. At least the kids would keep the energy flowing for a few hours. They were definitely looking forward to seeing Melia again.

He entered the restaurant, and by mutual consent, Michael Mason and he ate on the patio facing Mt. Hood.

Michael and Taylor had attended Berkeley together; they had actually been roommates. It was Michael who paved the way with his father for Taylor to take over their account when their old attorney died.

"I have to tell you that I'm considering taking over my grandfather's practice in Seattle," Taylor said as they sipped coffee.

Michael leaned back in his seat. "You've been Mason's attorney for six years. At this juncture, we don't want to change counsel."

"Would you consider moving with me?"

"I'll have to talk it over with my father first, but I'm sure he'll be willing."

"And thanks, man, for the offer of the cabin. We haven't needed it so far, but just knowing—"

Michael waved a hand. "Think nothing of it. You always have access to it."

"So I've been hearing rumors about your status as a single man changing soon."

"Now, who could have blabbed?"

"I have my sources. Is it true?"

"I haven't popped the question yet, but I plan to soon."

"I can't believe it. The last of the diehards."

"Hey, you're the last."

"Oh, well. Somebody has to hold out. Dad's working on his fifth. No way am I going through that."

"How old is this one?"

Michael scoffed. "Young enough for me. As long as he has money, he'll have young wives."

"What a waste," Taylor said. "I think he's still in love with your mother."

"As much as I love him, I don't think so. Mom has been happily married now for fifteen years. They're throwing this big shindig next month. She said she invited you."

"With the p.s. don't disappoint her. I'll be there."

Taylor's cell phone vibrated against his chest. He took it out and glanced at the number. "I have to take this."

He dialed Melia's cell phone. When she told him what had happened, he responded, "Be careful. I'll call Duncan and get you additional help."

"I have to leave, Michael."

"Anything wrong?"

"I'll tell you about it later."

"It looks primitive on the outside, but Taylor says it's a beaut inside—has all the comforts of home," Ronald said as Melia and Jessica exited the SUV and stretched their cramped legs. The temperature outside was measurably cooler, and there were even patches of snow in shady areas. Melia rubbed her arms. Nestled in a grove of trees, the cabin blended perfectly into the background. Mark would never find them there. And they wouldn't have to stay cooped up in the cabin. But they could not stay there indefinitely.

They unloaded the car, made the beds, and prepared dinner. Ronald made a fire in the fireplace. There were six bedrooms in the place. Ronald insisted on taking the bedroom next to Melia and Jessica's room.

After Jessica and Ronald turned in, Melia sat gazing into the flames. The last night she and Taylor had spent together, she could have sworn he'd said he loved her as she fell asleep. Ahh, that was only wishful thinking. He made no bones about the fact he had more wild oats to sow. Nervously, she looked at all the windows in the room. As gorgeous as the daytime view was, those windows offered scant protection against a lunatic. Especially when they were nestled in the middle of nowhere. Melia pulled a blanket around her shoulders and wondered when or how it all would end.

Another stressful week passed without incident. The U.S. Marshalls were beginning to think Mark had left the country. Or that he'd gone off to get another face-lift. They'd wait forever for him to make another hit. And they couldn't hide out forever.

One morning before daybreak, Melia was awakened by someone pressing a weird smelling cloth to her mouth and nose. She tried to struggle, but someone was holding her down. She tried not to breathe in the sickly odor, but she had no choice. Suddenly, she passed out.

When Melia awakened, Jessica was beside her and she couldn't move. Her mouth felt as dry as dust. It took a moment for Melia to realize they were tied to the those old-fashioned iron bed in which she'd slept. Where was Ronald? What on earth had happened? It was still pitch black. There was nothing to compare to the darkness in the wilderness.

"Jessica?" she whispered. Melia felt Jessica next to her, although she could barely see her outline. Jessica didn't respond. Melia panicked. My God. She wasn't dead was she? But her arm was warm. And then Jessica moaned. "Thank God. Jessica, are you all right?"

"I feel like crap. What happened?"

"I don't know." Melia heard a noise. "Somebody's coming." She pulled against the ropes, but they were tied securely.

She scanned the room, hoping to find something she could use to free herself. But what good would it do with hands and feet bound?

Suddenly, Mark appeared. "I see you ladies are awake."

"Why did you kill my parents?" If Melia was going to die, she wanted answers. It also gave them some time.

"Because Palmer wanted me to. Your parents were very stubborn about the land. And he had some debts that needed paying."

"You got rid of Palmer's problems. People mean nothing to you!"

"That's right. If that fool hadn't pulled you out of the way in the nick of time, you would have joined them."

So he was the one on the motorcycle. "Don't you have a conscience at all?"

"What do you think?"

"You've got money. Why did you want to kill Melia?" Jessica asked.

"Remember the robbery? I had millions that night. Millions." He nearly spit out the words. "And those guys knew it. But I don't have that problem any longer. I hunted the SOB down and killed him."

"He was one of your poker buddies," Melia said, suddenly making a connection. "All of those men were involved in the robbery? That man would have had to know in advance that you had so much money."

"Not the first few. It took a while for me to find the right one. I couldn't believe it. We had a credit card scam going, and we were ready to close it down. We had enough that none of us would ever have to work again. Roger decided he wanted it all for himself. As you can see, I disabused him of that notion."

"But you killed innocent people."

"Can't be helped."

"So now that you don't need Melia's land any longer, why are you here?"

"I came for you, darling." It wasn't an endearment. He leaned over Jessica, grabbed her chin in his hand, and kissed her. Jessica struggled against his mouth, but he held her still. "Nobody betrays me. Nobody," he whispered against her lips.

"You're going to kill us?" Melia asked. Really stupid question. Why else would he be there?

"Just an innocent tumble over a cliff. No one will miss you. Now, have I answered all your questions? I know you were burning for answers."

He leaned over Jessica again, and she turned her head to the side. He captured her chin, then kissed her again. Jessica moaned in pain.

"Leave her alone. You don't have to do that. You have what you want."

"I have to start all over again because of your mëddling. Of course, you'll pay for that."

Mark's glasses were gone, and she wondered how she could have ever thought he was a geek. There was nothing geeky about him.

Melia tried to think of a way out of their dilemma, but what could she do trussed up like a Thanksgiving turkey? Mark loosened the ropes tying them to the bed, waved a gun at them, and ordered them to rise. Their feet were still bound together with rope so they could only take halting steps. Their hands were bound, too.

"What did you do to Ronald?" Melia asked.

"That excuse for a bodyguard? He's alive—for now."

"Why don't you let us go?"

"Shut up and move."

They walked slowly ahead of him out of the cabin. Melia continued to look for an escape. She just wasn't going to fall down a mountainside for him. Or kindly stand there and let him push her without a fight. Finally, they reached the crest of a small hill. It was a very wooded area—enough trees to break a fall. Melia knew they wouldn't be able to get away, but maybe . . . All of a sudden, she fell into Jessica, and they both went tumbling. Then she heard the pop of bullets exploding all around them and wondered whether they'd been hit. She expected to feel pain, but none came. Melia quickly got to her knees, ready to take off, even if only with halting steps.

Then it came to her. She heard explosions coming from several directions, not just one.

"You okay?" Jessica whispered, hunched in a sprinting position. Both their hands and feet were still bound.

"Yeah . . ." Then she saw masked figures backing away, their guns pointed toward the ground. A minute later she heard the motors from several vehicles start up and then drive away.

The natural sounds of the area slowly returned. As if in slow motion, they began to see birds flying gracefully across the horizon. Squirrels began to scamper down trees. The sounds of leaves rustling sounded normal.

"See if you can turn around. I'm going to try to untie you." Her fingers numb, it took Melia several minutes to untie Jessica's ropes. Once free, Jessica quickly untied Melia's. Melia rubbed the abrasions on her wrists and ankles.

Together, they slowly walked up the hill.

"Oh, my God!" They both turned their heads too late to prevent the bloody mess of what was left of Mark's body from invading their dreams for a lifetime. His body was full of bloody holes. This was a nightmare from a movie, not real life, Melia thought.

"We have to find Ronald and get help."

"We can't leave Mark like this," Jessica said, her voice thin and reedy.

Melia glanced around, careful to avert her gaze from Mark. He was already dead. There was nothing they could do. But Jessica seemed to be going through an emotional crisis. "After we find Ronald, we can cover Mark with blankets from the cabin."

On shaky legs, they took measured steps toward the cabin. Inside they found Ronald bound and gagged, bleeding from a bullet wound in the shoulder. Jessica untied him while

Melia searched for first aid supplies. Melia patched the wound with a clean rag.

"He broke the cell phone," Ronald said through gritted teeth. "You two are going to have to go for help."

But when they went outside, they saw the SUV had all four tires flattened. And they couldn't find Mark's car anywhere. From how away far had he hiked in?

"We can't leave you here," Jessica said to Ronald.

"You don't have a choice. I'll be okay. Go. Go."

"We'll cover Mark when we get back," Melia said. Buzzards had already begun to circle overhead. They had better find help soon, Melia thought just before she dashed several feet away and retched. When she looked up, she saw Jessica had found her own patch to throw up in. It would take a long time for Jessica to recover from this. Melia believed that in her own way, her friend had loved Mark.

"Think you can walk?" Melia asked.

"If nothing else, we can support each other." Jessica glanced down at her bare toes. "Think we can scrounge up some shoes first?"

For the first time, Melia gave a lopsided smile. "It's required." Melia felt numb. She knew emotions would sink in later. But right now there were things to do.

After donning their shoes and jackets, they made their way to the road, very aware that night could close in before they made it to town. Nights were cold in the mountains, even this time of year.

They had walked at least four miles before someone in a pickup truck picked them up and carried them to the police station.

A phalanx of agents stormed the property.

Melia took them to the spot where Mark was covered up. Blood had penetrated the ground.

Taylor exploded down the hill toward them. Behind him, Melia saw Audie, Duncan, Leticia, and Earl.

"Damn it, you've got to marry me," Taylor said when he reached Melia and grabbed her roughly in his arms, holding her as if he'd never let her go. "You scared the life out of me."

"What?"

"Marry me." The steady thump of his heart let her know she was truly alive.

She couldn't think straight. Too much had occurred. "Ronald needs help."

"He's getting help."

She noticed an ambulance and heard the engine of a helicopter close by.

"Just say yes," Audie said, rubbing her back.

"Oh, my word. I will never forgive myself for setting this in motion," Leticia moaned, tears streaming down her face.

Melia didn't have the energy to deal with Leticia's guilt right then. It was all she could do to hold herself upright. But she recognized that Mark was evil on his own. Leticia hadn't ask him to kill anyone. She'd talk to her later.

"He's waiting for an answer," Audie prompted.

What answer? Melia thought. Then she found herself in Earl's comforting arms, and she remembered.

"Hurry up and answer. Blair's on the cell phone. He wants to talk to you," Audie insisted.

She glanced at Taylor. He was rubbing her back as if he had to have some contact with her.

"Yes." she said.

Epilogue

"Can the baby stay up here with us?" one of Taylor's nieces asked.

"She's with Grandma Leticia right now, and I think she's sleeping," Melia said. "You can see her when she wakes up."

"I want her to sleep up here with us," another niece said.

"Who cares about babies," Taylor's nephew muttered. "All they do is eat and cry and mess their diapers. Where's Uncle Taylor? He said he was going to take me fishing."

Melia rubbed the boy's head. "His flight was late leaving New York."

"Is he going to miss Christmas with us?"

"Hopefully, he won't."

"Okay, who's ready to play ball?" Audie said from the doorway.

"I am! I am," all the kids shouted at once. In less than a minute, Melia heard feet stomping on the stairway. She scooped up the children's games and piled them in the toy chest. Then she made her way downstairs to Leticia and Earl's room. Her baby was sleeping peacefully in Earl's arms. He was watching CNN with the volume turned down low.

She and Taylor had been married two years now. And little

Crystal was four months old. Even before she was born, Taylor had set up a crib in their bedroom on Bainbridge.

The family was gathered there—with Blair and Christina this time. Blair had spent the day inside. He still wouldn't go out for long periods, but he was improving slowly.

Taylor's entire family was there as well. Even his brother from New York and his grandfather, who had brought Mrs. Miles with him. Her grandson now lived in Seattle.

Jessica came out of the kitchen.

"Where's Duncan?" Melia asked.

"Playing pool with Blair and Grandpa," Jessica replied. Jessica and Duncan were spending the weekend with the Sieversons. "Do you think Mary will be all right by herself a couple of days?"

"You can't live at the store," Melia said. "Mary will be fine. You're a control freak. You can't stand to let anyone else take over."

"Buying Modern Gourmet is the best thing we've ever done, isn't it, partner?"

"I agree."

"I can't thank Taylor enough for working out the details with the U.S. Marshalls."

"They only wanted the money. They didn't really want to run the shop." The Marshalls wanted to recoup some of the money Mark had cost them and had seized his assets, but Taylor was able to arrange it so that Melia and Jessica could buy Modern Gourmet, which they renamed Today's Gourmet.

"So when is Taylor arriving?"

"Soon, I hope."

"With all those people he hired in the law office, I thought he'd have time to spare."

"Not likely."

"Well, Leticia is singing his praises. Northwest Coastal is really pleased with the way the community refurbishing project is going." They had taken Mel on as partner.

Duncan came out of the kitchen, eating a piece of berry pie.

The downstairs was filled with the smells of food. Everyone had been snacking all afternoon on huge apple and berry pies made from fruit they'd picked during the fall.

"You're going to ruin your appetite," Jessica said.

"Have you seen all that food in the kitchen? I'm going to have to jog five miles after dinner." He glanced at Melia. "Mind if I steal Jessica for a few minutes?"

"Be my guest," Melia said. As she passed the front door, it opened and a blast of cold air rushed in.

"I can't wait for the hot tub tonight," Taylor said.

Melia flew into his arms. "You made it," she said, holding him tight. His cheek was cold against her face.

"Couldn't spend Christmas away from my favorite ladies. How's the baby?"

"Sleeping."

"Think she'll sleep later on while we use the hot tub?"

"It's going to be a crowd in there." Melia kissed him. "I missed you."

"I missed you, too, baby. I'm telling them the tub's broken. We're going to sneak down after everybody goes to bed."

"That'll be the wee hours of the morning."

"Thank God, there are only two bedrooms on this floor. Whoever designed this house was crafty."

Taylor had moved into her condo, and Mrs. Emerline had purchased his, saying it was the perfect size for her. That woman was as ornery as ever. At that moment she was in the kitchen fighting with Mrs. Sieverson over holiday recipes.

"Think we can sneak into the bedroom for a quickie after I look in on Crystal?"

"Uncle Taylor! Uncle Taylor! You made it."

Taylor groaned. "So much for great plans," he said, and Melia chuckled as his nephew dragged him away.

Two hours later they were all seated at the huge dining room table. The house was filled with people again, and Melia couldn't be happier.

Not a day went by that she didn't think of her parents. At

one time, she had wished she could forget so the pain would lessen, but now she didn't want to forget. She wanted to remember and tell her children and grandchildren about the wonderful, strong couple and about all their other ancestors. She wanted to tell them about the stories her grandmother and grandfather used to tell her.

Besides, she thought as Taylor winked at her from the other end of the table, they had already started their own traditions.

Dear Reader,

I hope you enjoyed spending time with Melia and Taylor. I wanted to explore the complexities of finding family when those closest to you no longer exist. Even worse, Melia stood the chance of losing her second family. The wonderful thing is people are generous and willingly open their hearts to others.

Readers like you help me to continue working with the craft I love. Thank you so much for your support and for so many kind and uplifting letters and e-mails.

I love hearing from readers. Please visit my web page (www.erols.com/cpoarch), or write to me at:

P.O. Box 291
Springfield, VA 22150

With Warm Regards,

Candice Poarch

About the Author

Reared in Stony Creek, Virginia, nationally best-selling author Candice Poarch portrays a sense of community and mutual support in her novels. She firmly believes that everyday life in small town America has its own rich rewards.

Candice currently lives in Springfield, Virginia with her husband and three children. A former computer system manger, she has made writing her full-time career. Candice is a graduate of Virginia State University and holds a Bachelor of Science degree in physics.

Family Bonds is Candice's twelfth Arabesque novel.

BOOK YOUR PLACE ON OUR WEBSITE AND MAKE THE ARABESQUE ROMANCE CONNECTION!

We've created a customized website just for our very special Arabesque readers, where you can get the inside scoop on everything that's going on with Arabesque romance novels.

When you come online, you'll have the exciting opportunity to

- View covers of upcoming books

- Learn about our future publishing schedule (listed by publication month and author)

- Find out when your favorite authors will be visiting a city near you

- Search for and order backlist books

- Check out author bios and background information

- Send e-mail to your favorite authors

- Join us in weekly chats with authors, readers and other guests

- Get writing guidelines

- AND MUCH MORE!

Visit our website at
http://www.arabesquebooks.com